The Final Deception
A Quay Thompson Novel

Gail Lee Cowdin

© 2017 Gail Lee Cowdin   All rights reserved

ISBN-13: 978-1548834494

ISBN-10: 1548834491

**Library of Congress Control Number: 2017916003
CreateSpace Independent Publishing Platform, North
Charleston, SC**

No part of this book may be reproduced, stored in a retrieval system, or transmitted by any means without the written permission of the author.

CreateSpace Publishing 10/15/2017

This is a work of fiction. Names, characters, places, and incidents either are the product of the author's imagination or are used fictitiously, and any resemblance to actual persons, living or dead, business establishments, events or locales is entirely coincidental.

**For my husband Theo
and my children Michelle and Matthew
The loves of my life.**

Dear Readers:

Virginia Woolf's famous line goes, "A woman must have money and a room of one's own if she is to write fiction."

Well, times have changed. Thank heavens. Although I have neither of the qualifications Woolf lists, I do have another qualification: time. I am still able to write fiction at my leisure. So here we go again.

When I finished writing my first novel *Deception and Redemption*, I thought I'd finished the story, and that I was then finished with my novel attempt. (Pardon the pun.) But many of you kept asking for the rest of the story.

So here it is. What you have here in *The Final Deception* is the continuation of the story of Quay Thompson, Samantha Atwood, and Sunni Hyun.

As often happens when I write, the characters take over telling their stories. I am able to sit back and enjoy their story. This time as the plot unfolded, Quay's partner Samantha Atwood's voice became more dominant --for reasons you will understand as you read.

Another thing that I wanted to share with readers is that the CRISPR-Cas9 research studies described herein are real. In fact, CRISPR research was one of the candidates for Time Magazine's Person of the Year in 2016. The future is going to be interesting.

I'm glad I had the opportunity to share the rest of the story with you. I hope you enjoy the read. *-Gail*

CHAPTERS

CHAPTER 1 JANUARY — p.6
CHAPTER 2 A REST AREA KILLING — p. 9
CHAPTER 3 A NAME FROM THE PAST — p. 15
CHAPTER 4 SOMETHING FAMILIAR — p. 23
CHAPTER 5 THE DECISION — p. 39
CHAPTER 6 A DOG NAMED CHIP — p. 42
CHAPTER 7 ELUDING THE TRACKERS — p. 49
CHAPTER 8 THE SAFE HOUSE — p. 61
CHAPTER 9 SUNNI'S STORY — p. 83
CHAPTER 10 THE AMBUSH — p. 100
CHAPTER 11 NEED SOME GUM? — p. 110
CHAPTER 12 AFTERMATH — p. 122
CHAPTER 13 DAYBREAK AND DECISIONS — p. 135
CHAPTER 14 QUAY — p. 143
CHAPTER 15 THE REUNION — p. 151
CHAPTER 16 THE FIRST DECEPTION — p. 162
CHAPTER 17 TRUTH OR DARE — p. 170
CHAPTER 18 FILLING IN THE BLANKS — p. 182
CHAPTER 19 BOMBS AND BLIZZARDS — p. 192
CHAPTER 20 BREAKING THE CODE — p. 205
CHAPTER 21 LOOSE ENDS — p. 214
CHAPTER 22 SPINNING PLATES — p. 227
CHAPTER 23 FULL DISCLOSURE — p. 247
EPILOGUE — p. 261
ACKNOWLEDGEMENTS — p. 265

"Genome science will have a real impact on all our lives -- and even more, on the lives of our children. It will revolutionize the diagnosis, prevention and treatment of most, if not all, human diseases." - President Bill Clinton

CHAPTER ONE
January

Joo Jhim slowed his small sedan and exited from Interstate 94 into the rest area just west of Minneapolis. The caller had instructed him to pull slowly into the rest area lot and park near the back. He wasn't sure what to expect. His nerve synapses were exploding like droplets of cold water splattering into hot oil. As he edged his car into the lot, he carefully scanned each parked vehicle as he passed it. The rest area wasn't busy. They were here. He could feel it. He knew they wouldn't be out in the open. His anxiety centered on why they wanted to meet here. He pulled into an open spot near the end of the parking area as instructed.

After he parked, the six-month-old pup in the back seat excitedly jumped up and began happily pacing and turning around on the rear seat pressing its nose first to one frosty window and then to the opposite in hopes of being released. The dog's breath formed small, foggy clouds that wafted into the front seat providing Jhim with a good dose of dog breath. Jhim shouted in a commanding voice to the young pup, "Sit!" He turned and stretched his arm across to the back in an attempt to cuff the dog along the head. He missed. The pup, thinking he was playing, danced away from his slap, wagged happily, and then lurched back and jumped up with paws on the seat back, looking to give Jhim a quick slurp on the back of his ear.

"Chip! Sit!" Jhim ordered again as he ducked away from the dog's attack. This time he managed forcefully to shove the dog back with another shouted command to sit and stay. The young golden retriever cowered and crawled to the opposite corner of the backseat and curled into a ball.

That brief distraction had cost Jhim his life. He hadn't noticed the black car creeping into the parking area. Just before the bullet entered the back of his head destroying his brain, he'd wondered what moment of idiocy had made him bring the dog along.

The gunshot reverberated across nearby Rice Lake on the north side of the highway. Two teenage boys standing on the frozen lake next to a portable fish house had just finished drilling a hole into the foot-thick ice for late afternoon fishing. At the same time, a semi driver began applying his Jake Brakes to slow down his exit into the rest area off the interstate.

The boys' heads jerked up as they looked across the highway in the direction of a sound they both recognized. The singular sound of the gunshot had been distinguishable above the thundering of the trucker's brakes. Dedicated young hunters, they easily recognized the sharp retort echoing from the rest area as it had reverberated over the sound of the trucker's Jake Brakes.

Matt looked at his friend Brett. Brett turned to Matt. "That was a gunshot!" they said in unison. They dropped their ice fishing equipment and stared in curiosity across the lake in the direction of the rest area. As they watched, a dark sedan sped out of the exit onto the freeway and veered dangerously in front of a stream of oncoming cars. Both lanes of traffic slowed, cars swerved, and angry drivers honked as the black sedan sped away.

The boys watched as the semi driver noisily exited into the rest area. "I hope that trucker got the license plate of that car," said Matt as he took off running. Leaving their fishing hole and rods, Brett joined him in the race toward the highway and the rest area. As they ran, Brett pulled his phone out of his jacket pocket and began dialing 911.

CHAPTER TWO
A Rest Area Killing

Seconds later, Sunni Hyun also sped away from the rest area hoping to get lost in the tangle of rush hour traffic moving east into Minneapolis. She knew she could exit at the next ramp while most of the heavy traffic continued on toward the downtown area.

That had been too close. She couldn't believe she had just witnessed another killing. She was living a nightmare. Again! She flashbacked to the sniper murder at Cameron BioTech she had witnessed last fall. Now this. This was wrong. She was afraid for her life. She needed to find a way to escape from them, whoever they were.

Sunni's mind raced through the events of the afternoon. Just an hour before, Joo Jhim, her stepfather, who was also her control operative, had called her and ordered her to meet him at that very rest area. He'd said he had something for her and had ordered her to meet with him immediately. She hadn't known what he wanted, but she certainly knew what she had wanted. Seeking to end his control and manipulation, she had agreed. She had intended to tell him she was done. She wouldn't be taking any more orders from him or anyone else.

When she'd pulled into the rest area, she'd spotted his old, green Hyundai parked near the end of the parking lot. Suddenly a dark sedan had swerved around her and sped past. She'd watched in alarm as that car slowed to a crawl as it neared Joo's car. The whole thing had begun to evolve in slow motion as her mind registered what was happening. She'd watched in shocked disbelief as she saw the passenger window of the sedan roll down just a crack. A gun barrel had poked through the window. Then there had been the sharp retort of a gunshot booming above the noise of the highway. Her body had flinched in horror. She'd slammed on her brakes, and her trembling hands had covered her silent scream. She'd watched as the rear window of Joo's car shattered. And in the next second, the dark sedan had sped up and flown away down the exit ramp. The shooting had been quick and neat.

Stunned by what she had witnessed, Sunni reflexively swerved her car to the side and tapped on her brakes again so that she idled parallel to the curb while she caught her breath. Fear rippled through her. She'd spiraled into a full-blown panic attack. Gasping for air, trembling in uncontrolled terror, Sunni glanced into her rear view mirror. Who else had seen this? Were there others? She'd looked to the right and to the left, and then looked again in her rear view mirror. Nothing. No one. She'd realized she had to move.

She began to move forward in a steady route past Joo's car and through the parking lot to the exit. Once she reached the exit, she accelerated merging smoothly into the traffic. She hoped her vehicle had not been seen at the rest area. She could still see the black sedan ahead speeding down the freeway, weaving in and out of lanes, in the distance.

Sunni finished her merge into the rush hour traffic expertly and a mile down the highway took the next exit for Weaver Lake Road. Still trembling uncontrollably, she slowed and headed south. She couldn't believe what had just happened. An assassination. In another minute she would have been in the car with Joo. Had he been the real target? Or had she been the target? Did the shooter think she was in the car? Who had wanted to kill Joo? Was it a warning to her?

Why? She didn't like Joo, maybe even hated him, but she hadn't wanted him dead. And then there was the question of why he had wanted to meet her there in that spot, at that time. He had told her he had something for her. She had so many questions.

These thoughts raced through her mind, lingering, causing fear and blinding any clear analysis. She needed to stop somewhere. She needed to compose herself. She concentrated on slowing her breathing. First of all, she realized she needed to find out what was going on right now at that rest area. She took another deep breath.

Fortunately, she was familiar with the area. The Cameron BioTech research building where she had worked was about a mile down the road on the right. She continued down Weaver Lake Road past her former office. A small elementary school was just a bit further past Cameron BioTech. Sunni turned slowly into school parking lot. School would have ended for the day by now; students were gone for the day, but a few staff cars were still in the parking lot. She found an open space between two vehicles near the back of the lot. This was good. She could be anonymous here. She could think. She could pull herself together. She parked, feeling a bit more secure. She remembered a walking trail that led from this lot back about a mile to that rest area. This was all familiar territory. She briefly wondered if that was why Joo had wanted to meet her at that rest area. He knew the area, too. Maybe he'd planned another kind of ambush. Maybe he'd planned a quick getaway on the trail. Her mind was a jumble of thoughts, ideas, and fears.

She sat very still in her idling car. Her trembling had nothing to do with the extreme cold outside. She thought she'd heard the temperature was going to be in the low teens today. The winter air would be biting if she got out. She was sure she was alone here, and safe, but for now the question was what should she do? Where could she go that would be safe? Should she try to get back to the rest area to see what was happening? She was so very, very frightened. And not just frightened for herself. She also had her mother to consider.

Sunni's mother, June, had needed her after she became widowed, and she had needed her mother. In those years after her father died, her sole goal had always been to protect her mother. Her mother still believed Sunni held a highly respectable position in that big research facility, Cameron BioTech. Her parents had been so proud of her. She had always been their darling, perfect daughter. She was so thankful her mother had not discovered the truth about her activities.

Thinking back, Sunni realized her own personal nightmare had begun when Joo Jhim came into their lives. The events of the past several months flitted through Sunni's mind in a fast-forwarded video of nightmarish terror, angst, sorrow and guilt.

She'd thought that if she did what they wanted, it would be over and everything would be fine. It wasn't until after Joo had completely insinuated himself into their lives that she had learned how dangerous Joo was. She had learned that Joo was an operative for some North Korean group. Her mother hadn't known about that. June had liked Joo. But unknown to her mother, Sunni had been forced to become Joo's pawn. She had done everything he'd ordered. She'd had to. Joo had warned her that they would kill her mother if she didn't obey. She'd believed him.

As part of their plan, she had applied to and been hired by Cameron BioTech in Maple Grove as a research assistant right after graduating from Stanford. She had worked hard and had finally become a leader in the genome research program at the labs, just as Joo Jhim had wished. She had done her best to gather information and spirit out the most secret research findings on genome research from Cameron BioTech for Joo and his group, whoever they were. Joo's first demonstration of power over her occurred when she'd watched in shock last year as the Cameron PR director Karen Thompson had been shot by a sniper. She had tried to cover her fear. There was no doubt the group would not hesitate to kill anyone who didn't do as they ordered, including her or her mother. Joo had led her to believe that was true. So she had successfully completed his orders. At least, that was what she'd told Joo. But he hadn't known that she had not shared everything. She hoped he hadn't. She knew she had been playing a dangerous game. But as she thought it through, she was sure her plan had been her only way out. And it had become the only way to protect her mother.

Joo Jhim, the man she'd feared most in her life, had directed her every movement for months now. But now that someone had murdered Joo, she wasn't sure whether she should be relieved or perhaps even more frightened.

What would happen to her now? Who had done this? Why? Who controlled Joo? She believed someone had to be his international boss, but she had never known who it was. She had suspicions, but nothing was concrete. Were they going to come after her, too? And her mother? The questions tumbled into a messy, frightening heap in her mind. Her fear was amplified when she thought about the avenues of escape from here on out.

Her life had changed dramatically in the last year. Now Joo was gone. She sighed and took a deep breath. She had to make a decision. She needed to calm herself. She told herself she was strong. She was smart. She knew a lot. Not everything, of course, but a lot. Thanks to her work at Cameron BioTech, she knew a lot more than those murderers knew. And she had learned a lot about self-preservation in the last year. She had her own bargaining chips – real chips, powerful chips. There would be a way...

CHAPTER THREE
A Name From the Past

Detective Quay Thompson completed filing his reports on his latest case. He'd successfully closed that case. Time to head home. It was already late in the day. It had been a quiet day. The Minnesota BCA offices had now emptied out. Quay leaned back in his leather office chair, stretched out his lanky, six-foot-four frame and stared out at the winter landscape. Icy white frost etched delicate lace-like designs on the corners of his office window. It was peaceful out there, he thought, not unlike his BCA work the last couple months. That was a good thing. He'd needed time to get his life back on track.

After the craziness in October with the SPARTA case and its resolution, he'd needed time to sit back and review what he'd actually found out. SPARTA was The Strategic Populace Against Research Technology in America. What a crazy name, he thought. What a bunch of misinformed, obsessed, crazed people with over-active imaginations. Their protests and actions had created havoc and even murder on behalf of their misguided beliefs.

He reached into his pocket to retrieve a piece of wrapped bubble gum. The bubble gum had replaced his nicotine habit. Using gum to take the place of cigarettes had been his partner, Sam's idea. She'd convinced him that he needed something healthier than cigarettes, and something that would help occupy his hands, mouth, and psyche. It worked fairly well since it gave him a little sugar jolt and something to chew on besides his thoughts.

SPARTA. What a convoluted case it had been, he mused. He was pleased that he and Sam had brought a kind of conclusion to the case of the SPARTA involvement with the Cameron BioTech research thefts last fall. They had finally tied up some loose ends. He'd learned that the sniper who had gunned down his beautiful wife Karen outside Cameron BioTech was probably connected to that group's theft of data at that research facility. The BCA thought they knew the 'why'. The real questions of 'who and how' had still not been answered. Their investigations had reached a dead end. Quay and his partner Samantha Atwood had caught the small fries, a real odd couple; there had been that crazy Ernie Elson. And then there was Charlie Frank, an ego-driven, pseudo-security officer at Cameron. There had been some satisfaction in putting the two of them away. But those arrests hadn't totally solved the case.

Quay and Sam had worked their butts off on that case. The case had taken on so much significance for both of them. As it happened, Sam had nearly been killed near the end. One positive outcome of that case was that it had brought Quay and Sam closer, not just as partners, but also as friends. They had recently begun to tentatively explore where their friendship was going.

It had taken Quay time to move past his grief and anger over losing his wife Karen at the hands that unknown sniper. Both Quay and Sam knew and accepted that his love for Karen would never be diminished. She wouldn't be forgotten. Recognizing that had helped, and in the last months his friendship with Sam had helped him move ahead. He had finally come to some acceptance of the need to move on with his life. But he also knew that until her killer was identified he would never feel totally free from the duty he felt as a cop.

The jangle of his cellphone interrupted his thoughts. He looked at the clock as he reached for the phone. Five forty-five. Past quitting time. He almost let it ring, but at the last second decided to pick it up.

"Hello. Thompson here."

"Yeah, is this Detective Quay Thompson?"

"This is Quay. Who's this?"

"This is Officer Fred Nicholas. I'm with the Minnesota Highway Patrol. We just got a call to a shooting at the rest area off I94 in Maple Grove. Thought you might want to have a look at this one."

"Why is that?" asked Quay, his tone evidenced his disinterest. He wondered why he had been called about this particular shooting. A simple shooting didn't sound like something for the BCA to get involved in.

"Well, the BCA has had a BOLO out for a character who was connected to a case that I think you were associated with last fall. This shooting at the rest area may be of interest to you. Does the name Sunni Hyun mean anything to you?"

Quay abruptly sat up and reached for a note pad and pen. The BCA Be On the Lookout for Sunni Hyun hadn't turned up anything in the months since last fall after she'd disappeared. He'd almost given up hope.

"Sure does. We've had a BOLO on Sunni Hyun since the murders connected to Cameron BioTech last fall. How does she have a connection with this shooting you've got?"

"Well, the guy who was shot was parked at the rest area here in Maple Grove. He's a Korean looking guy. ID says his name is Joo Jhim, that's J-O-O J-H-I-M," he added, spelling out the name for clarification, "It looks like he was sitting in his car parked down at one end of the rest area. A couple witnesses say a dark sedan pulled through the lot and fired a shot into the back window of this Jhim's car. He's dead. The shooter fled."

"Okay," Quay said. His heart began to race. Memories flooded in. "So what's the connection with Sunni Hyun? Other than that he has a Korean name."

"We checked his wallet, ya know. Got his name. Then we noticed he had a business card on the seat next to him with this Sunni Hyun's name on it. It also has her picture on the card. It's the same pic that's on the BOLO. I double-checked just to make sure. The card says she's employed as a research tech at Cameron BioTech. It just rang bells. I remembered seeing the BOLO. And being she's Korean, too, and all, I just figured I'd give you a call. Your name is connected to the BOLO, isn't it?"

"Yeah, yeah, I get it!" Quay stood and in a fluid move grabbed his jacket from the back of his office chair. "You guys stay there. Don't move a thing! Set up a perimeter. I'll be there in no less than a half hour. I've gotta round up my partner. In the meantime, can you get witness names, and as much info as possible? Detain anyone who saw something. I'll see you soon."

"Sure, no problem. I'll meet you here. Name's Fred Nicholas. Ask for me."

As Quay hung up, he glanced at his watch. In quick, long strides, he stepped out of his office and turned to the right. He guessed Sam was finishing up her day, too. Samantha Atwood enjoyed shooting the breeze with their top techie Steve "Boogie" Schroeder. Boogie knew everything there was to know about past and current tech programs, and could retrieve just about anything they needed from the Internet. If they ever had a question, they knew Boogie could come up with a solution. Sam always turned to Boogie for the latest info on tech stuff.

As expected, Quay found Samantha leaning against the doorframe to Boogie's office. Her amber hair had been pulled back into a ponytail. She was wearing skinny jeans and a loose navy sweater with the tails of a long, blue denim shirt peeking out under it. It was the end of the day, and she looked relaxed as she visited with Boogie. Her tall, svelte figure was pressed against the door, her legs crossed at the knees with the tip of one booted foot wedged against the Obi-Wan Kenobi statue that acted as Boogie's doorstop. Slim hands were wrapped around a cup of steaming coffee. She had a sly grin on her face. Quay heard her say, "Oh Boogie, you will win. You always do. Those vultures will never take you down!"

"I'm not gonna let them!" Quay heard Boogie's deep, rumbling voice assuring her.

Quay knew they were talking about Boogie's computer gaming. Boogie had recently explained to them that Vultures were gamers who took spoils of war from other alliances who had fought for them. Boogie, the BCA head tech guy, was deep into gaming. And he hated Vultures."

Quay peered around the corner into Boogie's office and stepped up next to Sam. He took a panoramic view of the room, a room that was a mess in his mind, but one that was organized in Boogie's mind. Stacks of paper sat on every possible space including the windowsill. One laptop and two desk computers worked routinely displaying different programs running simultaneously. Boogie was leaning back in his swivel chair with Nike-clad feet resting on the corner of an open drawer, and a Coke in hand. He glanced over at Quay as he stepped in next to Sam.

"Hey, Quay! Good afternoon. Haven't seen you in an hour or so," he joked. Quay and Sam were his best customers. They kept him very busy doing research or just helping them search out backgrounds on their suspects. "What's up?" he asked.

Quay nodded at Boogie and turned to Sam. "What's up is that we have a possible lead on Sunni Hyun! Remember her?"

"Wow! Sure do!" said Boogie taking his feet down and sitting up at attention.

"Oh yeah!" Sam straightened, voicing her interest. "How did her name come up?"

"Got a call from an officer at a shooting in a rest area over in Maple Grove. Says the victim, some guy with a Korean name, had a business card on the seat in his car with Hyun's name and pic. Want to go see what we can find out?"

"Definitely!" Sam turned to Boogie. "Sorry, Boogie. Gotta go. You'll want to help us with this one, won't you?"

"You betcha! She's the one who took off after you nailed that what's-his-name for those murders connected to Cameron BioTech."

"A real piece of work, that one," Quay added.

"Yup! Now there's a real vulture!" said Boogie. "That guy hated you with a true passion, Quay. I remember he laid all the blame on you and that woman Sunni Hyun. Too bad we didn't catch her, too, to fill in all the answers."

"Well, this may be our opening," said Quay. "We'll keep you posted. Just be ready in case we need you to do some tracking, Boogie."

"Okay, man. I'll be here. I've gotta put in some late hours tonight anyway. I'll be waiting to hear from you. Go get her!"

Quay and Sam turned and walked down the hall. Sam ducked into a doorway next to Quay's office. Her office was smaller than Quay's, but neat and warm. A tufted chair with a soft green throw over the arm angled opposite her desk added a feminine touch. She retrieved a winter wool pea coat with a plaid neck scarf from the coat rack behind the door and pulled them on as she caught up with Quay. They continued down to the elevator together as Quay provided more details about the call he had received from officer Fred Nicholas. In minutes, they were on their way across town to the northwestern suburb of Maple Grove.

The BCA had lost all traces of Sunni Hyun last October. When they'd learned that the two men they'd caught knew only some of the story behind the murders in that case, they realized they still didn't have a complete picture and needed to find Hyun. There was more. Cameron BioTech had been operating on high alert since then. Hyun's complete disappearance indicated guilt in the mindset of the BCA and Quay.

And up to now, Sunni Hyun had not been heard of or seen. Sunni Hyun had vanished. Hyun had already cleared out her office at Cameron before they'd gotten back to the research facility that day after Sam had been kidnapped. The entry security officer said he had seen her leave. The security officer hadn't suspected anything at that point. So, they'd missed her by at least a few hours.

The BOLO for Sunni Hyun had been put in place shortly after the capture of the two men they'd arrested in connection with the case. Quay and the BCA team had tried to trace Sunni's address through her family, but that had led to another dead end. No one seemed to know a thing about her other than her exemplary education history and outstanding achievements as a researcher at Cameron BioTech. The people she'd worked with knew nothing about her personal life. Her address had been listed only as a post office box at the post office in Maple Grove not far from Cameron BioTech. Her father had died, and her mother didn't speak much English and claimed no knowledge of her daughter's whereabouts; she was a no one without any personal life. All they'd gotten were empty answers and dead ends. But one person, the man from Cameron that they'd arrested, had insisted she was a spy. He'd claimed she was his controller. He'd said she was dangerous. But they had no proof. They had no Sunni Hyun.

The most important question for Quay now was how was Sunni Hyun was connected with this Joo Jhim. Maple Grove was the location of the Cameron BioTech facility. And in fact, the rest area wasn't far from the research facility. It looked like the case was coming back to life. Sunni Hyun might be resurfacing again. For Quay, that was an exciting thought. It would great if they could tie up all the loose ends now because of this killing.

CHAPTER FOUR
Something Familiar About That Woman

Quay drove his pickup expertly around and through the rush hour traffic. He'd gotten the truck last fall. It still had that new car smell. His truck was his most precious and expensive possession. A sharp metallic grey, the double-cabbed short box truck had been decked out with all the bells and whistles as well as the extra necessities for a law officer: sirens, lights, computer, gun racks. As he sped toward Maple Grove, he turned on his lights, but not the sirens. No need. Quay knew how to maneuver through the braking cars to find the openings. Samantha Atwood sat back in her seat and gazed out the window at the snow-covered rooftops and quiet streets zipping by. The winter world seemed so peaceful, she thought. But she knew it was just an illusion.

The last two years had been quite a ride for the two of them. This latest call about a murder and the quiet, intense drive to the scene allowed her a few moments to call up memories. She and Quay had gotten off to a rocky start as partners. He had been a recent widower when they were first partnered up. He had a lot of baggage. The combination of his deep love lost and a cop's helplessness left him undone. On the other hand, Sam's life to that point hadn't been easy either. She had never been able to forgive herself for the loss of her stillborn baby. She'd blamed herself. Maybe she'd worked too late, exercised too much. Afterwards, her relationship with her husband had fallen apart, mainly because of the guilt that she carried over the baby's loss; her husband had finally left. But with some counseling and plenty of hard work, she had begun to put her life back together.

When they first began working together, they'd barely spoken to one another about anything other than work-related topics. They just did their jobs. There was no easy bantering and definitely no personal discussion. It was a perfunctory relationship, all work and no play.

But as months went by, Quay and Sam began to work more easily together. They gradually realized they had a lot in common with personal pain. Slowly, they began to respect and trust one another's expertise and experience. A few times Quay had even told Sam she had been right. That had made her laugh. She knew that had been quite an admission. And so it had been the beginning of a good-natured, ongoing banter developing between them. Frequent puns and even pranks centered on gender superiority. Samantha maintained that women had an intuition that made them better at handling perps in the field. Quay baited her by insisting that she was merely guessing, and that because he was a senior officer, he had a better sense of what was truly happening with perps. And he laughed when he got the expected reaction, and promptly blew a bubble with his pink bubble gum and popped it, as an end to the discussion.

His smoking had been another issue. Sam had announced that he needed to quit smoking, not only for his health, but also for hers. He'd finally conceded that he probably should quit but insisted he needed something to substitute for the smokes. He refused to try hypnosis, but he wasn't against trying the nicotine gum. Then it had turned out he couldn't stand the taste of the nicotine gum. So, as a joke, Sam had suggested he try bubble gum instead. "You know, you've got the bubble gum light on top of the truck, why not add the bubble gum to complete your whole image? I think it might work, Quay," she'd teased. He'd taken her up on it as a lark. And it had worked. He was still chewing his bubble gum, blowing bubbles, and grinning that quirky, lopsided grin every time he popped a huge, pink bubble.

He could be fun, but Samantha also realized that beyond being fun, Quay was an extremely smart, nononsense man. She respected him. He dug into a case and stayed with it until he had the last perp nailed. But underneath it all, she knew he was a very caring, sensitive man. He had built that protective armor around himself after his wife's murder. Now, in those moments when he allowed the softer side to come through, he was thoughtful, kind, and fun to be around.

Quay wasn't too hard to look at either, she mused as she glanced at his chiseled profile. Tall, with Scandinavian clean-cut good looks and apparently uncontrollable thick, blond hair, Quay's blue eyes could twinkle or pierce right through you, depending upon the occasion. He worked out regularly, lifted weights, and ran several times a week. When he was with Sam, he jokingly referred to himself as a lean, mean, bubble gum machine.

Sometimes, just to prove a point, he'd blow huge, pink bubbles and pop them. Of course, they would appear at the most inopportune times. The snapping crack of the bubble followed by a lopsided smirk totally disarmed her. Glancing toward her for a reaction, he'd break into a huge, happy grin. "You're impressed with my unique talent, aren't you?" he'd ask. She'd look at him and shake her head, but couldn't help smiling to herself.

After Sam's kidnapping near the end of the Cameron BioTech/SPARTA case, Quay had shared with Sam his fear of losing her, too, like he'd lost his wife. He had grieved for his wife intensely, and had no intention of going through anything like that again with his partner. He'd told her that he thought he was at a point where he could move on with his life, but he also needed to protect Sam so she was never in that kind of danger again.

There was still Sunni Hyun. The call Quay had just received was bringing it all back. Sam and Quay had assumed Sunni was the brains behind the whole scheme. Sunni Hyun had eluded arrest, and they thought she had probably fled the country; so, the case was only partially settled. Sunni Hyun was still on the Most Wanted list, and they had placed this BOLO on her. The sudden reappearance of her name had brought it back full circle. Finally, they might have a real lead on Sunni Hyun. That small woman was the enormous key to the entire Cameron BioTech case and the murders connected to it.

Sam glanced at Quay as he maneuvered his truck through the traffic on the freeway. Obviously lost in thought, Quay chewed his bubble gum and blew frequent bubbles. She laughed a bit.

"What a guy!" she murmured.

"What?" Quay demanded. "What'd I do now?"

"Nothing, Just watching you and your bubble gum!" Sam answered, smiling as she looked away and out the window.

Knowing Quay as she now did, Sam realized this final possible link to solve the Cameron BioTech case might provide the last of the answers they needed before they could completely move on as partners in life, too. They'd just have to see where this led them, she thought.

Quay spotted the rest area on the opposite side of the freeway, drove past it heading west until he could reach an exit to turn around and head back east to the rest area entrance.

"Looks like the guys have closed it off," he said as he pointed to the police cars down the road closing off the right lanes of traffic. Traffic was backed up and moving very slowly, giving the gawkers ample time to try to figure out what had happened.

Pointing to the lake on both sides of the highway, he said, "This has to be a bit of heaven in the midst of suburbia for these people. It looks like it's really built up around the lake. Shopping center back there. Big houses around the lake. Looks like the lake might even be fishable. Thought I saw a fish house back on the other side."

"Yeah, I don't get out this way very often. I drive by here if I'm heading to St. Cloud or west to Alexandria. It's a nice area. There are several lakes out here."

Quay unwrapped another fresh piece of bubble gum, carefully wrapped his used gum in the wrapper and tossed it in his trash bag next to the console before popping the new lump into his mouth. He signaled to the patrols as he pulled onto the exit to the rest area. Police cars blocked the entrance. He wound down his window, flashed his badge, and asked where he might find the State Highway patrolman, Fred Nicholas.

"He's near the back of the lot by the car with the body. Nobody's been through, yet," explained the cop as he pointed out the direction.

Quay thanked him and drove through to the back of the lot and parked. He and Sam got out, looked around spotting several uniforms and walked over to the car with the shattered rear window. Sam pulled her scarf over her face against the biting winter air.

"It must be near zero," she commented to Quay.

"Yeah," agreed Quay as he pulled his gloves on and pulled up his collar. He wished he'd worn his heavy down jacket and a cap.

A medium-built man with a State Highway Patrol uniform approached them.

"Quay Thompson?"

"Yes sir," Quay responded reaching to shake hands.

"Fred Nicholas. Glad to see you. You made good time."

"This case might be just what we've been hoping for," Quay commented. "This is my partner, Samantha Atwood," he said nodding at Sam by way of introduction. "She's worked on this case with me. Samantha, this is the man who called about the BOLO."

"Good to meet you," Fred said, shaking her hand.

"Can we get a look at the vehicle and the body?" asked Quay.

"Sure. Just come over here. Watch where you step. There's some glass here. We had to open the doors. Glass fragments all over."

"You had to open both doors?" asked Quay. "Why did you have to open the rear door?"

"Well, it's because of that," explained Fred as he pointed to a dog sitting in the back of a nearby patrol car.

"A dog?" said Sam and Quay in unison.

"Yeah. The guy had a dog in the back seat," explained Fred. "The dog was frantic. With the glass all over and the blood and mess, we decided we'd better get him out. Looks like a fairly young golden retriever. He's got a dog tag that says Chip. The dog seems to answer to the name. We put him in the patrol car to get him out of the way. He's pretty well behaved considering what he's been through. Don't know what we'll do with him, though."

"Poor thing," Sam muttered. "I can't imagine what it must be thinking. It must be scared out of its wits."

"Yeah, he was. He's calming down now a bit. We gave him some water, and the local K-9 cop came by with some treats. That helped."

"Any witnesses to the shooting?" asked Quay, turning back to the vehicle with the body.

"Not really. We had a few people pull in shortly after the shooting. They heard the dog barking and then saw the shattered rear window. They called 911. We also had a couple high school kids walk up. They were fishing across the lake and heard the shot. They are pretty shook up, too. We asked everyone to wait inside the building. Thought you might want to question them."

"Good. That might help, I guess."

Quay was bending over looking through the driver's side window at the body of the man slumped over the steering wheel. He appeared to be fairly short and slim. He had dark hair streaked with grey. Hard to tell his age, he thought. But maybe in his 40's. His face was pretty well gone. The shot had hit him in the back of the head and exploded out the front top of the skull taking a major portion of his face with it. He looked at the bits of bone, grey matter, and blood splashed over the dashboard and windshield. The shooter had to have been a pro to make that kind of a shot from a moving vehicle, Quay thought. It looked almost like a sniper hit. It was amazing the dog hadn't been shot. It must have been lying down at the time.

"You said you found a business card with Sunni Hyun's name on it?"

"Yeah, it was on the seat beside this guy. I opened the glove compartment and found the car registration. That's where I got the name. Joo Jhim. Says he lived in Otsego. That's not too far north of here. We haven't moved anything else."

"Okay," said Quay. "Let's get the BCA crime scene team in here to process it. We need to let them get their work done. Sam, will you give them a call, and then call Boogie and see what he can dig up on Joo Jhim. Then we can move the body to the morgue and see what we have."

"Yup. I'm on it. Let's go talk to those boys," Sam suggested as she pulled out her cell phone.

"Okay. Fred, will you wait around? I may want to talk to you some more, since you were first on the scene."

"No problem. I might wait in my car or inside. It's getting colder out here. I'm about frozen already!"

The lights had come on at the rest area. Night was definitely settling in. Temperatures were dropping to an anticipated zero degrees for the night.

"Sure. Come inside when you get everything set up. Let's keep the area closed off."

Quay looked at the young dog sitting up alertly in the patrol car. It stood as he walked by and gave out a short woof. The inquisitive gaze of the dark brown eyes followed him for several steps. Quay turned away and heard another short woof followed by a long whine.

He turned back and said, "I'll be back in a minute, buddy. Just lie down for a bit." He watched as the dog settled down onto the seat.

Two boys were huddled together next to the vending machines in one corner of the waiting area. Their white faces were plain evidence of the fright they experienced.

"Hi, I'm Quay Thompson," Quay said as he approached the boys. "This is my partner, Samantha Atwood. You must be the boys who heard the shots."

"I'm Matt," said the taller one.

"I'm Brett."

They stood at once to face Quay and Sam. "Glad to meet you," said Quay as he and Sam shook their hands.

Samantha took over the questioning. She and Quay intuitively understood that a woman would be the best person to ask the questions in this situation. She gathered name and ID information from the boys. Then she began to ask for details.

"So, where were you fellas?"

Brett spoke up first. "We went out on Rice Lake to fish after school. We usually fish over on the big side of the lake. It's deeper there, better fishing."

"What time did you go out?" asked Sam.

The boys looked at one another.

"I'd say we were out on the lake by 3:30," answered Matt. "We'd just set up our fish house. It's a portable. We were getting ready to fish, then the wind picked up. It almost blew the fish house across the lake with me in it. Brett had to chase me down." Matt smiled as he remembered the incident.

"Yeah, I'd gone out to check the pegs holding it and it took off with him in it." Brett smiled and the boys shared an embarrassed laugh. "We ended up a lot closer to the highway and the rest area than we normally go," added Brett.

"So when did you hear the shot? Do you have any idea of the approximate time?"

Quay was eyeing the boys with a steely look. They were good witnesses. They had obviously calmed down a bit now so that they could tell their story. They weren't in trouble. Sam's compassionate tone gave them more assurance.

Matt and Brett answered in unison.

"About 4:00."

"About 4:10."

"So sometime around four o'clock? Is that right?"

"Yes," said Brett. Matt nodded.

"And after you heard the shot, what did you do?"

Matt took over the story telling.

"Well, we were outside of the fish house, because we'd just gotten it stopped. We both recognized that the sound was a gunshot and not Jake brakes. The semis are always making a lot of noise with Jake brakes. But this wasn't the same. It was definitely a gunshot."

"We both hunt," Brett added by way of explanation.

Matt took over again. "So when we looked up at the rest area, there was a dark sedan that went racing out. I couldn't really tell what color. Black or dark blue or dark green, maybe."

"Yeah," Brett agreed. "We figured that guy must have been involved or the guy was scared and got out of there. There've been problems over here with drug dealing. We hear about that all the time. Our parents always say we're supposed to stay clear of the rest area. I guess we both thought that was what it was."

"Did you see where the car went?" Sam asked.

"Not really," said Matt. "It was just barreling down the highway. Cars on the freeway were slamming on their brakes all over the place because the guy pulled out right in the middle of traffic."

"Do you know it was a guy?"

"No. Not really. Couldn't see that well. Just thought it probably was."

"Okay. Did you see any other cars leave the rest area after that?"

Brett said thoughtfully, "Yeah, there was one other car that left after that. But it exited the rest area and wasn't driving fast or anything. Just drove up the road."

"Do you know what make or color that car was?"

"Not really," said Brett.

Matt added, "I think it might have been a Toyota Camry or something like that. It looked a lot like our car. It was dark colored, too. Maybe black."

"Well," sighed Sam, "you guys have really helped. We are so glad you came up here to tell us what you saw. That was good. We'll probably be in touch with you again. Do you have a way to get back home?"

"Not really," said Brett. "We hiked across the freeway and left everything out on the lake."

"We'll get a patrol car to get you back to get your rods and stuff and take you home. They'll get all your information, too, in case we need to talk to you again." Quay looked at his watch. "It's already getting dark. You can pick up the icehouse tomorrow. I don't think it's going to go anywhere tonight anyway," said Quay. "Thanks, guys. Like Sam says, we really do appreciate your help."

"Let us give you our cards," said Sam. "If you think of anything else, don't hesitate to call." She and Quay both handed each of them a business card. Sam walked the boys out to a patrol car and gave the officer directions to deliver the boys to their homes.

Quay returned to Fred Nicholas' patrol car. Nicholas was sitting inside with the car running. The young dog was lying down in the back seat. It had been sleeping until Quay got in.

When Quay climbed into the front passenger seat, the dog jumped up, placed its paws on the back of the seat, leaned forward, and planted a wet slurp up the side of Quay's face. Quay ducked, but made the mistake of turning at the same time to look at the dog. It managed to give him another sloppy kiss on the mouth. Its tail was wagging happily.

"Kisses, huh? Looks like he thinks you're his master," commented Fred. "Got any pets at home?"

"Nope, and I don't think I'd have time for any," said Quay wiping his face with his sleeve. "He sure is friendly, though. Considering what he's been through, I'm surprised he isn't cowering in the back seat." He reached around to the back to pat the dog.

"He seems to be pretty mellow. He must have been well taken care of. He listens to commands. I even got him to shake hands a while ago."

"Yeah?" Quay absently stroked the dog's head and rubbed its ears as the dog leaned closer in toward him.

"What'd you find out with the boys? Anything useful?" asked Nicholas.

"I think they may have been a little help. They said they saw two cars leave after the shot. The first practically smashed into oncoming traffic as it took off out of here. The second one followed soon after, but didn't seem to be driving as erratically. The one kid thought the second one might have been a Toyota.

"So, I had Sam call our techie. We'll try to see if we can come up with something on Joo Jhim. We need to get more info on those two cars, though. Are there surveillance cameras around here?"

"I checked just after we got here. Yes. There is one camera on each ramp coming in and going out, and there are two cameras for surveillance of the parking lot. We should be able to get something from that. I notified the state that we would need to get those films."

"Good!" said Quay. "Good job. As soon as the Crime Scene guys finish up, we can move the body out and load up the car. We'll have the car taken in for a more thorough look. It should only be a hour or so, and we'll be done."

"Okay. I'll check in with the rest of the guys and let them know. What do you want to do with the dog? We don't want to take him into a shelter this late," said Nichols.

Quay paused for a second mulling over the dilemma.

"I'm guessing the crew will want to check the dog out, too. It's strange that the dog was in the car with the guy. If he was just sitting in his car, he must have been planning on meeting someone. It's too cold to just park and sit here. We need those camera feeds to see how long he was here. I'll take the dog with me over to the offices. We'll figure out what to do with him from there after he gets checked out by our vet."

Fred was right, he thought. It was getting colder.

Quay jumped at a sudden, hard rapping on the passenger window next to his ear. In back, the dog gave one sharp bark in surprise, sniffed the air, and then began wagging its tail happily. Dark eyes of a small middle-aged Asian woman peered in through the frost-laced window. She wore a purple wool coat pulled tightly around her dumpling frame. A bright pink knit cap slouched down over her eyebrows. Wisps of grey hair framed her round face.

Quay lowered the window halfway. The dog edged its nose up to the window, sniffed out frosty puffs of breath, and then wagged happily. Quay reached back over his shoulder to push the dog down. The woman moved closer. He couldn't imagine that she could have gotten any closer as she leaned in toward him. She could have passed for Mrs. Claus, he thought, except for the glasses that framed her eyes with thick, round, bottle-glass lenses.

"Can we help you?" Quay leaned back a bit, his tone indicating he really didn't want to be bothered.

"Hello. I'm Mrs. Foster, Patty Foster." She glanced into the back seat at the dog, and then returned her attention to Quay. "I saw you talking to the boys back there inside. I asked the woman in there, but she sent me out here to you. Told me you were in charge. Are you in charge here?"

"I am. What can I do for you?"

"Well, I was just wondering if we could go soon? I was the last one to come into the rest area, you know. I got here after that mess happened over there. I really need to get home. But the lady said I had to ask you."

"Did anyone interview you?" asked Quay.

"Yes, one of the police officer's people asked me a couple questions. But I really didn't see anything. What happened, anyway? Was it a murder? Do you know who it was? Who did it?"

"We are really just gathering information right now. We don't have anything to report, yet."

"Well, I can tell you what it was," she interrupted. "I bet it was a drug deal gone bad! I hear there's a lot of that around here. Just last week, I heard from my neighbor that someone had been arrested up here for dealing drugs. You know the kids come up here all the time. They hang out. It's not a good place. Those teens, you know. Nothing but trouble. And all that..."

Quay cut her off. "Yes ma'am. We will check into all of that. Just leave your name, address, and telephone number with the lady inside." He tried to hide his grin. That would pay Sam back. She'd never get rid of this woman!

"Well, I tell you, this is no surprise," she continued without a pause. "We all know it. You need to do something about this. It's ruining the value of the homes around here!"

Before Quay could answer, she turned away pulling her coat tighter around her hunched over body, ducking her head into her collar as she shuffled up the icy walk to the building. The dog stood in the back seat and barked several sharp barks after her. Quay commanded it to sit and be quiet.

Quay had noticed the woman was wearing canvas clogs. No boots. That was unusual in this extremely cold weather. And she'd had small cotton gloves on her hands. Her hands looked too small, disproportionate with a body as large as hers. And her coat really didn't fit a body that large. She was pulling it closed in front. Interesting, he thought. Something off about her.

He raised his window and then decided to follow up on his hunch. Quay pulled his phone out of his pocket, and speed dialed Sam.

"Sam!" he said, before she even got the full word out.

"What?"
"That woman you sent out here?"
"What woman?"

"You know the one headed your way, coming up the walk now."

"I don't see her."

Quay looked back toward the building. He didn't see her either. Where had she gone? He turned and did a full 360 view of the lot. The woman was nowhere in sight.

"Fred, where'd she go? Did you see?"

"Nope, I was watching the dog. Not her."

Quay jumped out of the car and hurried over to a nearby patrol car. He knocked on the window and called with his demand at the same time.

"Hey! Did you see where that woman went?"

The officer looked up, startled, and rolled down his window.

"Uh, no. I guess I wasn't paying much attention. I was writing up a report on the computer here. Did she go in the building?"

"Nope. Not there."

"In another car?"

"Not sure. I can have the guys check the cars again. What'd she look like?"

Quay gave him a brief description and was already turning to walk away from the patrol car before he answered.

"Do that. Something familiar about that woman."

CHAPTER FIVE
The Decision

The winter air was biting at Sunni Hyun's exposed cheeks as she hurried along the snow-covered trail leading back to her car. She'd waited until she was out of sight of the rest area building before pulling the wads of cotton out of her mouth. She had stuffed her cheeks and lower lip with cotton balls to fill out her face. Blue contact lenses, thick black-framed glasses, a grey wig under the pink knit cap, and a blanket folded twice and belted around her mid-section, had changed her appearance completely. Her coat wouldn't button though. That had been a problem. But she'd managed to make it work. She was glad she always carried a bag with disguise material in it. Who'd have thought several years ago that she'd be in need of a disguise in the spur of the moment? It had come in handy several times already.

Chip, the dog had nearly ruined it, though, she thought. The golden retriever had recognized her. She was sure of it. But the officer hadn't picked up on his friendly wagging tail. Thank God! She wondered what would happen to the pup. Both she and her mother had truly loved that dog. She'd never had a pet before Joo brought Chip home as a small puppy.

Joo. She thought about him. Thought about his call. Joo was definitely dead. She had gotten the information that she needed for now. And she'd learned the cops had no idea why he'd been shot or who'd done it.

But then, neither did she. That was what she needed to find out. Who and why? It was entirely possible that she could be the next target.

She was fairly certain no one had taken notice of her driving through the parking lot just after Joo had been killed. Any other people in the rest area had to have been focused on the car with the back window blasted to smithereens. It would take them a while to find out that her car had also driven away. And with any luck, they would never find out anything. She began to relax.

Chip. There was the dog. She needed the dog. And, at the moment there was another special chip that concerned Sunni more. She shuddered as a chill ran through her body. This time it wasn't from the cold. She remembered the RFID microchip Joo had implanted in her upper arm. She guessed Joo must have had one, too. The Radio Frequency Identification microchip served as a tracker. When Joo had told her she would be working for him, he had told her that his boss had said she must allow him to place the RFID chip under her skin on the inside of her upper arm. He said no one would notice the slight bump. She knew it meant that she could be tracked wherever she went. They'd probably tracked Joo, too. Whoever they were. And they'd killed him. Now they could be tracking her, too.

She'd had no choice about the chip. He'd drugged her first. He had known she would never have allowed him to put a tracking device on her. She'd screamed and cursed while he laughed. She remembered the burning pain when Joo held her arm down and injected the chip with a small gun. She would never forget his domineering face and piercing black eyes. She knew the chip meant that she could never get away from him. He used that knowledge to remind her of his power over her. He would drop little comments into their conversations when her mother was present.

"Did you enjoy your trip to the movies today? Did you see...?" And then he'd name the current movies at the theater. Or he'd ask, "How fast were you driving on

I35W today? Were you going to your classes? Your mother worries about you, you know."

He'd always had enjoyed taunting her like that. He'd do it in front of her mother, sounding so interested and attentive. He'd wanted her to know that her mother just thought he was concerned. But Sunni knew he'd been reminding her that he knew everything she did. She'd lived in constant fear for so long now. Fear for her life, but also for her mother's life. She had no doubt that he would hurt her mother, just to keep Sunni in line.

Now he was gone. She couldn't imagine who had gotten rid of Joo Jhim, but she would be eternally grateful for that! Joo was an operator for powerful people. They were not only powerful they were also killers. That chip explained how they had known where Joo was. Her relief had turned to fear as she realized those people must have controlled Joo, too. They also had to have known the location was perfect for their ambush. Maybe they had set it up. She shivered. She had to figure out how to remove the tracking device from her arm immediately. It would provide her location to the killers.

Sunni was puffing in fear as well as anger by the time she reached her car. She climbed in and started the engine. She thought it would be best to let it warm up a bit before she left the school parking lot. She turned the fan and defroster on full blast to clear the frost from her windshield. It would only take a few minutes. A plan was forming. First, she would call her mother, tell her about Joo's murder, and reassure her that she was all right. After that, she would remove the tracking chip. Then she had another call to make. She'd decided that one was probably the most important call she would make.

CHAPTER SIX
A Dog Named Chip

Winter's night had settled in with its biting edge. Quay grabbed the collar of the young golden retriever and led it to his truck. The dog eagerly jumped into the back seat. As Quay slid into the driver's seat, the pup stretched across the seat toward Quay and gave Quay a quick slurp of appreciation on his ear. Quay jumped away, and turned to look at the pup; it promptly planted another wet kiss right on Quay's mouth, just as it had earlier.

"Ugh! Dog! What's that for? You're sure a friendly fella!" Quay reached around to the back, pushed the dog back, and scratched the dog's ear. The dog wagged more happily and slapped a paw onto Quay's arm as if it was holding onto him.

So they said the dog was named Chip. At least that's what the tag on his collar said. He happily greeted Sam with a wagging tail as she climbed into the truck. Sam turned in her seat to greet the pup.

"Hi, fella! You're a good boy. Now you need to sit. Can you sit?"

The dog looked intently at Sam with its liquid brown eyes and promptly sat.

"Awww, good dog!" Sam cooed as she reached back to pat the obedient dog.

"What are you going to do with him, Quay?"

"I don't have the faintest idea. We need to get him checked him out. I'll have to take him in to see if he's micro chipped. We assume the owner is the guy who was shot. We'll follow up. If he doesn't have a home, I guess we'll have to turn him over to animal control. They'll probably keep him at the Humane Society."

"He's so friendly and so cute! And seems to be really smart!" Sam said as she reached back again to scratch the dog's ears.

Chip wagged his tail harder and gave out a small groan of appreciation.

"Aw! Poor fella. He has been through a lot today. He's so sweet. I want him!!"

"Well, let's wait and see. Do you really think you have room for him at your place?"

Sam knew Quay had a small home north of the Twin Cities. She only had a two-bedroom place on the third floor of a small apartment complex.

"Well, no, I can't have a dog there." Sam paused and then brightened. "But you could take him! We could share him." Sam emphasized the 'you' as she smiled at Quay.

"Right! Like I'd have time to care for a dog. Let's just find out what they tell us about him first, before we make any decisions or claims."

Quay turned to the dog and said, "You'd better sit down, Chip. We're going for a ride."

Chip gave out a soft woof and settled down contentedly on the backseat.

Quay was just about to put the truck in gear when the phone in his pocket rang and automatically transferred to his audio on the car phone. Quay looked at the ID and sighed. He didn't recognize the number, probably a misdial or one of those irritating robo calls. But he clicked the answer button on his steering wheel anyway.

"BCA, Thompson," he announced.

"Is this Quay Thompson?" The soft voice was a woman's.

"Yes. What can I help you with?" His voice didn't hide the irritation he felt.

"I need your help. They are going to kill me! I can't get away from them." The voice was breathless, whispered, feminine. Frightened. She had a slight accent. Maybe Asian. The l's came across as a soft 'r' sound.

"I know you have been looking for me," she continued. I have information you want. I can solve one of your cases. Just help me, please!" Her words were rushed and running together.

"Who is this?" Thompson demanded. "This had better not be a prank. How'd you get this number? I'm not in the mood for pranks tonight."

"Sunni Hyun." She paused and repeated, "This is Sunni Hyun."

Quay Thompson sucked in his breath and looked at Sam. She had been listening to the phone call, too. They turned simultaneously to scan the area. Where was she?

"Sunni Hyun? Sunni Hyun. Really? I'm supposed to believe that. You're calling me?" Quay's voiced skepticism was real? "Why? How do I know it's really you? And how did you get this number?"

Thompson felt like his heart had just stopped. The dog raised his head at the different tone in Quay's voice. Quay reached around for the pup absently reassuring him with a few strokes on his head.

The call out of the blue was more than just unexpected. Why would she call him? She had been on the run for several months now. If this was really Sunni Hyun, it was an unimaginable stroke of...what? It was more than a stroke of luck. It had to be a trap of some kind. If this truly were Hyun on the phone, it would be the biggest catch of his career. She was at the top of his Most Wanted List. She was the key to many of the questions they still had about the Cameron BioTech case.

She had to know that. Why would she call? And why now?

"I need help! Now! Please! I can give you information." Her urgent pleading came across in a shrill voice. It certainly sounded real enough. Whoever this woman was, she was clearly frightened. "They are going to kill me if I don't get to safety," she continued. "They have been following me. Someone has already died today. You know about the shooting at the rest area in Maple Grove."

"Yeah! I know about it."

"I have information. I need protection. Please!" The woman's voice rose in pitch with each plea. She was panting and nearly whimpering now.

Thompson paused a full fifteen seconds as he listened to the caller's labored breathing. He looked again at Sam silently questioning what she thought. She nodded. He made his decision. This was all or nothing.

"All right. Where are you? How will I meet you?

The caller let out a huge sigh of relief. She continued to speak in a soft voice rushing her words.

"You can find me in the parking lot of an elementary school off Weaver Lake Road in Maple Grove. Drive into the lot. Park your car and flash your headlights twice. I will come to you when I think it's safe. Don't bring anyone. I will get into your passenger seat."

Quay processed the scenario. Not really safe. He needed to bring Sam. Samantha Atwood was the one person who knew how important this move would be.

"Can't do that," Quay responded.

The woman began to object with another urgent plea. He interrupted her.

"I will bring my partner. She'll be in the back seat. You get in the front passenger seat. Do you have weapons on you?"

"No weapons."

"Make sure you don't. My partner will have you covered. How will I know you?"

"I'll be wearing a navy blue pea coat with a white scarf."

"I'll be there in a truck. It'll take me a few minutes to get there. Can you hold on that long?"

"I think so. I hope so. They are looking for me, but I don't think they know what I'm driving or what direction I went after the hit."

"The hit? You mean the shooting at the rest area?"

"Yes. It was a hit. I think I'm next."

"Stay put. Keep down in your car. I'll be driving a dark grey Toyota Tundra. I'll pull in to the back of the lot and flash my lights twice when I pull in."

"Hurry." It was an urgent demand. Then she hung up.

Quay hung up and turned to Sam.

"Sam? What do you think?"

"I think we're going for a drive."

Sam quickly popped her door open, got out, and moved to the rear door of Quay's truck. She opened it carefully, not wanting the dog to jump out and run. The pup got up. seeming to know what to do, moved over to the opposite side of the seat and sat down. It had made room for Sam.

"Wow! Look at that, Quay! I'm impressed," Sam marveled. "We really have to keep this dog," The dog leaned toward Sam and slurped her on the cheek.

"Okay, good boy. Now lie down. We're going for a ride," Sam told the dog. Chip looked at her intently and obeyed as if he understood this was important.

Quay pulled out onto the freeway.

"We have to keep him with us for now. I don't have time to drop him off. I can't believe we just got a call from someone claiming to be Sunni Hyun. Do you think it's real, Quay?"

"Well, she said she knows about this shooting at the rest area. She said she thinks she's next. Wants to come in for protection. And she wants me to meet up with her. I guess we can't take a chance that it's not for real. Just be on guard."

"I know. Can you believe it? Quay, this could be a trap. Let's be very careful."

"Let's do a drive by first. Take a look at the scenery. Then we'll decide what to do."

"Should you call it in?"

"Not yet. I want to check it out without making a big scene. I have a hunch we need to keep this quiet for now."

"I'm just trying to wrap my mind around this. Sunni Hyun completely disappeared after we nailed the insider from Cameron BioTech. He claimed he didn't know where she went. So she's been on the run since October. Where's she been? Why come in now?"

"Good questions. That's what I want to ask her. If it's really her, she's got a lot of information that we want. And we might not want others to know we've got her until we know what we've got."

Quay exited the freeway and turned right onto Weaver Lake Road. Another mile down the road they saw the signs for the elementary school. Quay slowed and scanned the lot. He counted eight cars in the parking lot.

One car was set apart at the back of the lot. No one appeared to be around or in the other cars.

"That must be her at the back of the lot," said Quay. "That's the same kind of car one of the boys said he thought he'd seen leaving the rest area. What do you think, Sam?"

"Looks okay right now from what I see. There's nothing else around here. It's all marshland across the road. What do you want to do?"

Quay continued past the parking lot entrance. "I think we'll turn around down here and stop. I need you to keep that little Chipster quiet. I want Hyun to get up in front here. But you cover her. You think that will work?"

Sam nodded. "I think we can make it work. What's the plan once we get her? You gonna take her back to headquarters?"

"We've gotta take her someplace secure. Let's find out if we've got a safe house somewhere around here. Let's call in now. Will you? Then we call Super Mike. I'm sure Mike will give us permission to hold her. If we get Hyun, we can take her to a safe house, but we can't let it get out that we have her. "

CHAPTER SEVEN
Eluding the Trackers

Joo was dead. They had found him and killed him. Sunni Hyun huddled down behind the steering wheel. If she couldn't get rid of her tracker, she knew they would be after her next. She had escaped--–for now. She had not started her car. She didn't want anyone to spot an idling car. It would raise awareness she didn't want.

She was shaking from the freezing cold; but more than that, she was shaking from pure terror. The more she thought about Joo and the shooting, the more she realized how close she had come. Her life was in danger, too. Whoever they were, they had known where he was. She was supposed to have met Joo at that rest area. They must have known that. They must have been worried about something not going well. Maybe it was because Joo hadn't given them what they wanted, or because she hadn't come through for Joo. Maybe they had discovered that she had held back information. Maybe there was even more she didn't know about Joo. Maybe…

Now Sunni had decided she had to move quickly. She must do one thing before she left the car–before Quay Thompson came to pick her up. She reached for the fanny pack she carried and rummaging through it found what she was looking for. She carried a small pocketknife with her at all times. It was amazing how often it came in handy.

Slipping her wool coat off her left arm, she pulled her arm out of her sweater sleeve. She pressed her trembling fingers on her upper arm, feeling for the lump under her flesh. She found it on the inside fatty part of her arm. It was a small pencil eraser size bump. She pushed on it. She tried to slide it around. It moved a tiny bit.

Flipping open the pocketknife with her right hand, she used her index finger to pinpoint the spot. She held her breath, and then she used the knife to make a small pin-sized incision on top of the bump.

This was going to hurt all right. But being shot wouldn't begin to compare to this little nick. It had to be done. She took a deep breath, held it, and made two quick slashes into her skin marking an X over the top of the chip. Hissing a puff of foggy, cold air through her teeth, she peeled back the corner flap of skin and dug the point of the knife under the chip. Warm, red blood was trickling down her arm now. The pain was intense, and she began to sweat. She lifted the chip with the knife, and her vision blurred as she became light-headed.

Must be shock. I can't pass out now, she told herself. Gritting her teeth and sucking in her breath, she placed the point of the knife deeper behind and further under the chip and gave it a quick, sharp tug. The chip tipped up, but didn't come completely out. Retching with the pain, she made one more stab at the chip, catching it again with the tip of her knife and carefully lifting it up and out. She released the breath she had been holding, and sat back panting. She'd done it. The small metal square looked non-threatening. It looked deceptively innocent, but she understood the enormity of what that tiny thing could do.

Her arm throbbed at the cut, and her blood ran in small, red rivulets down her arm. She reached into her fanny pack for her packet of tissues. Pulling a wad of tissues out, she used her free hand to fold them and press them over the wound. She would have to sanitize it later. She held the tissues tight for a minute and then pulled the sleeve of her shirt carefully over the tissues and pressed harder on the soggy lump. Holding the tissues in place under her sleeve, she thought about what to do with the chip. There would have to be someone close to her to get a reading on it, she thought. She was fairly certain they hadn't followed her yet, but they would certainly begin by searching the immediate area. And if they were as advanced as she feared they were, a tracking device would eventually zero in on the chip, especially if they happened to drive by during their search. She palmed the small device. Maybe the best thing would be to destroy it. Or maybe she should throw it out the window. She couldn't decide.

Headlights flashed on her windshield. She watched the oncoming lights find their way. A truck was pulling into the parking lot. Sunni sank down further behind the steering wheel, peeking through her passenger frost-rimed window at the truck as it slowly moved to the back of the lot near her car. Then the headlights flashed twice. This was it. It was Quay Thompson. She was almost safe. She hoped this was the right decision. She thought to herself it didn't really matter; either way, she could be dead. This option, she decided, gave her the best chance of survival that she was going to get. This nightmare had to end.

She flashed her lights in return and waited as the truck pulled in next to her car.

Sunni watched the truck's darkened driver side window slide down revealing the face of BCA detective Quay Thompson at the wheel. She lowered her window to look up at Thompson. She recognized his face. His expression was unreadable. He was staring at her with piercing blue eyes, searching her face and the interior of her car. Holding her breath, she inched up in the seat.

Her arm was aching now. Blood had begun to seep through the wadded tissues and through her sleeve. She could feel warm wetness dripping down her arm.

"Sunni Hyun? Are you ready to go?" Thompson's voice was deep, demanding. He'd spoken in a terse, no nonsense voice.

This was it. She had made her decision. She was going to save her mother and maybe even save herself, too. Overall, she was worried about her mother more than herself. If they got to her mother, she knew they would try to use her mother as a bargaining chip to get to her. They were cruel. They had no moral conscience. She'd just witnessed that. She had to convince Thompson to help protect her mother, first.

"Yes, I'm ready," she answered firmly with a confidence that belied her fear. She raised her window, grabbed her things, pushed open the door, slid out, and paused to look once more at Thompson. He nodded at her in approval and agreement. She moved quickly around the truck to the open passenger door and scrambled into the front seat. A dog gave a sharp woof from the back seat as she climbed in. Sunni turned to eye the dog with surprised recognition showing on her face. "Chip!" she exclaimed in delight and relief.

Sam leaned forward, pushed the dog back onto the seat, and brought her left hand holding a small gun around from the back of the passenger head rest, raised it to Sunni's line of sight and dug it solidly into Sunni Hyun's shoulder to let her know she was under guard.

"Good evening, Sunni. I'm Samantha Atwood, Quay's partner. So glad to have you join us. Are you armed? Do you have weapons?" She reached around the seat and firmly patted Sunni Hyun's chest and sides.

"No. I have nothing. I'm not armed." Her voice was soft but her slight accent made the 'r' sound like 'h'. Sam thought she sounded like she was saying she wasn't *ahmed*.

Thompson turned to study the young woman as Sam finished the pat down. She appeared to be a mere slip of a young woman, almost girlish in appearance, with porcelain skin and dark eyes. Wisps of jet-black hair circled her face beneath her knit cap. She wore an oversized quilted jacket with a fringed winter scarf wrapped around her neck and pulled over her mouth. Dark eyes returned his scrutiny with a defiant glare as she lifted her chin. He reached out to her, pulled the scarf away from her face, and then grabbed her arm. She winced and yelped as he stretched it toward him, and he saw the bloody material of her sleeve.

"What happened? Are you injured?"

"Nothing major. I'll explain when we are out of here. We don't have much time. I think we'd better get away from here. They'll be coming."

As if to provide veracity to her statement, headlights from a car suddenly flashed through the windshield as it pulled slowly into the parking lot and drew their eyes back to the entrance. Then it paused. Headlight beams streamed with laser-like precision toward one another across the empty lot. Quay and Sunni turned to look at one another and then looked back toward the idling car. It took only a mini-second before they both realized what was happening. Someone had indeed tracked them. The now-idling vehicle facing them had effectively blocked the driveway entrance.

After some thawing during the day, the parking lot had refrozen with the dropping evening temperatures. Tire track slush now formed ruts of packed ice. Quay's quick shift into gear and sudden acceleration spewed ice and gravel up peppering the underside of his truck with a pounding pop, pop, pop as they thumped over the ruts.

The dark car at the parking lot entrance began moving forward directly towards Thompson's truck. Then it accelerated, its tires spinning making the car fishtail wildly on the iced pavement.

"Get down! Get down! All of you! He's losing control!" Quay yelled.

Sam grabbed the collar of the dog and pulled the animal down onto the floor behind the driver's seat. Sunni immediately clambered down onto the floor of the front passenger seat. She curled up covering her head with her hands.

"Go! Go! Go!" she screamed.

Quay gunned the truck and steered directly toward the oncoming car. It was a game of chicken now. The headlights of the sedan were lower than those of Quay's truck. He knew he could blind the driver. He flipped his light beams up on bright. The approaching car blinded by the glaring lights swerved again. It was enough. Quay slammed on the accelerator and maneuvered past the oncoming car. Pops from a gun reverberated in the winter air as he passed the car. Sunni squealed. Quay flew out of the parking lot wheeling left onto the four-lane Weaver Lake Road. It had all happened in a flash, but it had seemed like a slow-motion action sequence. Quay steadied the truck and began moving north on the road toward the freeway.

A stream of flashing lights paraded toward his truck on Weaver Lake Road, sped past and swerved into the parking lot. The cavalry had arrived. Quay sped on toward the exit ramp of the Interstate ahead.

"Sam, you called for back up?" Quay asked.

"Yup! Just had a hunch we were going to need some help in case company came. Looks like it was a good hunch!"

Quay grunted and then grinned. "You and your hunches. Gotta love it, Sam!" He continued accelerating down the road and exited onto the Interstate safely away from the attackers. Sunni Hyun hadn't been kidding. Someone wanted her. Whether they wanted her dead remained to be seen. Now he needed to get her to safety.

Quay turned to Sunni as she crouched on the floor. "You can get up on the seat now. Put on your seat belt!" Sunni crawled timidly onto the seat.

"What the hell are you into?" he growled at her.

"I told you. They want to kill me!"

"It looks like it! Who are they?"

"I'm not sure. I think they are from some North Korean mob. I don't know more. They think my life is theirs. They are very dangerous. Please help me! And I've got to have protection for my mother. They will go after her just to get to me."

"I'll see what we can do about that. Give me her address. Where does she live? Is she home?" Sam asked.

Sunni rattled off an address in White Bear Lake, a suburb north of St. Paul.

"First, give me your phone!" Sam ordered Sunni. "I need to take the SIM card out so you can't be tracked. Then tell me your mother's number. As soon as we can, we will have to call her using my phone. You will warn her and tell her we are sending someone for her, but you can't use your phone."

As Quay raced down the freeway, she obeyed Sam's order, handing her phone across the seat back to Sam, wincing as she reached across the seat.

"There's something else," Sunni whispered.

"What?" demanded Quay.

"My arm. It's bleeding because they'd put a tracker chip in my arm. I dug it out. But they can follow me as long as I have it."

"That's your injury?" asked Quay.

"Oh great!" Sam moaned.

"Give me the chip first, and then I'll look at your arm," Sam ordered.

"We've got to ditch that chip! They'll track us, like they tracked her," said Quay.

"We can't, Quay. If we toss the chip, we could be losing a ton of information. Can we use it against them? Maybe we could we lure them in?" Sam asked.

"I'm not sure. What's going on with our back up? Can you find out if they got the guys at the school?"

In an instant Sam had her phone to her ear. She was listening intently. "Okay, good job, guys. Thanks for the support. Keep us posted."

Sam looked up from her phone. Quay glanced at her in the rear view mirror. She nodded.

"They are blocking the cars at the I94 intersection and at exits on down the freeway. One guy got away. They tried to break through the blockade at the school parking lot. Smashed up their car and ours. Two guys in the car are headed to the hospital. One guy ran. They're searching the area. There's nowhere he can go. Besides, it's too cold. If he's got any injuries at all, he'll freeze to death out there."

"Okay. I'm going to head to St. Paul. Call in the address for Sunni's mother, and get someone over there to pick her up." Quay ordered. Then as an afterthought, he said, "Did you get hold of Super Mike Bergman? We need to bring him up to speed on what's happening and find out if he's still with us on this. Gotta get clearance on all of this. Gotta figure out what to do with her tracking chip, too. Damn! What a mess!"

"I called before we went in. Had to leave a message. I'll try again. We've got to find a safe house for her, too. Super Mike will support this and us," said Sam nodding toward Sunni. Mike Bergman was the BCA Superintendent in charge of all BCA operations. They referred to him as Super Mike, because he could line up just about anything they asked for. This looked like it was going to be a huge operation. Sam absently patted the dog that was now laying its head in her lap. For some reason, this had a very calming effect.

"What time is it?" Sunni asked softly.

"It's about seven, why?" answered Sam.

"My mom."

"What about your mom?"

"She's going to be coming back from grocery shopping. She told me she was going to the store to get the week's groceries for the restaurant. They'll be looking for her. They might even be waiting for her."

"Okay. Let's use your phone, Sam! We can get Super Mike's okay later. I think he'd approve the call. Let Sunni call her, now. Tell her not to go home. Tell her to go to the Ford car dealer on White Bear Avenue. Pull into the lot and park by the front door. They won't find her there. We'll have someone pick her up."

Sam handed Sunni her phone, and Sunni punched in the number for her mother.

While Sunni was placing the call to her mother, Sam looked at the small chip she was holding.

"Quay," she said, "if this is truly a tracking device, it won't matter where we go with Hyun. They'll find her. I've got an idea. Let's assume this chip has a GPS tracker in it like she fears; let's use it. It'll just take a minute to meet up with the county sheriff's patrol car on the second roadblock at the 169 exit. We're almost there. The freeway will be a quick entry and exit for us, especially if they've got it blocked. We can give the chip to the sheriff. He can take it to BCA headquarters. The bad dudes won't go in there. And they'll assume we've got Hyun under guard there. They'll be stymied for a bit, and it'll buy us some time."

"Sounds like a good plan, Sam. Get hold of the sheriff out here at the 169 southbound ramp. We can transfer the chip there and then get right back onto the Interstate."

Quay was dodging slower traffic as he headed toward the ramp. Leftovers from rush hour, he thought, and the roadblock was having an effect. He checked his rear view mirror. Red lights flashing all over the place in the distance. Good! The sedan behind him had slowed. He couldn't wait around to see the outcome. He pushed on, swerving around a slow van in the lane ahead of him.

The county sheriff's patrol car had blocked the southbound ramp and another sheriff's car was waiting for them at the bottom of the ramp on the edge of 169. Quay pulled alongside the patrol car. Sam jumped out and handed the chip in the bloody tissue to the officer sitting at the wheel of the car.

The young officer looked at it, grimaced, and asked, "What is it?"

"It's a very important tracking chip. We think a bunch of bad dudes back there are going to be coming after it. So what we need is for you to hightail it to the BCA headquarters and deliver it to a fellow named Boogie. Deliver it personally. The fewer people who handle it the better. And you're going to have to step on it, because those guys are tracking it. We can't let them know that you've got it. Can you do that for us?"

"No problem," he answered. "My name is Alex Boeser, by the way. Glad I can be of help. I'll have this guy Boogie give you a call when he's got it, okay?"

"Thanks, Alex. That'd be great. We're gonna get moving. You gotta go, too. Thanks again for helping us out."

Sam turned and quickly jumped back into Quay's idling truck. With a quick wave, Quay pulled back onto the highway and sped south. While Sam was talking to the sheriff's deputy, he'd gotten his call and approval from the BCA Superintendent. They had approval for the plan and had their safe house. It was in southern Minnesota. They had a drive of about an hour ahead of them. He was going to turn on his lights and move out as fast as possible. The evening rush hour was over. He hoped they'd have clear roads and smooth traveling with no one following. He was thankful the MNDOT crews had been out sanding the roads.

"Sunni, let me see your arm. Are you still bleeding?" said Sam as she reached over the back of the seat to pull on Sunni's arm.

Sunni turned in her seat to hold up her arm. She pulled away the wad of bloody tissues. The wound was small. It appeared that the bleeding had slowed if not stopped. Sam reached under the seat in front of her and felt for a first aid kit she knew Quay kept there. Finding it, she pulled it out, opened it, and found a bottle of sanitizer, a rolled package of gauze, and a large bandage. It took her seconds to wrap the gauze around Sunni's arm and secure it with a bandage.

"There. That should hold you for a while. It doesn't look too bad."

"Thank you," whispered Sunni as she turned back in her seat to face forward. She settled back into the seat and seemed to shrink into a small, soft ball.

CHAPTER EIGHT
The Safe House

Quay had used his navigation system to enter the address for the safe house. He was heading for the small town of Janesville fifteen miles east of Mankato in Southern Minnesota. Super Mike had told them that the BCA kept a small home on Lake Elysian outside of Janesville.

Shortly after Quay had entered the address and taken off, he'd received a text from Super Mike with more background information on the place. He handed his phone back to Sam, so she knew what to expect.

"Will the place be stocked, Quay?" asked Sam.

"I'm not sure. Mike didn't say. It'll be after nine when we get there. Maybe there's a little Quik Stop or something open on the outskirts of Mankato. We can pick up a few necessities for the first night there. We need to get some dog food, too."

The pup sat up in the back seat, stretched and gave out a little whine, bringing the small group to his attention.

"Quay, do you think we can stop for a second to let the dog out? I think he's got to go!"

"Oh! I forgot about him. Do we have a leash?"

Sunni sat up and turned around to Sam.

"I have a leash in my fanny pack. You took it and put it in the back when you searched me. May I get it out?"

Sam and Quay turned to look at Sunni with questioning eyes.

"No! I can get it. But why do you have a leash?" asked Quay. "Do you know this dog?"

"Well, yes, actually. He's my dog," Sunni confirmed in a soft voice.

"What? How? Why? What was he doing in Joo Jhim's car?" asked Sam skeptically.

"I don't know. I think Joo must have taken him along to upset my mother. He knew that my mother loved this dog. She wouldn't go anywhere without Chip. So Joo used Chip to control her."

"Okay," Sam said, dragging out the word with a tone of disbelief. "We'll need to talk some more about that. In the meantime, the Chipster here needs to take care of his business. Let's pull into the rest area up ahead."

Quay stole a quick glance at Sam through the rear-view mirror. She looked back and nodded her agreement. They were on the same page. They would need to call Boogie the tech guy to help do some background work, and also get some people from the Mankato Bureau to join them at the safe house as soon as possible.

When Chip had relieved himself and gotten a drink from one of the bottled waters Quay bought from a machine at the stop, they got on their way again. The dog settled down in the back seat with its head once again lying on Sam's lap, eyes closed, breathing contentedly.

The occupants of the vehicle rode on in silence, each lost in thoughts anticipating what lay ahead. Quay focused on his drive. The snowy winter freeway roads had been cleared pretty well, he thought. Quay knew that wouldn't necessarily be the case when they reached the county roads by the safe house. The wind was picking up swirling some light snow across the highway. Black ice could be a possibility if it kept up. His dash thermometer said it was 10 degrees outside. With wind chill, it could be somewhere below zero. Minnesota, he thought. Gotta love it!

His thoughts switched to their passenger. He wondered what other surprises Sunni Hyun had in store for them. She could be a real wild card. He was anxious to get her settled at the safe house and to start questioning her.

Focusing on what they were going to do with the dog at the safe house, Sam was mentally organizing the events for the evening and the next day. She also wondered how Quay was going to hold up emotionally with their questioning of Sunni Hyun. There was a lot at stake personally for him. She hoped he would finally get the real answers about why his wife had been murdered by a sniper at Cameron BioTech that day she'd prepared to deliver that major research announcement at the press conference. It had happened right in front of him. They both believed Sunni Hyun had the answers. Now at last, answers...maybe.

While Quay and Sam thought ahead about Sunni Hyun and what she knew and how they would handle her, Sunni was thinking about her mother, and hoping against hope that the BCA people had been able to rescue her. She worried that her mother would be confused and frightened. She wished she could talk with her. She was pretty sure her mother had no idea about the real Joo. She would be shocked to learn he was not only dead, but that he had been murdered in front of her daughter. And then when she found out that her daughter had been involved with his terrorist group, it was going to be an even bigger shock and a humiliation. Sunni had brought dishonor to her family name. What would her mother think? And then she was worried about what was going to happen to her. Was she guilty not only of theft, but also accessory to murder, or treason? She was frightened beyond anything she had felt before, even Joo's threats. How did this ever happen to her, a smart, young girl who had had such a promising life ahead of her? Her parents had given up everything for her. Her father had adored her. She was his shining star. And now it was all lost.

Quay found a little general store just outside of Mankato. They stopped to pick up a few groceries: food for the dog, milk, water, cereal, eggs, bacon, bread, soup, and munchies. It would be enough to help them get by until Boogie and the other team got there in the morning.

Situated on several acres along the shoreline of Lake Elysian, one of many lakes in south central Minnesota, the house nestled deep into woods near the lake just three miles northwest of the small town of Janesville. Frozen over at this time of year, the lake was known for its good fishing in both winter and summer. This winter, they would find the lake dotted with small fish houses owned by the local sportsmen. The background on the house said the BCA had acquired the house about twenty years previously when the owner died and left no family to inherit the property. It said the house was nondescript, but well kept up. A mailbox with the house number 1998 identified the property. They would find information about the house in a folder attached to the underside of the mailbox.

It was a quarter past nine when Quay's headlights reflected the numbers 1998 on a grey metal mailbox standing sentry at the entrance to the drive. Quay pulled up close to the mailbox allowing Sam to reach through her rear passenger window for the packet under the box. She found it, pulled it out, raised the window back up, and wordlessly nodded at Quay. Turning right into a long, narrow drive, Quay's headlights illuminated a drive that stretched through a thick arbor of pine and cedar trees interspersed with bare-branched oaks, and white-barked birch. The tires crunched along the snow-covered gravel driveway interrupting the stillness of the evening. The drive had been plowed, giving the appearance that the place was occupied. About thirty yards in, the drive opened to a large, recently cleared parking area with piles of banked snow at its sides. A small, white two-story house and another small outbuilding that appeared to be a garage emerged side by side to the right of the parking area. A winter moon glimmered brightly amidst ribbons of stars dotting the black winter sky. The natural illumination provided the only exterior lighting for the property.

The trio in the truck fell silent as Quay edged his truck up toward the house and waited, his truck idling as they surveyed the property. Even the dog sat up as they slowed to turn in and now sat perfectly still curiously eyeing the new scene. A troop of trees off to the left paraded in a jagged line along a path down to a lake near the back of the property, preventing a clear view of the outermost surroundings. Near the lake, Quay spotted the roof of a small shed partially hidden by bushes and snowdrifts. Must be a boathouse, he thought, as he pointed it out to Sam. She nodded, indicating she had seen it, too. He looked to his right, scanned the house perimeter, and decided it was safe to move into the house.

Sam opened the packet from the mailbox, and scanned the top sheet.

"It says there is a key code security box attached to the inside lip of the egress window by the door. You'll need to enter the code before inserting the key into the lock. Here's the key," she said reaching across the seat with a key she'd pulled from the packet.

"Okay," Quay said as he took the key. "You two wait here. Give me the number. I'll get the door open and get the house cleared." Quay climbed out allowing a whoosh of icy, cold air into the cab's interior. He paused for a second to survey the area once more before closing the door and moving toward the house.

Sam sat alert and leaned closer behind Sunni Hyun who sat rigidly straight in the front passenger seat. Sam aimed her gun carefully covering Sunni while Quay walked slowly up to the house.

The egress window protected by a raised metal edge was sunk next to the double steps into the house. Quay had to kneel on the frozen ground, feel inside the egress, and run his gloved hand around the bottom. On his second pass, he found the small box and lifted it from its hiding place. He entered the code and a green light appeared on the box. He climbed two steps, opened the storm door, inserted the key and turned the lock in the entry door. The slight click gave him satisfaction, and his grimace turned to a smile. He opened the door and felt to the left for a light switch. There were three switches. He flipped them all on. A light in the center of the kitchen ceiling, another over the sink, and a single spotlight over the exterior steps by the door provided the illumination they would need. He gave a cursory look into the kitchen and the other rooms he could see before entering. After entering and doing a quick search, he decided it was clear. Returning to the door, he stuck his head out and waved an all clear at Sam as he walked back out. Sam waited for Quay to return to the truck and open the passenger door for Sunni Hyun. He grabbed her arm in a firm grip and led her up the steps to the door. Sunni didn't resist, but let out a slight groan when he pulled her from the vehicle. Sam grabbed the dog's leash, hooked it to the ring of the dog's collar and held the door for him to jump out. The pup happily sniffed the ground racing to and fro at the end of the leash, and then promptly found a small bush to relieve itself on.

They settled into the house, hanging their coats on pegs by the door. The dog wagged happily at Sunni as they moved themselves and their supplies into the kitchen. Sunni settled at the kitchen table while Sam explored the house and returned with a report that it was a three-bedroom house. One bedroom was downstairs; two were up. It had a main floor bathroom as well as a full bath upstairs. The bathrooms were both stocked with soap, toilet tissue and towels. Sunni remained silent as they explored the contents of the kitchen cupboards and refrigerator.

"The information in the packet says there's enough food and other household supplies to last a couple weeks, at least," said Sam. "We will need to talk about what's going to happen to you," she said to Sunni with an edge in her voice.

Sunni made no response as her dark, liquid eyes stared briefly at Sam and then looked down. She reached for the dog, and patted its head. The dog edged closer to Sunni, and laid its head on her lap.

"It's been a long day, Sunni," said Quay. We will wait until tomorrow to talk in detail. We have someone joining us tomorrow, to help sort everything out. I do have a couple questions tonight, though. First, were you the woman who came out to the police car asking questions about when you could leave when we were at the rest area?"

Sunni looked up at him and slowly nodded.

"I thought so. You seemed familiar. We'd met when I came to Cameron last fall investigating a break in, right? We will need to talk about that, too. Next, is there anything else we need to know to keep you safe tonight?"

"My mother?" she asked looking plaintively at Quay.

"She's being taken care of. She's been located and moved," Quay assured her in a perfunctory tone. His deep voice expressed neither emotion nor concern for her. "We'll know more tomorrow. For now, we believe you will be safe here tonight. You can sleep in the bedroom down here. Ms. Atwood and I will take turns standing guard through the night. You will not be leaving at any time. Understood?"

Sunni gave the slightest nod. She looked at Sam and then at Quay and gave him another slight nod seemingly affirming her agreement.

"Let's get a bite to eat first. I'll see if we can warm up that frozen pizza we picked up," suggested Sam. "Then we'll let her settle in."

"I'm not hungry," Sunni whispered. "I think I'd just like to lie down."

"Fine," Quay muttered. He turned away from her, walked to the bedroom and opened the door. "The door stays open. The bathroom is right there," he said pointing a few steps away. "Sam will stand outside the door while you are in there. There is no window in the bathroom, so don't think about that. The bedroom windows are sealed and locked. The building is protected by alarms."

"I understand," said Sunni. "I'm not going to try to leave. I've got my mother to think of."

"Hmmm," replied Quay. "We'll see."

Sunni turned for the bedroom. Quay and Sam looked at one another and turned back to the kitchen table.

"It's going to be a long night," Quay grumbled. "How do you want to do this?"

"Let's grab a bite and feed the dog, first. Then we sleep in shifts, if that's okay with you," suggested Sam. "I'll do first watch, and I'll wake you about three. Then, Ican catch a few winks before everybody shows up in the morning."

"Sounds good," agreed Quay. I'll go pull the truck into the garage and walk the dog around the perimeter first. I think it'll help settle him for the night."

Sam got up and walked to the counter. She grabbed the bags they'd brought in and began to put things away. She found the pack of bubble gum Quay had purchased along with the supplies and smiled.

"Quay?" She held out the pack to him. "I think you're going to want this."

"Yeah?" he said, turning around. Seeing the pack, he reached for it and smiled. "You might be right. This is one of those times I really wish I still smoked. I could use a cigarette tonight."

"You've gone too far to start up again now, Quay. You've been doing really well." She laughed as she added, "Just keep popping those bubbles."

"Oh, right! Like that helps," he said, but he grinned at her when he said it and pocketed the pack of gum before heading out to move the truck.

It began as an uneventful stay, but neither Sam nor Quay was able to doze in more than a light sleep that night. Neither of them trusted their guest. Plus, they were both busily reviewing the day's events and their mounting questions about Sunni Hyun. They had no idea who she truly was, and what was really behind her call to Quay.

Quay's mind was running non-stop with concerns. Who was this woman? Who was her control? Was it Joo Jhim who controlled her as she'd indicated or someone else? Who was Joo Jhim? How was she involved with Joo? She seemed to be afraid of him.

He knew Sam was thinking about Sunni, too, but on a more emotional level. Sam did that. Sam had noted that Sunni seemed to have a lot of fear for her mother's safety. She shared her theories with Quay about why and how Sunni Hyun had gotten involved in this conspiracy with Cameron BioTech. Sam didn't think Sunni had ever been in charge. Then there were many questions about what had really motivated Sunni. They'd learned last fall that she was a top researcher at Cameron. She was supposedly very intelligent. She earned an excellent salary. So most importantly, Sam wondered what Sunni Hyun knew about the motive behind the shooting of Quay's wife, Karen, that day over two years ago? What had been going on at Cameron? What did Sunni Hyun, a.k.a. Cameron's top researcher, know and have to gain? What was her true endgame? Had she really come clean with them? And most importantly, would she? Sam had voiced all of her questions to him, and he had agreed with all of them.

It seemed like only minutes had passed when the morning sun winked through the windows; the day began still, cloudless, and cold. It was another bitter, teeth-chattering morning.

Sam, awake from sitting the last watch at the kitchen table, put together a small breakfast of scrambled eggs, bacon, and toast before waking Quay and Sunni. They were eating breakfast in silence when two men from the Mankato BCA pulled up at 8:30. They hadn't heard the car right away, but Chip who had been asleep on the floor near Sunni's feet under the kitchen table, had gotten up suddenly, let out a low, deep growl, and had run to the door. He had evidently heard the vehicle just as it pulled off the road to the driveway.

Quay met the men at the door. Two men bundled up in matching navy blue BCA parkas stood on the step. The tallest man, in his thirties, blond, blue-eyed, solidly built flashed a BCA badge. The second man stood slightly behind him and a step below. He appeared to be a little older, in his mid-forties perhaps. His close-cropped greying hair and dark brown eyes set in a square clean-shaven face gave him the intense look of a seasoned law enforcement officer. They each shook hands with Quay in friendly recognition. They'd worked with Quay before. Besides, Quay's name was well known in the BCA rank and file. Quay ushered them into the small kitchen and introduced them to Sunni and Sam as Drew Thurston and Dan Young.

"Just call us Double D," smirked Drew after the introductions were done. "That's what everyone else calls us."

Quay raised an eyebrow.

"I'm almost afraid to ask what that stands for," said Sam. "Diabolic Dan and Drew? Or maybe it could be The Dazzling Duo?"

"Oh, how about Dainty Duo?" Quay smirked as he popped a new square of bubble gum into his mouth. "I know these two, Sam. Be careful. They'll prance around you and look all innocent-like, and then suddenly you're in a smack down. No warning! Drew may look like an old guy, but don't underestimate him. And Dan, there. He looks all innocent and baby-faced, but he's really the devil in disguise. He's just plain wicked!"

"Aw, shucks, Mr. Thompson. Now you've gone and ruined our routine," chuckled Drew. "You were close, Miss Sam. It's really nothing too serious. We are just Dan and Drew, aka the Dangerous Duo."

"That's it!" exclaimed Quay. "That's it in a nutshell!" They laughed and slapped one another on the back. The tension broken, the four of them pulled up chairs around the kitchen table. Sunni, who was to be the center of attention, was invited to sit next to Sam. This afforded her a bit of comfort by seating her next to the only other female of the group.

Quay began by providing Sunni Hyun's background to Dan and Drew, as they knew it. Sunni sat with her head down and shoulders hunched, making no eye contact while occasionally stroking the head of the attentive dog, Chip, who had settled down after greeting each of them. Chip stood by her side with his head in her lap.

Sam looked outside to see a light dusting of snow that had begun to fall as the temperature rose with the sun.

Steve Boogie Schroeder, the BCA tech expert, had called Quay at seven that morning, telling him when they could expect him. He pulled into the drive at nine to a loud woofed greeting from Chip. Sam escorted Boogie in quickly. His clothes carried a crisp smell of the frigid, outside air. Stomping his boots, Boogie shrugged off his parka and hung it on the peg by the door. As he struggled out of the boots, he brushed fresh snow off his jeans. His well-worn sweatshirt with an Apple Logo on the chest loosely topped a blue-green plaid, flannel shirt. His jeans were typical Boogie attire, displaying a rip over each knee. He stepped to the side to give an inquisitive Chip an opportunity to complete the sniff test and provide a wag of approval. Waiting until the dog was finished, he reached down and patted Chip's head.

"Good boy! You're a beautiful dog," he said. "He's quite the fella," he said to Sam. "He could be a show dog with those long, blond feathers on his haunches and chest, and with that broad chest and big head." He squatted putting his face on a level with the dog while rubbing the dog's ears. "You're a good-looking golden retriever. Yes, you are!" he said to the dog in a happy singsong voice. The dog wiggled faster, nuzzling his neck and hands. "And you're a friendly dog. Bet you're wondering what's going on, right?" The dog seemed to understand. His dark eyes, gold-flecked with intelligence looked intently into Boogie's eyes, and he reached out to surprise Boogie with a quick slurp on the chin. Boogie stood and looked at Quay and asked, "How's he handling all this?"

'"Pretty well, actually," said Quay. "He slept on the floor next to the bed in Hyun's room last night. Seems to be a well-trained dog. He's pretty laid back. Considering what he's been through with the shooting, the transport in a strange vehicle, and then being reunited with his owner, he's doing great!"

"His owner, huh?"

"Yeah. She claims he's her dog. I don't think we've gotten the whole story of why Joo Jhim had her dog with him, though," Quay said as he turned to look at Sunni. "Come on Boogie, sit at the table with us. We're just getting started. You know Dan Young and Drew Thurston from the Mankato branch?"

"Yeah, we've done some work together. Hi, guys! Good to see you again." He gave a small wave as he moved to join the group at the table.

Boogie found a spot to set up his laptop on the table, and they all became quiet. Boogie began by pulling up the information on the chip that Sunni had cut out of her arm.

"Okay. Here's what I've got on the chip. Maybe you have all heard of the RFID microchip?" he began as he pushed a long strand of dark hair back away from his face. He rubbed a big hand across his face, rubbing his bristled cheek.

He was met with hesitant nods.

"Sort of. We know about tracking chips. Is that what it was?" asked Quay. "That's what she's claiming it is." He turned to look at Sunni and then back to Boogie.

"Cool! Yeah. She's right. These RFIDs or Radio Frequency Identification microchips have been around for some time now, but the RFID chips and other under-the-skin implants have only recently had more widespread with humans. I've heard there is even a high-tech office somewhere in Sweden that is implanting its workers with computer chips like these under their skin. The place is known as The Bio Complex."

"Sounds a bit like Cameron BioTech in Maple Grove," mused Sam.

"Yeah, but not totally. The workers in Sweden are actually tracked, or controlled you might say, by dog-style microchips inserted under their skin to help them do all sorts of things—almost like droids. The workers can also use them to unlock doors, operate photocopiers, and share contact info without using a PIN number. Their ID is the chip."

"That's sort of what we have here, I guess," said

Quay. "Ms. Hyun says a chip was implanted in her arm that allowed her superiors to track her. They knew where she was at all times. She told us this morning that they controlled her and forced her to do their bidding at Cameron BioTech while she worked in the labs there. The ME called in this morning to tell us that Joo Jhim had one implanted on him, too."

Sunni Hyun's head popped up. She stared at Boogie for several seconds and then shook her head.

Boogie looked from Quay to Sam. He was barely containing his excitement. "Wow! This is going to be fun! Sounds like this was a high tech group." His stocking clad feet were shuffling side to side. He stood and bounced up and down on his toes, looking somewhat like an excited child opening birthday gifts.

"Maybe," said Quay. "In the case of Ms. Hyun, here, we will need to talk to her about how and why she had a chip implanted."

He looked over at Sunni Hyun who was sitting across the table with her head and eyes cast down. Her fingers nervously rubbed over the bandage covering the cut in her arm. She shook her head as tears began to fall.

Sam glanced at Hyun and then focused on Boogie. "Did you disable the chip? Did we get any information or data from it? Will we be able to use it to help us get them? Can we backtrack with it?" The questions came in a barrage from Sam. She was already jumping ahead as usual, thought Quay. But in this case, it was a good thing. Sam was relentless when she got started. These were the exact questions he had.

"Well, we have the chip locked up in a secure room at headquarters that will block all signals," explained Boogie. "They won't be able to get any tracking from it while it's in that room. The room is built to totally block everything, even hacks, either incoming or outgoing. That way we can analyze it without any interference or threat. We've already started to work on it. We will see what information we can get from it and whether we can track it back to the owners. We'll pull in the chip that was on Joo Jhim and look at that, too."

Sunni interrupted with a tearful question. "Is my mother okay?" she asked in a soft, trembling voice.

Quay looked to Boogie. "Were you able to follow up on that before you left? She's been concerned about her mother."

"Yup. BCA had a car meet her mother in that parking lot like you suggested. No problems. The guys said she came along willingly. She's worried about her daughter, too. They told her that she'd be able to talk to her sometime today...if that's okay with you. We've got her mother settled in at another safe house in the Twin Cities. They said it's best to keep them separated for now."

Sunni sighed, and leaned back in her chair. "Thank God," she whispered.

"Yeah, we'll set that up later. A lot depends on how cooperative you are," Quay said, sending Sunni one of his piercing ice-blue stares.

"Sunni, do you know if your mother was chipped?" asked Boogie.

Sunni looked up shaking her head. "My mother doesn't know about any of this. She thinks she met Joo by accident. She had no idea he was using me and controlling me. That's how they blackmailed me. He was always nice to her. He was the one who bought her this dog. She enjoyed the company when she was home alone while I was away at school. I think she would have told me if they had tried to chip her."

"Well, that's another thing we need to check on. Maybe the Double D team, here, can do a follow up with the mother," said Quay. Turning to Sunni, he explained, "They will follow up with her. Boogie will be the conduit between your mother and you, because he's got the tech equipment to set that up. What's your mother's full name, Sunni?"

"Her name is June Yung Hyun. My father died several years ago. She's a widow. She's fifty-five. Life hasn't been easy for her." She paused, and seemed to hiccup before she said, "I've totally dishonored my parents!" Tears began to stream down her cheeks again, as she tried to choke back outright sobs. She covered her face with her small hands. Her dark hair hung in strings over her hands as her shoulders shook.

"It's okay," Sam said, looking at the men while reaching for a tissue box on the kitchen counter. She placed the box in front of Sunni and spoke in a calming, but firm tone. "We can deal with all of that later. Let's start talking about what we have here. Sunni. " She placed her hand on the girl's shoulder, "Look at me, Sunni."

She waited for Sunni to get control of herself. The young woman wiped her eyes and looked up.

"We have a lot of questions. You have a lot of answers. Boogie here is our top tech guy. He's going to be listening very carefully to your answers about what your role was at Cameron BioTech and how you got information out of there. He's going to know if what you're telling us could be true and make sense. Got it? There's no room for lies now."

"Yes, I've got it. I know I'm in a lot of trouble. But what I want you to know is that I also have a lot of information that can help you catch some very bad people. I was used. I wasn't able to break away. But I did my best to prevent these horrible people from having success." Her r's began to slur into w's again as she spoke more quickly. She gulped before continuing. "I think that may be the reason Joo Jhim was murdered." She paused, looked at Sam with her intense, dark eyes, and said slowly, "That is also why I know I will be next. I'll help you. But I want your guarantee that my mother and I will be protected from these animals. Forever!"

"Sunni," began Sam, "what we can do for you depends upon what you do for us. We will talk about those options after we know what you know. In the meantime, we must tell you that you can have a lawyer. You have a right to a lawyer. And you do have the right to remain silent. Having a lawyer may provide you some guidance, but it will also delay what we can do for your mother in the meantime. It'll take a while to get someone lined up as your counselor."

"I know my rights. I think a lawyer would tell me to tell you what I know. We can work out the deals later. I'm going to trust you. I have to. So no lawyer. And I pray it will be all right."

"Okay," said Quay as he sat down at the table directly across from Sunni. Boogie had pulled his laptop on his lap. He was clicking away. Quay glanced at him with a bit of an annoyed look on his face.

"Boogie! Are you with us?" he snapped.

"Yeah, man. I'm here. I've got to get some of this stuff entered so we can follow up on it. I just got some info on the guys who tried to take you out at the school last night. They're in the hospital, but they aren't talking. The one that ran has disappeared. So keep going. I'll listen with one ear. I'll catch up."

Drew and Dan looked from Quay to Sunni and

then to Sam. They were surprised at Quay Thompson's intensity. The Quay they knew was normally more laid back.

Sam could tell Quay was beyond stressed, and he was obviously tired. His neck muscles were flexing, and so were his fingers. He had just popped a new piece of bubble gum into his mouth and was chewing fiercely. The bubbles would start popping soon. Sam knew he wished he had a cigarette about now. Good thing he still used the gum instead of cigarettes, or the room would be filled with smoke.

Quay stared at Sunni Hyun. "Better start talking, and don't leave anything out. What do you know? You've got five good witnesses here. We will know if you stray away from the truth."

Sunni Hyun took a deep breath.

The group sat back as she spoke. They observed her demeanor, analyzed her behavior, and listened carefully. Boogie took notes on his computer, while at the same time, getting online to run initial fact checks on everything she said.

Sunni began at the beginning when she'd first been hired at Cameron right out of college. She explained that she knew that Cameron BioTech had been working for over four years on a project originally begun by scientists Emmanuelle Charpentier and Jennifer Doudna and built upon by other researchers later. Simply put, the Cameron BioTech research centered on a system to alter human genes. If successful, the possibilities became endless. She added that the introduction of the technique they called CRISPR-Cas9 made it possible to add to or remove genetic material in any system. She explained that Cameron research was taking everything a step further. With the right formula they would be able to create a perfect human, a disease-free world, and more.

"Before that press conference when my wife was killed, she told me that Cameron was on to something really big," interrupted Quay, looking around the table at Dan, Drew, Sam, and Boogie. "She was their PR person, and she was so excited. But she wouldn't tell me anything more until after the press conference. It was top-level secrecy until they had the patent locked up." He turned to Sunni. "And that's the big announcement that my wife was going to make at that press conference when she was killed by the sniper?"

"Yes," said Sunni. "It was, and continues to be, a very big deal. And there were others who didn't want that information out there. Not yet. It was important to these people to stop it until they could get all the information for themselves, and then they would patent it first."

Quay slumped back into his chair and rubbed a hand across his forehead. Then with a sigh, he ran his hand through his thick blond hair, and nodded to Sam.

"Tell us more about it," insisted Sam.

Boogie looked up from his laptop. "I just Googled it. It's out there now. This is a big deal. It's made news all over the scientific community and even showed up in Time Magazine. The public knows. So why, if it's public knowledge, is it still a big deal?"

"What does the acronym stand for anyway?" asked Quay.

"It's all about the details—and the all-important patent—which hasn't been filed, yet," said Sunni. "CRISPR stands for Clustered Regularly Interspaced Short Palindromic Repeats. In 'science speak' it means we basically can make changes in acquired immunity in DNA. Using CRISPR, we can direct the DNA inside a cell of an embryo, a person, or a plant to do just about anything. All diseases can be eradicated, not just some. It can be used to alter crops and affect the food chain. The possibilities are endless. On the extreme end, it would even be possible to revive previously extinct species like the wooly mammoth using frozen DNA. In addition, the world ecosystem could be changed. We could use CRISPR-Cas9 to develop perfect disease-free plants. It is very exciting work. But in the wrong hands, in the hands of an evil person or nation using it for their power, money, and ego, it is more than frightening. For example, it could be used to create a perfect new species! And the patent is the key. If one group has the sole patent on this technology, they could control virtually every aspect of human life and world ecosystems."

"My God!" exclaimed Sam.

Quay was leaning across the table mindlessly drumming his fingers. He suddenly sat back and reached into his shirt pocket. Pulling out another small square pack, he held the wrapped piece of pink bubble gum at the ready in his hand. Rolling the piece in his hand, he began actively chewing on the piece in his mouth, blowing and popping small bubbles while thoughtfully staring at Sunni.

"So you had access to this information?" he asked.

"Yes. I have all the information, all the data. Every last bit of research! That's what they want!"

Quay noticed the change in verb tense.

"You *have* the information? My god, woman! What have you done?"

"Let's go back to the beginning, Sunni," said Sam, laying a calming hand on Quay's arm. "Tell us about yourself and how you came to get involved with Joo Jhim and all of this."

CHAPTER NINE
Sunni's Story

Sunni's thick-lashed brown eyes looked at each of them intently. She nodded her head briefly in understanding and consent. The dog, sensing that Sunni was calmer now, nuzzled her hand and then settled onto the rug at her feet. This time, Sunni began her story with her personal background to help them understand. They leaned forward intently listening to her soft voice. The room fell silent with the exception of Sunni's voice and the sound of the winter wind now howling with its hard sheets of snow peppering against the windows.

Sunni Hyun started with her birth in South Korea. She and her parents had moved to the United States when she was still a toddler. Her parents placed a high value on her education. They spoke mostly Korean and some English at home. When she entered kindergarten, she went to the American school five days a week, learned English from her dedicated English Language instructor, and studied nightly to maintain her position as the top student in her class. In addition, she also attended a special academy on Saturdays to develop her talents in math and science. Even though she was a girl and not highly valued in her native country, she said her father and mother expected nothing less than the highest achievements from her. She was their only child. And because she was a girl, an extra responsibility rested not only on Sunni, but also on her parents. She had to be their perfect child. They had emphasized that because she was their only child.

And as she told it, Sunni had succeeded in becoming the perfect child in every way.

It made sense thought Sam. Sam noted that Sunni was remarkably tall for an Asian girl. She wore her beautiful, shiny black hair in a ponytail with a fringe of bangs that offset her porcelain skin and huge dark eyes; she had become a stunning young woman. Her evident intelligence completed the perfect package.

She talked of her school experiences. She'd had a few casual boyfriends in high school. She'd taken part in the normal high school activities: attended prom, been active in debate, ran for and was elected president of the student council, and worked on the student paper and yearbook. She'd had a bit of a social life. Her teachers and others told her she was mature for her age. And to support that opinion, her eyes were focused more on her future than her teen years. She had promised her father that she would make him proud of her.

So, Sunni had excelled in all her school accomplishments including being fully bilingual in Korean and English, and winning academic accolades. She had performed as was expected in a good Asian family. She had made her father and mother proud.

Then, just after she'd graduated, her father had died suddenly of a heart attack. He had been a small man who carried the weight of supporting his family in a new country. He'd worked two jobs. He'd managed everything for Sunni and her mother June. Sunni had adored him.

Suddenly he was gone. Sunni had just turned eighteen. She was thankful that her father had been there to watch her accept her diploma and scholarship awards. He had even hugged her after the ceremony, a display of affection rarely shown in an Asian family.

Prior to her high school graduation, Sunni had applied to and been accepted at several top-ranking colleges. As a minority student and an academic all-star, she'd won scholarships and grants that would fund her college education. Her parents were grateful and relieved, since they did not have the money to send their daughter to college. It was something they had hoped, planned, and wished for since she had been born.

In the end, she'd chosen to attend the University of Minnesota. The U of M allowed her to be close enough to be home on weekends, and it had still offered her the education she needed in her undergraduate career. The location had also allowed her to work with her newly widowed mother on weekends. The two of them had managed. They'd missed her father. But they knew he'd have wanted them to be strong.

Shortly after Sunni's father died, her mother had begun a job as a waitress at a local Korean restaurant. It didn't require much English, and she was good at waitressing. Sunni was proud of her mother. June's determination and hard work opened doors for her, and she quickly worked herself up to become the manager of the restaurant. The Korean owners shared how happy they were to have found June.

So it was that Sunni and her mother survived those first few months after her father died. They'd supported one another emotionally and physically by working hard.

Then Joo Jhim had come along. Knowing what she did now, Sunni said she wished they had never met him. And she wondered now, about the coincidence of his entering their lives. Joo Jhim had introduced himself as a friend of a friend of her father's. But she didn't remember him as someone she'd known. Sunni had not felt comfortable with him from the start. She'd shared her ill feelings about him with her mother.

"Either my mother could not see it or didn't want to see it," she said bitterly.

Joo Jhim was tall for a Korean man. When he stood ramrod straight as he usually did, Sunni estimated him to be at least five foot eleven, and had guessed him to be in his mid-to-late fifties, perhaps about the same age as her father would have been. His granite face bore a thin, dark scar over his left eyebrow from some long ago injury. A stub nose centered on his pock-marked cheeks. He slicked his dark hair back from his forehead and on the sides emphasizing the sharp, menacing profile of his dark face. His sideburns revealed a few gray streaks, but the rest of his hair remained dark. Sunni guessed that perhaps he colored his hair. She'd never really been able to decide.

When she was first introduced to him, Sunni had felt uncomfortable with what she felt was Joo's insincere flattery and fawning behavior toward her and more especially her mother. Sunni suspected that he had ulterior motives for insinuating himself into her mother's life, and hers. She couldn't prove it, then. It took awhile, but before long, she was sure Joo Jhim was going to bring nothing but trouble to their household.

He'd shared very little about himself. He didn't own a home of his own. He had been living in an apartment when Joo and June met. He'd begun working as a cook at the restaurant just a few months previously. Sunni tried to believe her mistrust and fear were simply false paranoia, but still she worried about the direction their life appeared to be taking.

In a matter of a few short months, Joo declared himself a caretaker for Sunni's mother June. Then he quickly proposed marriage to June. Sunni felt she had realized far too late that Joo had taken advantage of her mother. Because she had been away at college, Sunni suspected her mother had been alone too much and had been lonely since her father died. That was the only way she could explain the sudden relationship. Joo had made himself indispensible to the middle-aged, widowed June.

Sunni knew she shouldn't fault her mother for responding to Joo's attentiveness. But she also couldn't understand why her mother hadn't been able to see through his façade. Maybe her mother hadn't wanted to see it. There had been times Sunni had tried to discuss Joo with her mother; June had dismissed her as being too suspicious and accused her of perhaps being even jealous of a new man in the house.

June and Joo had sneaked away to marry. Sunni hadn't even been invited. They had just informed her that the marriage had occurred. As soon as Joo and June married, Joo had moved into their home.

Sunni soon observed that Joo became more and more demanding, seeming to constantly direct and control every aspect of June's life. She watched as her mother left their home very early in the morning to go to work at the restaurant while Joo hadn't left until lunchtime for his duties. Then, exactly at five p.m., Joo escorted June home. Later, he returned to the restaurant to finish his shift.

"My mother wouldn't leave the house without him. When I came home on the weekends, I observed my once lively, beautiful mother begin to wilt under his apparent domination. She became quieter. She didn't laugh anymore. She just went to work and then came home to do more work--her regular housework," Sunni explained, looking from Quay to Samantha, then Boogie and the Double D men. "I felt like there was nothing I could do."

"Did you try to talk to her about it?" asked Sam.

"I wasn't home a lot. I was at school. When I was home, she only wanted to be sure I was getting my schoolwork done. Mother was very serious about my education. She placed more stress on me than she had when I was in high school!"

Sunni continued, explaining that she had completed her undergraduate studies with high honors at the University of Minnesota. Then she had been accepted at Stanford University in California. Stanford, one of the world's leading research and teaching universities, was a feather in her hat. Sunni was elated. Once again, her mother told her how she was so very proud of her daughter. She also added that her father would have been so very proud of her, too. Sunni knew it was true, but it made her sad to remember the kind, loving man who had been her father, and then make the comparison with the man who had replaced him. Joo did not make her mother happy. In fact, Sunni had seen that he had the opposite effect.

Sunni left that fall for Stanford with mixed emotions. She had been excited to begin her studies at such a prestigious college, but she worried about her mother, too. She'd been afraid of what might happen to her while she was away.

Sunni had only come home for holidays. She had called and emailed frequently, trying to keep the line of communication open with her mother. But she noticed that when Joo was present with June, the messages were more reserved and less frequent.

During the times when Sunni was able to come home, she felt very uncomfortable. She saw, too, that Joo had become more controlling. Once when she'd come home, she noticed her mother's arm had been in a sling.

When she had questioned her mother about it, she found June to be evasive.

"I tried to sound nonchalant when I asked her what happened to her arm. I told her it looked like it hurt."

She had quickly responded, shrugging it off, "*Oh, I just fell last week. I tripped on the stairs and just went tumbling down. It's okay.*"

"I asked if she'd seen a doctor. She said she just went into the drug store and bought herself a sling. She said it'd be okay, that it was nothing. She looked at Joo when she said it. He just nodded.

"Then Joo said she'd be okay and didn't need to get it checked. He just brushed it off! He told me not to get her all worked up. He said I didn't know everything. Then he sneered, actually sneered when he said, 'You just think because you go to that fancy college you have all the smarts. Well, guess again! I can take care of June without any help from you.'"

He had glared at Sunni, and she had returned the glare. That was all.

She had watched her mother carefully, though. And with each visit, she became more observant of Joo's activities.

During later visits, she explained that she'd turned around and caught him staring at her several times. Just staring. Then he'd begun asking her questions about her studies. What was she doing at college? What classes was she taking? What kind of grades was she getting? What type of job could get with her degree? How fluent was she in her native Korean language? Had she learned any other languages?

Finally, he had nearly demanded that she begin moving toward science research in her studies. He explained to her that it was her duty to find an area where she could make top dollar and support her mother.

Sunni said she'd found herself wondering more and more about Joo. Who was this man? What was he doing in their lives? Where was he really from? And above all, how safe was her mother? She'd suspected him of physical abuse. But her mother would not divulge anything about their relationship other than that Joo was taking care of her. Sunni paused and took a sip of water before continuing her story. The group waited in silence.

During one winter vacation at home, Sunni woke in the middle of the night and heard Joo on his cell phone. He had spoken a different language. It wasn't Korean. She knew she would have recognized that. She assumed he must have been speaking some sort of dialect. Perhaps it was a Korean dialect. She knew there were many dialects in Korea.

At first, he'd sounded like he was giving orders to someone. Then his tone changed and became more hushed. It was as if he was reassuring the person on the phone of his ability to do something. Even though she couldn't understand the language, Sunni could understand the inflection. Her fears grew. Joo Jhim was up to no good.

During that visit, she'd heard Joo make several late night calls. Each time, Joo sounded very agitated. His voice would begin as a whisper and suddenly would rise louder and become threatening. And then he would hang up and return to her mother's bedroom.

Silently Sunni slipped back into the security of her own bedroom and worried about this man who had come into their lives. Sunni had wondered if her mother heard his calls in the night. She'd wondered if she should talk to her mother again about Joo. She knew she needed to find some way to check into his background. She didn't know how. The Internet wouldn't provide much.

Sunni had finally decided to put it all on hold for a while and returned to Stanford to complete her studies. After graduation, Cameron BioTech, a scientific research lab in the Maple Grove suburb of the Twin Cities, had quickly hired her. She had been so happy to be back in her home state and especially to be closer to her mother. She had hoped now she would be able to keep a closer eye on what was happening between Joo and June.

It was shortly after she returned home that she discovered just exactly who Joo Jhim was, and what he was doing in their lives. It was after Sunni had secured her place at Cameron BioTech that Joo laid out his plan for her and for himself.

He had approached her not long after she'd started work. She remembered clearly how he had taken her aside one afternoon at the house and told her he needed to speak with her privately. He suggested they meet for coffee at the local Starbucks. When Sunni pulled into the Starbucks parking lot that afternoon, she'd spied Joo sitting in his car at one side of the lot. He flashed his lights and signaled for her to park near him. After she had parked, he walked over to her car and climbed in with her. Sunni had been startled. She remembered the conversation clearly.

"I thought we were going to meet inside and have coffee," she said.
"I think it'll be better if we just sit out here and talk for a bit. I really don't want to take the chance that our conversation will be overheard.

"*Really? What is so important that it can't be heard? Is this about my mother?*

"*In a way, I suppose this could affect your mother.*" His tone sounded almost threatening, dark.

Then he added, "*And your sister.*"

Sunni had been astounded. "*My sister? I don't have a sister! What are you talking about?*"

"*I'm talking about the sister your father left behind in Korea. The little girl who had not even been born when he left. She was the love child of your father and a girl named Jaemee Wan Park. Your father had an affair.*"

"*What? I can't believe--you can't be serious! He would never have done that to my mother. How can you say that?*"

"*I can say it, because I know it's true. Jaemee is my sister. Your father had an affair with my sister Jaemee, broke it off, and left the country. My sister suffered in disgrace bearing the child of a married man who had disserted her! Believe me. It's the truth. I know.*"

"*Did my father know she was pregnant? Did you tell him? Did Jaemee ever contact him to tell him? Who knew besides you and Jaemee?*"

"*No, to all those questions. He didn't know. Jaemee didn't want him to know. She knew he would never leave your mother. So she had the little girl and later married an older man who was willing to be a sire to her daughter. He was a very good man. Your little sister Eun Wan Park is alive and doing well. For now. The rest is up to you.*"

"*What do you mean?*" Sunni was overwhelmed, confused. "*If all this is true, why are you coming to me now? What's the point of bringing it all up and creating all this hurt? You haven't told my mother, have you? You won't tell her?"*

"No, I don't plan on telling her anything." He emphasized the word 'plan' and then continued. "That is, as long as things go as I want them to. You are going to go to work for me, little Miss Smarty Pants."

"What? Why? And how would I do that?"

"Because, you see, if you don't do everything I'm going to be asking of you, your mother will learn about Jaemee and your sister. And I will personally see to it that she learns that you knew about it all along and kept it from her. She will be told that your father shared everything with you. Your father even shared pictures of your sister with you. And you even sent money for your sister."

"But I didn't! I wouldn't! I couldn't! That's a huge lie."

"But your mother June won't know that, will she? She will believe me. And she will need me to console her. You will be gone. Finished. Out of her life. And I will be most important to her."

"No! I won't allow that!"

"Oh, but you will." Joo Jhim sneered as his lips curled into a smile, but his hard eyes exhibited no kindness.

"And if you don't, I will not only reveal everything to your mother, but I will make sure she has an 'accident' that will take her life. Your mother has come to respect my power. She knows what I can do to her. I daresay, you do, also. So your dear mother will not only be hurt emotionally, but she will also be hurt physically, and perhaps even die. Do you want that, my dear Sunni?"

Sunni sat stunned for several minutes, saying nothing. A tear threatened to escape from her left eye. She quickly swiped at it, determined not to let this man see her as weak.

Why was Joo doing this? How could she determine if this was the truth? She needed to find a way to get DNA done on that little girl. She had to hire someone who could go to South Korea and find the truth. And she had to protect her mother. She had to get her away from him. She couldn't trust this man. He was not just cruel; she was sure he was dangerously crazy!

Sunni turned to look at Joo who had been staring out the window at some distant object. He had a sharply etched profile that gave him an even more sinister look. He had slicked back his sparse black hair on the sides and pulled strands of hair down down onto his forehead giving an appearance of ruggedness. His eyebrows furrowed as he turned to look directly at Sunni. He was clearly unmoved by her shock or pain.

She took a deep breath. "What do you want?" Sunni whispered, trying to keep her voice steady.

Joo smiled again, the same nasty smile.

"I have many reasons to be here in this country. The least of which is to share this joyous news of your long-lost sister with you. That is just a small part of my plan.

"You are now working for a giant research lab. You must realize the result of the research in that building at Cameron Bio-Tech is worth millions, if not billions. It is research that will help the United States become a leader in gene-alteration research. My country-our country," he corrected himself, "wants that research. We will steal it from the United States and our country will become rich and powerful once again. You

are going to discredit that facility and send all of that research to a specific lab in North Korea."

Sunni ended with a sigh, her face crumpled into a mix of anger and sadness, as glistening teardrops streamed from her eyes.

"That was the beginning. I didn't know where to turn, how to escape, how to deny him. This man would ruin my mother and me. And I knew he had been hurting my mother physically, already. I didn't know how much more she could take.

"I did everything I could do to protect my mother," she continued, "while at the same time appeasing Joo Jhim. Then, Joo began to complain that I was moving too slowly at Cameron BioTech. He said I wasn't doing enough to discredit the lab. I wasn't able to get into all their research files. He was always angry. Always threatening. I became more and more afraid for my mother. But last week I did something to protect my mother and myself. I think maybe Joo or his operatives above him found out."

Sunni stopped talking, took another sip from her glass of water. Quay looked at Sam and Boogie. He shook his head.

"So did you kill Joo to protect your mother? To end his hold over you? Is that what you did, Sunni?" asked Sam.

"No! No! I could never kill anyone! I would never..."

"But you hated him. You hated what he was doing to your mother. You admitted that you hated the control he had over you. You had every reason to kill him, Sunni. And you were there that day."

"But I didn't kill him!" Sunni's voice rose in a high, insistent plea. "I didn't!"

Drew was standing, leaning across the table, with his face directly in front of Sunni's. "So we have a man who was killed, in a parking lot just before you arrived, and you're saying he was killed by someone who knew about that chip in your arm, and about the information you had access to at Cameron BioTech? Sunni! Would you believe that if you were me? How can we believe you?"

"Let's take a step back," said Quay. "Let's assume for now, that maybe she is telling the truth. We can proceed safely, I believe, as long as we have Sunni with us. She can verify or deny whatever we discover. "Miss Hyun, you aren't going anywhere for a while. Not until we settle this murder and this case. Do you understand?"

Sunni nodded, wiping her teary eyes with the back of her hand.

"This is going to have far-reaching repercussions," Sam said. "Let's put double security on her mother right now. Make sure you've checked everything, Boogie, okay?"

Boogie nodded, grabbed his cell phone and walked to the bedroom to place a call.

"Okay," Quay almost growled. "Let's hear the rest of it. What did you do with this CRISPR research at Cameron?"

Sunni looked directly at Quay without wavering under his steel blue glare. A sly smile began to emerge.

"I stole all the research data and studies on CRISPR-Cas9. I gave Joo some bits and pieces. Never all of it. And I hid the rest of it. Right now I alone have all the information that can change the world. The data and research is on a microchip. That microchip, as I explained, if placed in the right hands, could end not only modern diseases, it could also lead the entire world in a hyper jump into the future with increased food production from perfect non-diseased plants. Think about what that means. Or consider the opposite. The information from this study could destroy civilized society if it falls into the wrong hands. I couldn't let that information go to Joo Jhim. His would be the 'wrong hands'. Yes, Cameron BioTech also has the information, but it isn't completely patented yet. It won't be patented until they complete all their tests. That will take a while. Tests must be done. Human trials must be completed. Then patents must be applied for. In the meantime, I can protect it myself by keeping it away from people like Joo."

Quay and Sam groaned in unison. Drew and Dan stared at Sunni with matching glowering expressions. Sunni Hyun was telling them that she had the power to decide into whose hands her chip would fall. She could destroy Cameron BioTech by releasing the data to another agent, or she could save Cameron BioTech by protecting it. It was an enormous coup.

"Talk about letting the chips fall where they may. Literally! She's doing it. There are too many loose ends. We'd better get going," announced Drew. "It's been a long day. It's getting late. We've got a lot of background to check on. Boogie can send us what he's got. We can do the follow-up on Ms. Hyun's mother and possible sister. We'll coordinate with you Quay. We'll check in as soon as we have more info. We're going to head back to the Cities for her mother, first."

"Sounds good," said Quay. "Boogie will do most of the online digging. He's good at finding stuff nobody else can! We'll have him work with you."

Boogie walked back into the room, heard the last bit of the conversation, and nodded in agreement. He then looked directly at Quay catching his attention and nodded once more in what appeared to be another kind of acknowledgement, sat down, and looked around. "What'd I miss?" he asked looking from Sam to Quay to Sunni. Sam and Quay shook their heads.

"We'll be in touch," said Dan as he and Drew pulled on their coats and walked quickly out the door.

Quay stood and stretched. "It's gonna get dicey! Dan and Drew are taking off. They'll keep in touch. I've got to get some air. It's been a long day. Want to go for a walk out to the lake, Sam?"

"Sure!" Sam was on her feet reaching for her jacket before Quay could get to his.

"Boogie, will you stay with her for a few minutes? We need a break. Maybe she and the pooch need a bite to eat," he added as a seeming afterthought.

Quay pulled on his jacket, and added a stocking cap on his head, before reaching into his pockets for leather gloves. He looked down at his hands and saw the square, wrapped, pink pieces of bubble gum he had stashed away. His whole frame was tight and tense. He began unwrapping a piece of gum before pulling on his gloves. He opened the door for Sam, popped the gum in his mouth, gave another glowering glance at Sunni, and nodded to Boogie with a wink. Boogie nodded back in understanding. It was a "Watch her and beware!" look.

Sunni smiled now as they walked out and reached down to pat her dog at her feet. She ran her hand through the soft golden fur behind his ears and on his neck. The dog raised his head and gave his mistress a quick nuzzle while wagging his tail happily at his owner.

Sunni continued running her hand over the dog's head and back. She couldn't feel it, but she knew it was there. During her time working as a research assistant at Cameron BioTech, Sunni Hyun had carefully stolen and hidden away all the data and studies she could access; she placed everything on a special microchip that was also embedded under the skin of this friendly golden retriever sitting at her feet. She'd named him Chip for one very important reason. He was her security. He was her everything – in many more ways than anyone suspected. She was happy for so many reasons that he was with her now. It was all so perfect. She was sure it would work out. Joo was dead. The BCA was involved and would protect her and her mother. They would find out who these people were and stop them. And she would finally be able to get her life back on track. It had to work!

She straightened, placed her hands around the warm cup of coffee Boogie had poured for her, and smiled at him as he filled the dog's dish with fresh kibble. Boogie watched her with a puzzled expression. She smiled again and bent to pet Chip. "You are such a great dog, Chip," she said as she rubbed her hand again over his back.

CHAPTER TEN
The Ambush

They'd parked their vehicles in the double garage next to the house. The night rolled in silently. The sky was clear now. A luminous white, full moon lit up the frozen lake ahead of them. Tight, thick stands of pine, oak, and maple trees lined each side of the path leading to the lake. A trail had been cleared through the woods, not by nature, but by man. Several trees had fallen in chaotic angles off to the sides of the trail. Weeds and bushy branches spiked up in shining silver slivers that reflected the moonlight. They flourished in bushy spheres over and around the path.

Quay led the way from the house with Samantha following in silence behind him. The subzero night air etched their faces with brisk pinpricks. In typical Minnesota form, they had each ducked their heads into the collars of their coats, chins down into the neckline. Quay wore a dark blue parka that blended into the night. He'd pulled the hood up and forward over his stocking cap and pulled up the inside collar to shield his face from the cold. Sam pulled up the collar of her wool pea coat, and wound the fringed green plaid wool scarf around the collar pulling it tightly up over her nose and mouth. A dark knit cap covered her loose auburn curls allowing only her eyebrows and eyes to be exposed to the air. Their breathing pushed puffs of white air ahead of them.

"Damn, it's cold!" muttered Quay. He looked up. Ice crystals circled in a blue arc around the moon. Not a good sign. Common lore was that ice crystals around the moon meant a storm was brewing.

"That's not good," Quay noted.

"What's not good?" Sam looked up to follow Quay's gaze. "Oh," she said in understanding. "The moon, huh? Haven't heard a weather report. Maybe a storm coming. What are we doing out here, Quay?" Sam's voice trembled now as she shivered not from fear, but from the cold.

Quay looked at her and then motioned ahead of them. "I saw a small building down here by the lake when we pulled in last night. I'm guessing it's a boathouse."

He was talking a bit loudly, she thought. His voice would carry in this cold. "Just a place to get away, find some shelter, and privacy. We need to talk about this," he continued, almost projecting his voice.

She understood now. She played along. Over the last two years, they'd begun to sync with one another; lately, they innately understood each other's mannerisms, reactions, and cues. They'd spent so much time together they acted almost as one. Right now, they were in tune on hyper-alert.

They continued walking, now side by side, on the path leading to the lake. The snow had been brushed away and a set of fresh tire tracks led the way down to the small shed.

"It must be a boat house down here. Looks like they drove down here not long ago," Sam said in her pseudo-loud voice. In a quieter voice she said, "But don't you think we could have sat in your car and turned on the heat? This is a bit remote to be walking around out here at night. We don't know who's around here."

An owl's hoot from a nearby tree seemed to emphasize her point. She jumped.

"My thought exactly," responded Quay in a gruff whisper. He directed her, steering her walking more to the left of the path. "We don't know who's out here." Suddenly, he reached out to grab Sam's arm, quickly pulling her close to him as he ducked behind a tree off to the left.

"Quay!" she pushed against him whispering in a low growl.

"Shhh!" He put his mouth over hers.

Sam responded, then pulled away whispering, "What's going on? What are we doing? Did you see something?"

Quay leaned to her ear, pulling her close again. "I'm pretty sure we've got company." Sam looked up at him inquiringly. "Listen to me," Quay said. "You saw the nod from Boogie when he came back after the phone call? They've tracked us. Gotta be another tracking chip. She must have another chip on her."

She nodded and slumped against him a bit. "Rats! So now what? Did Boogie call it in? How long before we get backup? Any idea?" She whispered and peeked over Quay's shoulder and surveyed the yard behind them.

"Not sure about time. But help is on the way. We are just decoys to lure them away from the house. I'm hoping our trackers won't want to have us out here if, or when, they decide to attack the house and go after Sunni. Put your arms around my neck. But keep your head down. If they are here, we want them to think we are just de-stressing, so-to-speak."

The sound one makes when walking on snow in sub-zero temperatures echoes and crunches much like walking on a bowl of crispy cereal. Quay and Sam stiffened as they heard the rhythmic crunches at the same time. They each tensed in readiness as footfalls in the snow approached nearby. Someone across the path and to the right of their position was making a poor attempt of sneaking up on them.

Sam pulled her scarf down under her chin. She smiled up at Quay, looked into his steely blue eyes, and pushed Quay back against the tree as she snugged in tighter.

"Just in time," she murmured. "Let's do this!" She moved her hands up his back and pulled tightly around his neck closing the space between their bodies. Quay slowly slid one hand down his side between them to reach into his holster for his Glock 19. He pulled it out while carefully controlling his movement. Sam slowly caressed his face, and then dropped her hand between them to pull her own Glock from her holster.

"Oh my dear," Quay chuckled softly in her ear, "what smooth hands you have. Want to put them to work?"

"Why, of course, sweets! Let's show them what we can do," Sam murmured.

"Wait for it," Quay muttered softly.

"Always," Sam whispered with a sly smile.

Another louder set of footfalls joined in unison with the first ones as the hunt party grew and neared.

They could almost hear the hunters breathing.

Quay whispered again in Sam's ear. "Maybe two, possibly three." The cold air was forcing the visitors to breathe open-mouthed. Sam was holding her breath. She nodded slightly at Quay's observation. Quay was breathing slowly and easily. She could feel his chest rise and fall with each breath. It was a moment of comfort before the battle.

Suddenly two sharp, slapping retorts erupted from the house.

"Now!" Quay whirled around moving to the left away from the tree, shouting. Sam turned, ducked and slid right. Their moves were well-practiced choreography. They fired precisely at the same time at opposite targets. Quay had fired off to the left. She had dropped while firing to the right in a diagonal direction.

A brief responding muffled rat-a-tat-tat confirmed that their assailants were intent on taking them out. Sam felt the hiss of bullets flying past her ear and heard the thunks in rapid succession sink into the trunk of a nearby tree. AK47 she thought.

She aimed again in the direction of the shots and fired twice before rolling back behind the tree. She thought she'd gotten one. She'd heard the sound of his 'oomph' and then a crunching fall into the trees. She hunched herself into the smallest ball she could make and listened for another noise or shot. Quay hadn't made a sound. She'd heard other shots echo out into the night from nearer the house, but she hadn't heard Quay return fire nearby after the initial volley. She wondered how many trackers there were. She thought only three. If she'd gotten one, and another was near the house, maybe Quay was sighting the other one. She didn't dare call out. Quay might be crawling behind any shooters.

She decided to slide straight back into the brush behind her so she could begin circling around toward the house. Ten feet back and another set of bullets buried themselves into the snow bank next to her, kicking up ice chunks just where she'd been. She made a dive again for the brush, whirled and fired several shots back in the direction of the shooter. That would be guy number two, she thought. Still, there was no indication if she'd gotten that one or not.

She could hear Chip barking madly in the house. The dog was still inside and alive, but he was definitely upset. He didn't sound at all like that friendly pup they'd left a few minutes ago. His vicious snarls and barks also meant at least one of the shooters had probably tried to get into the house to Boogie and Sunni. As long as Chip was still barking, that was good, she thought. They'd take out the dog first, if they got inside.

Sam realized that Boogie would have locked the house up tight as soon as Quay and Sam walked out the door. The windows of the safe house were bullet proof; the doors were steel. Boogie knew when he should take Sunni and move to the safe room in the house. The dog's barking indicated they hadn't moved to that safe room, yet. Boogie was waiting. Or he was talking with command about how they should approach this sudden assault. There was no way these attackers were going to get Sunni Hyun. They could count on Boogie to keep her safe.

There was still no reaction from Quay's area. What was going on? Where was Thompson? She usually knew where he was. It was too quiet. She wondered if she should work herself over to his last location. Then she decided against it. "He's a big boy, " she muttered to herself. "He can take care of himself."

As she continued to circle forward toward the house, she thought Quay must have been doing that, too. In the meantime, she decided to send an alert. She ducked down again into the weeds and brush and pulled out her phone. A speed dial sent an SOS to the BCA. She was sure Boogie would have sent out an alert. But another wouldn't hurt. The SOS simply sent the signal that officers were under fire and gave a GPS location. She knew help would begin arriving in minutes. Local departments would respond first. Then others. She and Quay had to be patient now and hold them off. She listened for more movement.

Then the crunching came again. Footsteps. She thought it was a single person. A barrage of shots rang out, a voice bellowed in shock, a grunt nearby. She watched in horror as her partner and friend, Quay Thompson, crashed through the brush, stumbling into a slow motion fall just three feet away from her.

"Quay!" she screamed. She began laying down cover fire in the direction of the shots as she scrambled through the brush and snow to Quay. Return fire sprayed the ground into her previous location just behind her. She heard sirens. There was help coming. Shots still rang out, but they seemed to be pulling back away from her and Quay and away from the house. Maybe they were covering their retreat. Car engines revved, and the roar of the motor began to recede. Then silence. They were gone.

Samantha Atwood couldn't remember a time that she had ever been this frightened. Even when that crazy security guard had kidnapped her last year and taken off with her in that wild chase up north, she hadn't felt this weak and helpless.

She couldn't be positive they were in the clear yet, so she belly-crawled through the snow and brush toward Quay. Blotches of snow sprayed from the low branches blinding her. The dry branches scratched at her cheeks and caught in her loose curls pulling her hair out from her knit cap. She reached out to touch Quay's arm. He wasn't moving.

"Quay?" she whispered. "Quay, I'm here."

She heard a low moan.

Then, "Yeah, 'sgood," he mumbled.

"Quay, they're going. Help is here. Just hang on. Where are you hit?"

"Dunno. Hurts."

Samantha Atwood took on a new role as Samantha, the protector. Quay had previously held the protector role. Now it was her turn. She scanned the area one more time. It appeared clear now. Laying her gun down next to Quay, she reached to him, feeling cautiously, probing.

"Where, Quay? Tell me where. I need you to stay with me. Talk to me."

Quay groaned. She heard a muttered, slurred word that sounded something like, "Leggg." There was no other response.

"Leg? Is that it? Let me see." The moon dappling through the trees served as her only light as Sam slid her hand down from Quay's chest over his abdomen and further to his left thigh and leg that was nearest her. Nothing there. She moved her fingers across to the right thigh. Quay jumped reflexively and groaned.

"Oh, God! Don't!" he commanded.

"It's there?"

"Mmmhmm." His voice was a low pain-filled growl.

She removed her glove and ran her fingers lightly over the thigh. It was a sticky wet. Pulling her hand away, she held it up to the moonlight. Blood. He was definitely bleeding. She examined further. A lot of blood. Her first thought was femoral artery. If Quay had been hit in the upper leg, the bullet could have hit his femoral artery. He would bleed to death if they didn't get help soon.

She scrambled up on her knees and pulled off her scarf laying it across the injured leg.

"Quay, I'm going to wrap my scarf around your leg. I've got to stop the bleeding. I'm going to have to move your leg a bit to do it. Hang on!"

Quay nodded. His eyes were closed. She could see he was clenching his teeth.

"Want some bubble gum?" Her voice was strained; she was trying to take his mind off the pain while she slid the scarf under his leg.

"Oh, don't think so! Maybe something a bit stronger!" he groaned and half-chuckled. He reached out to grab her arm as she finished tying the scarf.

"That's good." At least she'd gotten a bit of a laugh from him. That was a good sign, she thought. "You'll be okay. Just hang on Quay. Help is coming. I sent out the SOS."

She pulled her phone out of her pocket again and dialed Boogie.

"Yeah," Boogie answered on the first ring. "Where are you? What's happening out there?"

"We are in the woods to the back left of the house, Boogie. We're about twenty yards out. Quay's been hit. He needs help in here right away. What's going on there?"

"We are clear. I think most of them cleared out when the local department started pulling in. There may be one or two down by the door. I don't know. Stay low. Wait. I'll get someone in."

"Hurry, Boogie! There isn't much time. He's bleeding a lot. It's bad!"

"On it!" Boogie hung up. Sam dropped her phone back into her pocket, and lowered her head to Quay's face.

"We've got you covered. You just need to concentrate on staying with me. Got it?" She brushed a few errant leaves and gathering snowflakes away from a gash on his forehead caressing his face with soft feathery touches. "Quay? Quay? Answer me."

"Yeah, I'm trying." He was whispering. "It's awfully cold, Sam."

Samantha inched closer laying her head next to him with her arm across his chest. "It'll be okay. It'll be okay. I've gotcha," she whispered.

The ambulance EMTs arrived just after the local sheriff and two other local city patrolmen pulled in with their lights flashing. The three vehicles led the way for the ambulance. The ambulance followed them into the parking area and idled. Boogie sprinted out of the house and motioned to the vehicle. He pointed and directed the EMTs to Quay and Sam. Sam stepped forward, called out, and began waving her arms. "Hurry! Hurry! Over here!" she called. A spotlight from one of the patrol cars found her.

She held her hand up to shield her eyes. It looked like three people were getting out of the vehicle carrying a gurney and walking toward her while scanning the area. It looked like two men and a woman. They must wonder what they've walked into, thought Sam.

CHAPTER ELEVEN
Need Some Gum?

"I'm Ann," said the sturdy, dark-haired woman who stepped out in front of the group of EMTs. "This is Brad," she said motioning to the tall, young man on her right. "Jay, my husband, is driving tonight. We're here to help. What have we got here?"

"Thank God you're here! We're BCA. I'm Sam. It's my partner, Quay." Sam had stepped up to meet them and quickly shook their hands. She turned and pointed toward Quay. "It was an ambush! I don't know what you've been told, but my partner Thompson has to be your first consideration. He took a hit. Gunshot wound. It's his right leg. We can take care of the others after we get him on the way."

"We'll take care of him," Ann said with matter-of-fact authority. "Let's get him loaded and then on an IV." The EMTs quickly loaded Quay onto a gurney and carried him to the ambulance. Sam followed and waved at Boogie. "Take care of him," called Boogie. "We'll take care of this end. I'll see you in a bit."

Sam crawled in by the front of the gurney to stand along side Quay's head. The man named Jay continued to the cab of the ambulance, climbed behind the driver's wheel, started it up, turned on the lights and began to pull out.

Boogie understood she needed to be with Quay, Sam thought. He would head up the situation at the house. A clean up crew would be called in. Sunni Hyun had to be moved again. And scanned again. She was sure Boogie had calculated what she and Quay had already figured out. There had to be another tracking chip! Whether Sunni knew about it or not, was a question she would have to answer. Right now, saving Quay Thompson's life was the first order of business.

She reached across and through the wires now attached to Quay and grabbled Quay's hand as two of the EMTs began to work on cutting away his pants leg. She felt his fingers give a slight squeeze of her hand. He knew she was there.

"His name again?" asked the EMT.

"Quay Thompson. It's Quay. I know it's an odd name. Q-u-a-y," she spelled. "Thompson with o-n. Quay was his mother's maiden name, ya know? I can't remember his mother's first name. His dad died when he was in his teens. He lost his wife when a sniper killed her while she was delivering a big scientific breakthrough announcement at Cameron BioTech in the Twin Cities. He's been on the hunt for her shooter since then. You might remember that..." Sam suddenly realized she was rambling. She stopped abruptly and looked from one to the other of the medics. They glanced at her, nodded and continued working.

"Mr. Thompson, Quay, can you hear me? Can you open your eyes and look at me?" Ann asked.

"Yeah," mumbled Quay as he opened his eyes into narrow slits and looked at the EMT through what appeared to be a haze of pain.

Sam squeezed his hand. "That's good Quay. Stay with us."

Brad said, "We're going to begin an IV on you. We'll get another going that will ease your level of pain soon. Looks like you've lost some blood. Can you tell me where you feel pain?"

"My leg, I think. Hurts like hell. Just so damned cold all over." Quay's body gave an involuntary shudder as he spoke.

"We'll warm you up. You're in shock. We can help you. Just relax, fella," Brad said, patting Quay on the shoulder.

There was so much blood. She didn't think it seemed to be spurting, but what did she know? Hopefully, it hadn't hit the artery. The emergency techs didn't speak as they worked together with calm precision.

"His GAWK, gunshot wound, is near the side of the right femur," commented Brad, clarifying the EMT jargon for Sam. Ann pulled a small iPad tablet from her jacket pocket and began to fill in data. "His femur may have been hit. We'll know better after we get him to the hospital. We're going to apply a tourniquet proximal to the injury to control the bleeding. Mark the time as 10:35 p.m.," he said to Sam and looked at Ann who nodded and continued writing in the chart.

The two of them worked as a unit and quickly applied the tourniquet, while talking constantly to Quay. They needed him awake. They checked his vitals: blood pressure, pulse, and respiration. Ann continued to enter each number on the chart in her tablet.

Jay called to his crew in the back with estimated time of arrival at the hospital. "We've got open road on highway 14. No snow. With lights on and light traffic, we should have arrival in ten minutes."

"That's good! Let's get his clothes off," said Brad, as he began tugging at Quay's jacket. "I see he's got a good gash on his forehead. We need to see if there's another wound anywhere."

While Ann and Brad worked efficiently together, Sam sat back feeling a bit more at ease accepting that Quay was in good hands. She listened as they continued to talk to Quay while they worked, making sure he was maintaining consciousness.

"Bullet is not in the leg. Looks like a through-and-through," Ann said perfunctorily, looking up at Brad. "It may have cracked the femur."

"Let's gauze the opening and wrap it tight," decided Brad.

The lights of the ambulance flashed, tinting the passing snow-covered fields with blurs of red and blue. Sam watched the undulating white snow drifts and rust-colored weeds spiking through the snow as they flew by. They were running silent with no siren.

As Sam listened to the EMTs work as a team, it brought to mind how she and Quay had become more and more comfortable with each other working together. They were a good team, she mused. Then her mind jumped to the events of the last hours. Maybe they shouldn't have split up tonight. If she had stayed with him, she could have covered him. It had all happened so fast. She wasn't even sure how many attackers there actually were. She thought she'd gotten at least one. She didn't know if Quay had gotten one or not. Boogie had said there were one or two up by the house. He must have found a way to fire on them. It had all happened so fast, she thought again.

Poor Boogie, she thought, abruptly. He wasn't a field guy. He was an inside guy. He was their top tech guy, not a shooter. He'd been trained to shoot, but it wasn't what he knew or wanted to do. He just happened to be in the wrong place at the wrong time. She wondered how he had protected Sunni Hyun. Had he ever gotten to the safe room? Maybe he had been the one who managed to take out one of the attackers. Knowing Boogie as she did, he must have been in a chaotic, but ordered panic. It was an oxymoron, but so was Boogie. Poor guy. They had needed him there for the tech analysis. He understood exactly what Sunni was talking about. But this action definitely wasn't his field of expertise. She and Quay had been trained. They knew what to do.

And still, she hadn't been able to protect her partner. She shook her head and looked over at Quay. He was deathly white. She needed him to be all right. She needed him to be strong again. She. Just. Needed. Him.

She began to review the night. It all made sense now. The nod from Boogie indicating they had company, the Double D team rushing out the door, Quay leading her on a walk to draw off the attackers. There was the question of how they had been discovered. How had they been tracked to the safe house? They'd thought when Sunni gave them the chip she'd removed from her arm, that it was all clear. Had she lied to them? If Sunni had lied to them, the big question was why? She had called Quay for help. And then she had lied. What was going on?

Returning to the present, she decided first things first. She needed to make sure that Quay was going to be okay. She'd stay with him as long as was necessary. She could call Boogie and the BCA Superintendent after they got to the hospital. Jay, the driver, had said they were headed to the closest hospital. That was the Immanuel-St. Joseph's Mayo Hospital in Mankato. She'd contact the Double D team and Boogie when she knew something about Quay. Then she'd find out what was happening with everything else. But, first things, first.

Fighting to stay aware of his surroundings, Quay listened to the man and woman working on him. They were good, he thought. He tried to puzzle out what had gone wrong tonight. He had known the attackers were nearby. He'd heard them. The frigid night air had even carried the sounds of their muted breathing. Sam had leaned against him. She'd heard it, too. They'd practiced the routine many times in training. This time it had been time to put it to actual use. He'd reached for his gun; she'd reached for hers. He remembered shouting, "Now!" and diving low to the left while Sam dove low and right in their oft-rehearsed choreography. The men, whoever they were, had AK47s, he thought, and they had suddenly begun firing on him and Sam with precision. He remembered that it was almost as if he and Sam had a spotlight shining on them. They knew exactly where to aim.

Those guys were good. He'd aimed in the direction of the incoming shots and heard a target go down with an "oomph" and crunch. The shooter fell, but had continued firing as he fell. Quay remembered thinking the guy must have had his finger stuck on the trigger. The rat-a-tat of the automatic rifle continued for several seconds. Quay had belly-crawled to the cover of a nearby shrub while scanning the area for another shooter. He thought he had found the guy. Then he thought he'd heard Sam move over closer to his right. He had just begun to move to better cover behind a nearby tree when the remaining shooter began setting down a blanket of fire in an all-out assault. The tree had taken several direct hits, with bark chips flying off creating mini-wooden missiles. One had gotten him on the forehead. Just as he dove for cover again, he'd felt a sudden knife-hot pain catch him in the thigh. His first thought was to wonder if it was another one of the bark missiles from the tree.

But the power and speed of the hit took his breath away. It felt like someone had jabbed a hot poker through his leg. He'd been shot. His body had gone into instinctive survival mode as his training instructor's orders popped into his mind. Get down! Stay Down! Don't move! Listen!

Where was that SOB? Had any of his own shots hit the guy? Where was Sam? Had she been hit, too? Questions had spun through his mind while he'd visually searched the area. The pain...

God in heaven, he remembered how his leg had hurt. The arc of pain spread all the way up to his midsection. He hadn't been able to move his leg. Then he had felt the cold creeping up from his toes. His body had begun instinctively shuddering as his arms and legs vibrated in continuous spasms. He was cold, but that wasn't the cause of the uncontrolled shaking. Had he lost a lot of blood, he wondered? He just couldn't force his body to stop the relentless, awful trembling. He'd wondered if he was going into shock. He hadn't been able to see anything. It was so dark in those woods. He'd begun to feel light-headed. It had gotten so quiet. So still. He'd wondered if everyone was gone. Had they left? No. He knew Sam wouldn't leave him. She was near. He'd known it, felt it.

He was gathering himself and pushing through the pain to pull himself semi-upright when several shots zinged by his head. He'd slunk down into a mound of snow again. He thought he'd heard Sam call out to him after that as she returned fire. Pain smothered everything, and he'd helplessly begun to fade.

The next thing he remembered was Sam crouched next to him running her hands over him, searching for the wound. She'd said something about blood. So much hurt. Then came the lightening strike of scorching, throbbing pain when she touched his leg! The searing heat of a white hot branding iron arced through his entire body!

The last thing he remembered before the darkness enveloped him was Sam saying, "I've gotcha."

The ride to the hospital had taken less than ten minutes thanks to a very professional driver. A crew of doctors and nurses met the ambulance at the door ready to relieve the EMTs. Sam thanked Ann, Brad, and Jay and crawled out after Quay when they unloaded him. She watched the hospital staff whisk him away into the emergency room while she stayed in the reception area to give the admitting staff Quay's information. When everything was completed, she settled in for the wait.

A light snow had begun falling again. She looked out the window at the white flakes drifting down. The winter night was quiet like the hospital. It was deceptively peaceful, she thought. She knew she would have to be patient. She had steeled herself to be ready for whatever news the doctors brought. She glanced at her watch and noted the time. Just past midnight. It had been a long day. Time to begin the calls.

She spoke with Dan from the local BCA first. She quickly gave him an update on Quay's status, and then she asked for a run down on Dan and Drew's part in the evening's events. Dan told her he and Dave were running the clean up at the safe house. He explained they were nearby when the dog had alerted on the noise outside and had begun setting up such a fierce warning. He said they'd seen two men near the house trying to gain entry. Dan and Drew had called out and the men turned to them and pulled weapons, so he and Drew had fired on them. The two men were both dead. That was when a second crew had begun the attack on Sam and Quay in the woods. He told her they'd found another body in the woods after the ambulance left with Quay.

"We figured you or Quay took out that one. It sounded like quite a firefight out there. They were using suppressed rounds. But your return fire came through loud and clear."

Sam nodded and paused as she remembered. Finally realizing she needed to give voice to her thoughts, she said, "Yes, we had a battle on our hands. Quay and I were both receiving and giving fire. Quay took one out, first. I think they got Quay in one of those volleys. I wasn't sure where Quay was for a bit there. I was able to lay down cover fire, so I could get to Quay once I determined that he was down. I don't know what happened after that. It got quiet. I was busy trying to take care of Quay."

"The one fellow who was left tried to circle around the house," Dan explained. "Drew caught him just as he was sneaking out of the woods. He ran; Drew fired, took him down. He's gone, too. We don't have anyone who can tell us anything, now. I'm sorry. The bodies were clean. No information on any of them. We'll try to ID with fingerprints, but don't expect much. They were well armed, had a couple AK47s, and some smaller revolvers. We found their car parked off the road in a field driveway about a quarter mile up the road from the house. It was a rental."

"Bummer that we can't get anything on them. Be sure to sweep the car."

"Yeah, we are already on it. We've got the clean up crew in working already. Boogie is in charge of the woman and the dog for now. He'll move them to our location in Mankato. We figure there must be another tracking device on the woman. She's got some explaining to do. We aren't going to let it slide after they tried to take you and Quay out. She's got a lot of talking to do! We've got her locked up at the Mankato bureau right now. You can talk to her when you get here. Drew and I got here about thirty minutes ago."

"Thanks, Dan. I agree about Ms. Hyun. I'm glad you guys are on it. I'm going to wait it out here with Quay until we get the all clear. He's going to be fine. I'm not going to believe anything less. He's tough. But I'm pretty sure he's going to be out of commission for a while. I'll meet up with all of you as soon as I can. Keep me in the loop."

"Will do," said Dan.

"Oh! And will you get in touch with Super Mike at the BCA? We're going to need another safe house, and clearance to keep moving on this."

"I'll be on it first thing in the morning. No point in waking a sleeping grizzly bear tonight," he said with a smile in his voice.

Sam knew what he meant. The Superintendent was going to be spitting tacks!

Sam had just curled up on the waiting room sofa, and nodded off into an uneasy sleep when a doctor came through the ER door.

"Miss Atwood? Are you with Mr. Thompson?" he asked.

"Yes, how is he?"

"Does he have family we can call?"

"His wife is dead. He has a brother, John, who's a county sheriff up at Lutsen. You can call him, I can give you his number, but I know he'll give permission for me to sign for Quay and get info until he can get here. I'm Quay's partner. The Bureau has us sign papers that will allow me to stand in for his family. So, what's the prognosis?"

"We'll call the brother just to let him know. But I suppose I can fill you in now. He's lost a lot of blood; we had to give him several pints. His wound will heal. He was one lucky guy, though. The bullet barely missed the femoral artery. It also missed the bone. That's almost a downright miracle. It was a through and through, but it did do a major tear up of muscle, ligaments, and tendons. Now that we have him stabilized, we will need to head to the operating room and go in to repair the muscle and torn ligaments and tendons. He's going to be here for a few days. After that, he's going to need rehab for that muscle. All in all, though, your partner is lucky to be alive. He's one incredibly lucky fellow."

Samantha Atwood said a silent prayer of thanks, wiped the unbidden tears from her eyes, and impulsively stood and hugged the doctor.

"Thank you! Thank you! Thank you!" she smiled up at him. "Is he conscious? Can I see him before he goes to the OR?"

"He's drifting in and out. You can see him just for a couple seconds. We've got to get going into surgery. Follow me."

Sam hurried after the doctor as he led her back into the emergency room cubicle. She saw a washed-out version of Quay lying on the bed. Wires were attached to his chest, and IVs were attached to both arms. She thought to herself, this wasn't real. It wasn't really Quay. Quay was strong. Quay was invincible. But this version was barely there. This was an unrecognizable body dangerously in peril.

"Quay?" she whispered bending near his ear. "Quay? Can you hear me?"

One blue eye opened in a small slit, peering out at her under thick lashes.

She placed a hand on his head, running her fingers carefully through his thick, blond hair. It was a caress of caring that she hoped he could sense.

"Quay, I'm so sorry! I should have stayed with you. I shouldn't have gone the opposite direction. This shouldn't have happened. I'm so sorry." She was fumbling for words, her voice quivering with emotion.

Quay shook his head slightly and forced out a gravelly, "No! Not your fault! My stupidity."

"We are going to make this right! I'm going to follow up with Sunni Hyun. We will get them. This will be ended. You need to be strong. Concentrate on healing that leg. I'm going to see Boogie. I'll be back after your surgery. You understand? I'll be here!"

Quay nodded and closed his eyes, with a mumbled "Okay."

Sam patted his shoulder, squeezing a bit for encouragement, and turned to go.

"Sam?" Quay said with a slightly stronger urgency to his voice.

She turned back, staring at him, the worry resonating through her face. He stared directly at her with those fierce blue eyes. Something was different, though.

"Yes?"

"I'm going to want some bubble gum when I get out of surgery. And some beer. Better bring lots of both."

She laughed for what seemed like the first time in hours. The old twinkle was still there in his eyes. She knew he was going to be all right.

CHAPTER TWELVE
Aftermath

Sam was on her phone as she walked to the waiting area. Someone needed to pick her up and get her to Boogie and Sunni. It took only ten minutes before the local police squad car pulled up at the entrance to pick her up. It was a local officer on night duty. He introduced himself, and they sped away.

Her first questions were about Sunni, the dog and Boogie. The officer assured her they were headed in that direction. It was four a.m. in the dead of night. The quiet city lights glowed over the streets directing their way. The night was still black, but soon the sky would begin its morning greys, pastel blues, and pinks as the sun began to rise. She hadn't slept but for a few minutes while waiting for the doctor in the ER. She was tired, but her adrenalin still had her in hyper-drive. She needed to get at Sunni Hyun. She thought...she couldn't think...there weren't any words to describe what she'd like to do to that lying, conniving, evil, crazy witch-bitch of a dragon lady! She was so tense and keyed up, she didn't even know where to begin. Drew, Dan, and Boogie might have gotten more out of Sunni Hyun. She hoped.

Sunni Hyun was sitting on a chair at the end of the table in the upstairs conference room of the Mankato BCA headquarters. Her chin rested on her chest. She appeared to be dozing. The dog, Chip, sleeping soundly, was curled up near her feet.

Boogie, red-eyed and haggard looking, his long, brown hair hanging loosely across his forehead almost covering one eye, lay on the leather sofa. With his lanky body resembling a roller coaster track, he'd propped his laptop against his folded up knees. Boogie focused intently on the computer screen defiantly punching at the keyboard. It was obvious he was not only tired, he was angry. Not a good combination.

Drew, with experience born of dealing with pressure, had just brewed a fresh pot of coffee. Its aroma permeated the room. Dan sat at the other end of the conference table opposite Sunni.

Samantha Atwood took it all in with a single quick surveillance of the room. She closed the door behind her with purpose, walked directly across the room to Sunni Hyun, grabbed a handful of hair and pulled Sunni's head up, and slapped her with one resounding, forceful, solid smack across the right cheek. Sunni's eyes flew open in wide-eyed shock and fear as her head whipped to the side. She reflexively held her hand up to her cheek and turned back to stare at Sam with watery eyes.

"What did you think you were doing?" Sam asked in a very still, quiet voice. "Did you think you could get us all killed, and you would be free? What kind of game are you playing, lady?"

Drew stood and moved toward the two women. Boogie stopped jabbing at his computer keyboard, and Dan moved behind Sunni. Chip yelped, jumped up and skittered back away from both of them.

"I didn't know," said Sunni returning the angry scowl at Sam. Her voice shook. "I had nothing to do with what happened out there. I didn't know!" she repeated.

"Well, someone knew something. And it almost got Quay killed! He was trying to help you. That's what you wanted, right? Or was it that you wanted to get him killed? Let's get some things clear here, Sunny, or Sooni, or whatever you call yourself. We are going to get the truth from you, and we are going to get those bastards behind that attack that came in tonight."

"It's pronounced Sooni not Sunny," Sunni said quietly. "I will help you any way I can. I just don't know how they tracked us. I thought I had removed the only tracker I had on me. You saw that. I didn't think there was another."

Drew stepped in closer, bent over toward her, his face near hers. His dark eyes met hers as he said, "Sunni, there's a lot going on here. Let's back up. You said you have stolen all the research data from Cameron BioTech, right?"

"That's correct," said Sunni, looking up at him directly. "I took everything I could find."

"And what did you do with it?"

"Well, first I copied it and took it out on a flash drive. Two flash drives, actually. Then I transferred everything to a microchip."

"What did you do with that microchip, then?" asked Sam.

Sunni paused, looking from one angry face to another scowling, angry face. She took a deep breath before she exhaled and said, "I tried to tell them," she answered, pointing at Dan and Drew. "They told me to sit here until you came." She sighed and then continued, "I went to a vet with Chip one day to have him micro chipped for identification. That was when I realized what I could do to protect the information I'd stolen. I paid to have the vet put in the dog's ID chip, and then I told him I'd pay him extra if he'd implant a second chip in my dog. I told him it was my personal information that I wanted placed on my dog for his protection. He agreed, and the vet planted the data chip on Chip, too. Actually, that's why he's named Chip. Joo Jhim may have thought the dog was his idea, but his name was my idea." She paused, thinking, and then continued in a thoughtful tone, "Maybe he used Chip to implant a another chip to track me, but he never knew that I used the dog to hide my data on a chip, too."

The four of them looked at her in silence. Finally, Boogie said, "So you know for sure that this dog, Chip, has two chips implanted on him? One for general pet ID and another with the data you stole from Cameron BioTech?"

"Yes, that is correct," she answered in a soft voice. "That chip is what they want, but what they don't know is that I've hidden the research data I stole on a chip I had implanted on my dog. They will never know. They want it, but they must not get it. Ever. You've got to help me." Her voice rose to a fervent pitch.

Samantha Atwood looked around for the dog. Chip was sitting across the room watching the events guardedly. Sam squatted down, considering the pup and beckoned, calling the dog in a soft, friendly voice.

"Chip. Come, Chip. Come here, sweet puppy."

The pup stood, wagging its tail at the friendly recognition. Still not quite sure as he hesitated before coming near Sam, he finally lowered his head in a submissive bow, and stood before her. Sam scratched behind his ears and talked soothingly to him. "It's okay, fella. You're a good fella. Let me pet you, okay?"

She ran her long, slender fingers over his back and down the sleek, silky feather-covered haunches of his legs and then, under his tummy. He really was a beautiful dog, she thought. She finished her examination and patted him. The pup leaned forward and gave her an appreciative kiss on the nose. Sam laughed lightly and gave him another gentle pat.

"Dan, Drew, " Sam said, looking from one to the other, "do you think we could perhaps scan Chip while we're here to see if there's another tracking chip on him?"

"Definitely need to do that!" interrupted Boogie. "I'm thinking this dog is a walking information factory. He could probably be a bona fide science reference guide and atlas. Maybe he's even got a Farmer's Almanac on him!" His little joke broke through the tension. Sam gave out a brief chuckle and patted Chip, who wagged happily.

"We've got the equipment downstairs to run that check. Let's do that with Chip and let's also do Ms. Hyun one more time, just to be safe," agreed Dan, looking intently at Sunni. "If either one has a tracking chip, should we remove it?"

"Can you tell the difference between the tracking chip and the ID or data chip?" asked Sam.

"Should be able to," responded Boogie. "I can go along to be sure. What do you want to do with the data chip?"

"Let's leave it in place, for now," suggested Sam looking to Dan and Drew for agreement. "It's about as safe embedded on Chip as any place. But we really need to remove the tracker chip. Until that is done, none of us is safe. Let's remove and save the tracking chip, if you can. Boogie can work on the original tracker chip from Sunni, and if there is another tracker on Chip, compare it to this one, so we can continue to pull information from both, right Boogie?"

"Yeah. That should work," agreed Boogie.

Drew slipped a leash on Chip, and led him out the door. The dog looked back at Sunni with uncertainty, until she followed and encouraged him telling him, "It's okay, Chip. Let's go!" Dan and Boogie walked out, side by side with Sunni.

It was still very early in the pre-dawn morning. Sam knew they needed to find a new safe house, but for a few hours, she felt the BCA office was safe. There would be no way of tracking anything or anyone to this location. It would block signals and was totally secure. The adrenalin was wearing off. Samantha's body ached. She couldn't begin to imagine how Quay's body must feel about now. She needed to see him, after a little sleep for herself. She reached for her coat picking it up from the floor where she'd dropped it when she had blown into the room, looked at the small leather sofa, settled down into it, curled her legs up, pulled her coat over her, and closed her eyes. She needed sleep. They could wait a few hours here, but she wanted to move Sunni out before full daylight. She wanted to be ready for the next move.

When Boogie walked through the BCA office door an hour later, he found Samantha Atwood curled up on the sofa in Drew's office, sound asleep under her coat. She had curled into a small comma. He decided it would be better to let Sam sleep for a bit. She'd been through a lot. And there was more to come. They were going to have a busy day once the sun came up.

He looked around the office. Dan's corner office was a fairly large room with high ceilings and a set of six windows that hung from the ceiling and dropped down in narrow three-foot panels. The obvious effect would be for indirect daylight lighting that allowed for privacy but plenty of illumination. The room was spacious enough to hold a black leather sofa where Samantha now slept, a rather large modern looking glass-topped desk, a small black table with two chairs, and a credenza holding a flat-screened TV. Next to the table and chairs, a medium-sized recliner had been angled to face the TV for screening.

Boogie guessed they could spare about an hour and a half for Sam to sleep. Dan and Drew were still doing the final follow-up and processing in the lab with Sunni Hyun. He knew he needed sleep, too, but he was so keyed up about what they had discovered, he just wanted to get online and begin searching.

It had turned out Sunni Hyun was tracker free, just as she'd claimed. She was an enigma, though. He just didn't know what to make of that little Korean woman. She seemed to be tough while appearing fragile at the same time. What were they going to do with her?

Then there was that dog. It had turned out that poor dog had had three data chips embedded under his skin. One was the typical ID chip on the back of his neck registering the dog's name and owner in case it was lost. The second chip appeared to be the data chip with all the information from Cameron BioTech that Sunni had asked her vet to embed in the dog. They'd discovered that chip farther down Chip's back just above his right hip. The third chip was another tracking chip similar to the one Sunni Hyun had dug out of her arm yesterday. They found that one above Chip's left shoulder. As long as they stayed here with the dog, any signals would be blocked by the building's security system. But once they left, all bets would be off. The dog and they would be open targets. The tracking chip would have to be removed before they left the building.

My God, he thought. A lot had happened in the last twelve hours. Had it only been late yesterday afternoon when Quay had gotten the panicked call from Sunni Hyun? He yawned and settled his lanky body into the leather chair at the desk. As he pulled his laptop up onto the desk, he began reviewing the events from the time Quay said he had received the call from Sunni Hyun pleading with him for protection from some attacker and asking him to let her turn herself in. After Quay and Sam had picked her up at the school, there had been that incredible race to the safe house in southern Minnesota. Sunni had also demanded that they protect her mother. Boogie had done the background on that one, and found and placed her mother in another safe house. There was more to be done with her, though. Sunni's link with her mother seemed to be very important.

Quay Sam, Dan and Drew spent that first day grilling Sunni for details. She was elusive; sometimes she appeared confused, sometimes confident, and other times she was cagey, and obviously evasive. At times she'd glowered with those big, dark brown eyes aimed directly at Quay for what seemed like minutes on end without saying a word. It was as if she'd been challenging him to doubt her. Then suddenly she'd begin to cry and put her head down on the table. Sam was the one who had been the best at pulling Sunni back to the story she'd been telling. She'd handed her tissues, placed an arm around her shoulders, cajoled, whispered, assured, and encouraged, until Sunni began talking again. Sam had a touch, no doubt. Sometimes, when she was angry, it wasn't such a light touch either, Boogie thought, remembering the later incident when Sam barreled into the office early this morning. He smiled to himself remembering Sam smacking Sunni Hyun. She'd reached her boiling point right then. No doubt about it. But maybe that was good.

But thinking back to last night, he realized it had all fallen apart in minutes. He believed much of what happened was thanks to Sunni Hyun not being truthful. Last night--was it only last night, he thought again--when they'd been at the safe house, after they'd taken a break and had pizza for supper, the dog had started acting funny. Chip wouldn't lie down and had paced from room to room. Then the dog began listening to something; he'd finally sat and begun looking up at the ceiling, cocking his head as though listening to a strange sound. At one point, he'd even jumped up onto the sofa, and stood alert with paws on the back of the sofa, ears up, head tilted, eyes up. They hadn't known what to make of it. Quay had even commented that maybe there were squirrels up there. Quay had probably said that to throw the others off to what it might be. That was when Boogie had been fairly sure there was going to be trouble. He hadn't thought Chip was listening to squirrels, either.

Then he'd gotten that look from Quay, and the slight movement of his head told Boogie he wanted him to check in with headquarters. That move was their agreed upon signal to one another. Time to check in. He had just excused himself and gotten up when his phone buzzed with a message from the headquarters tech. It was a signal for alert and emergency! When he called the office, he had been informed there was reason to believe the safe house had been exposed. The high tech security system of the safe house had sent off a silent alarm to headquarters alerting to the presence of a drone in the vicinity of the safe house. That's what the dog had heard. Bless those canine ears! The dog had tried to let them know.

He had headed back to the kitchen to alert Quay. It had been Quay's plan to have Boogie check in with the security team if anything felt amiss. If the news was bad, all he had to do was look at Quay and nod once. Quay and Sam would take it from there. Boogie had sent the request for backup immediately after the emergency alert. It was a good plan. But it had taken some time to fall into place.

In a matter of minutes, the events of the evening had been set in motion. Thank heavens Quay had been his usual calm and controlled self. Quay had picked up right away on Boogie's nod of a warning. Boogie had to smile as he remembered Quay reaching into his pocket for his square of bubble gum. He was a good man. He'd stood there intent on unwrapping it and then popped it in his mouth with a wink before turning to hold the door for Sam. Quay had used the pretense of getting fresh air for Sunni's sake. But Boogie double locked the door behind them.

The two of them had put their lives on the line to distract the ambushers and give Boogie time to safeguard Sunni Hyun by moving her quickly to a special panic room in the house. He'd felt somewhat safe because he had already sent out an alert for emergency help to the local BCA and police when he received the message about the drone. They hadn't thought a drone could hurt them. They'd decided Boogie would keep the dog with him. He didn't know why they'd made that decision. It just seemed to be the right thing to do. Maybe it was another bit of protection. Keeping the dog with him had turned out to be a good decision.

That beautiful, intelligent animal who had displayed such a loving, gentle disposition earlier in the day had snarled a warning before Boogie had even heard a sound. That added to his understanding of how important a canine officer could be. Chip behaved like a sweet-natured pup with them, but it soon became clear he was also a well-trained, incredibly talented watchdog.

Chip had protected them by alerting to the prowlers with his initial growl and then had continued setting up a barrage of fierce barking and snarling when one of the ambushers tried the door. Most perps don't want to deal with vicious dogs. These guys probably had had no idea that mild-mannered Chip would react as a loyally, protective force.

The attackers had moved away from the door and had begun to circle the house. He knew that because he'd gotten a message from Dan and Drew who said they were following some men through the woods from the south. He'd texted back that someone had, in fact, been circling the house. The next few minutes had flown by like an action movie on fast forward. The flashes and automatic rifles' rat-a-tats were strobe-like staccato explosions in the winter night. That echoing gunfire combined with the shots fired close to the house made it sound like a full-scale firestorm outside.

The first shots had driven Chip into an even wilder frenzy. Boogie grimaced when he remembered the scene. That dog had turned into a wild attack monster the moment the first shots had been fired. He'd growled, snarled, scratched at the door, and paced from one window to another while whining and barking furiously. He remembered seeing the flash of Chip's muscled, tense body whipping past as he had raced to look out of one of the living room windows. At last the shooting outside had stopped. A deathly pall had fallen over the house. Chip had come to his side, panting, whimpering softly and nuzzling his hand, seeking approval and security. They had waited, side by side.

Chip was a smart dog. When it became quiet outside, Chip quieted, too. He was still very frightened, but he'd stopped pacing. Boogie had sat down at the dining room table and called the panting pup over to him. It would take a while to calm the young dog. It had been a dual effect to run his hands over the back of the dog's soft fur. The stroking calmed the dog and Boogie, too. He'd petted Chip and talked to him in soothing tones. Their panicked, rapid breathing had slowed.

It had been an eventful night for the dog, and there were probably more to come. That poor dog had had a very rough forty-some hours, just like the rest of them, he thought. That dog had been in the line of fire twice now and had held up remarkably well. For a young pup, he'd stood up to a perceived enemy, and his instincts had led him to know which humans he could trust. That was amazing. He was going to be a great dog for someone.

The aftermath of the firefight had been followed with Quay being taken down. He would never forget hearing the "Man Down" call from Sam. The skin along his neck and down his arms tightened as chills ran over him all over again.

That attack at the safe house had happened so fast late last night. Everything had seemed to fly by in a flash. He, Dan and Drew had discussed it and decided that whoever had been looking for them hadn't followed them directly to the safe house. The chasers must have been searching for them.

As he thought about it, he shook his head. It was overwhelming. Their questioning of Sunni had begun that morning just after he'd gotten there. Boogie had tried to put together all the information that Sunni Hyun spilled out. There had been so much information to process beginning with the stolen research at Cameron Bio and following with Sunni's alleged attackers. The BCA would need to assign someone at the main headquarters to follow up on that information. Maybe he could suggest Lex Ellingson. He was good, he thought. He would be free to combine what they knew down at this office with that information from Lex. It had become a massive case. And it had all developed in the last twenty-four hours.

Boogie yawned. What a night it had been. He was shutting down. Soon they'd be following up on Quay's condition, getting on the road moving Sunni, deciding on what to do with the dog, and tracking down the man or men who had gotten away. Boogie yawned again, stretched his lanky arms over his head, dropped them and folded them on the glass-topped desk. He bent forward laying his head on his arms. His long brown hair fell over his face, and he closed his eyes. He was bone-weary tired. Sleep closed in. He didn't fight it.

CHAPTER THIRTEEN
Daybreak and Decisions

At six a.m. the sun had just begun to peek over the horizon to shoot tinges of coral and pink into the morning sky and form a soft reflection through the darkness in the high office windows. Boogie and Sam were still asleep in Drew's BCA office. Boogie's soft, rumbling snore was interrupted when a warm nose pushed against his arm and a wet tongue began gently licking his hand. Boogie opened one eye to see Chip happily wagging his tail in a morning greeting. "I think you're happier to see me than I am to see you," muttered Boogie.

Sam heard Boogie groan and grumble. She stretched her long legs out, pulled her coat over her head, and whispered, "Shhh. Not yet. Be quiet!"

Seconds later, Drew escorted Sunni Hyun into the office as Dan provided the wake up call. "Wake up, team! Rise and shine, you sleeping beauties. You have company, and we're ready to roll!"

Drew pointed Sunni to a chair in the corner. Sam struggled into a sitting position and regarded Sunni's pale, haggard appearance. Her face clearly revealed the strain of the night's interrogation. Dark, stringy strands hair hung loosely to her shoulders. With no sleep, dark plum-colored bags under her eyes anchored the red-veined road maps in the whites of her eyes. Sunni sat stiffly in the chair and clutched her coat and scarf close to her chest using them almost as a shield. A fresh, clean bandage covered the wound on her arm where she'd removed the RFID chip.

Dan pulled a nearby chair up to the desk, and nudged Boogie again saying, "C'mon, man. We're going to need you today! Gotta pull it together."

"Okay, okay. I'm awake," Boogie mumbled through a suppressed yawn. He leaned back and looked around the room. When he turned to pat the dog happily nuzzling him, he spotted the bandage on Chip's back hip.

"What'd you do? Take out the data chip?"

"Yeah," replied Drew, lowering his voice to a whisper so Sunni couldn't hear their hushed conversation. "We decided we'd better take out both the tracker and the Cameron BioTech data chip, too. We can retrieve the data, copy it, and store it here safely. That's the first order for you. We need you to make a copy of the stuff that's on that chip, so we can get Cameron to check it out. We'll store the original in our safe. We need to verify if Miss Hyun here has what she says she has." He paused and looked over at Sunni. She didn't raise her head to look at or acknowledge him.

"Okay, I can do that, but what have you decided to do with the tracking chip?" asked Boogie.

Sam pulled herself up and leaned closer to the men. She'd moved across the room and had been straining to hear. "I can help with that decision," she whispered. She reached behind her head to pull the hair in her ponytail tighter, and then gave her auburn hair a slight shake, glancing at Sunni, who still didn't appear to be paying any attention to them. "I did a lot of thinking about this situation last night. I think we need to keep that tracking chip active. You've removed it from the dog, but can still use it to lure them in. Let's let them think we still didn't find it. They think we're stupid anyway. We let them try to ambush us, for crying out loud! That makes me furious that we didn't think of that. Let's turn it on them. We'll be ready for them. Keep Chip here where he can't be seen for awhile, until we can get Sunni to a new safe house. They won't know where we put the dog.

They'll think we are all still here. We need to move her mother in with her, too. Keep them together. Then we won't be so spread out. You guys will have to make sure the dog is safe and taken care of here. It'll just be for a couple days. Can we do that? What do you think?"

"That sounds like a decent plan. I agree that we should keep the chips here. We will definitely need time to move Sunni first. We've got to get her out of here soon!" said Dan.

"And that'll give me time to do some heavy duty work on that tracking chip Sunni removed from her arm, as well as the one from the dog," said Boogie, looking at Sunni. "We might be able to do a reverse track on the chip that she dug out of her arm. That would be my first order of business. We can set up a trap. When we have everything in place, we can bring the dog and the chip in to the location. They'll think they are tracking everyone again. So, I'll keep the tracking chips and the data chip here. That way we would be in total control."

"That sounds really good, Boogie!" agreed Sam. "So do you think it would be okay for you to stay in the BCA headquarters here in Mankato and work from here? No need to go back to headquarters in the Twin Cities?"

"I think I'd like to stay here for now. Besides, I don't think we can move the chip out of here without them knowing. They'd zero in on it right away. We move the chip when we 're ready. In the meantime, we've got it locked up here. I can do as much here as I can up in the Twin Cities, thanks to the Internet, our technology and that cloud in the sky. I also want to do some searching to see if I can verify the story Joo Jhim told her about her father having a daughter with another woman. We need to verify that. And," he paused, "would it be okay if I take total charge of the pooch here for the time being? He and

I have kind of bonded. I'd like to just keep him nearby for company, too. Maybe we could even get Quay over here after he's released. He could spend some of his rehab time here with me and the pooch."

"That would be great!" Drew said with a note of relief in his voice. "I wasn't sure how we were going to handle the dog and still have time to do the follow-up work we need to do on this case."

"Cool!" Boogie smiled while rubbing his hands together in happy anticipation.

"Let's get started!" said Sam, speaking up so Sunni would hear her. "Dan. Drew. Were you able to get a new safe house set up for us?"

"Yes, we found a place back up in the western suburbs not far from Cameron Bio Tech in Maple Grove, actually. It just opened up. There's even room in the place for Sunni's mother, too. We've already made arrangements to have the place staffed with our people 24/7," said Drew.

Sam looked at her watch. It was 6:30 a.m. It would be full daylight soon. Thank heavens for the long nights of winter, she thought. It wouldn't be fully light for about an hour, yet. Dawn was just beginning. Right now they needed the cover.

"Should both of you head up to Maple Grove with her?" asked Sam.

"Yes, the Double D team will need to do double duty, just in case," answered Dan. "There will be staff coming in here about eight. So, you'll want to get yourself set up in our office here before they come in, Boogie. I'll send out an email to the staff before I leave explaining that our office is going to be used by Boogie and his friend Chip for a few days. They don't need more information other than it's a high level job. I'll ask them to give you the run of the place and to support you in whatever you need, Boogie."

"That'll be cool, man. Thanks. Is there some place I can take Chip out to do his business without worrying?"

"Well, we have a fenced perimeter. I think he'll be safe to do his business behind the building. Just make it quick. Short visits, you know? There's a workout gym downstairs with a track if either of you needs to run."

"That will work!" agreed Boogie.

Sunni Hyun had been following their conversation, looking from Dan and Drew to Boogie with a panicked look on her face.

"NO!" she suddenly shouted. "You can't keep Chip! He needs to be with me! I keep Chip!"

Everyone turned to look at her. She hadn't evidenced that much emotion anytime during the entire ordeal.

"What? What do you mean? Don't you understand? He can't stay with you, Sunni. There's another tracking chip. You'll be tracked again!" said Sam. It was obvious, that Sunni hadn't heard any of their conversation. That was good. Sunni thought the dog's chips were still in place. "I thought you were afraid for your life. Are you telling us you're not? Was this all a big scam? What's going on, Sunni?" Sam's voice had risen with each question. She was angry now.

Sunni looked at Sam, and shook her head. "It's just that he's my dog. He's been with me since he was a puppy. I know he's scared and confused. My mother loves this dog. It will help her."

Sam wasn't convinced. "You didn't have Chip with you when Joo was shot! Chip was with Joo! How do you explain that?"

"Joo took him! He must have taken him away from my mother's house. He told me he might take him. He thought I loved Chip. He knew how my mother felt about him, too. It was his control tool. He used stuff like that all the time. Blackmailed me and tried to scare me with his little threats. He said I could get Chip back when I met him at the parking lot. I didn't know what he had planned. I certainly didn't know that there would be an attack."

The men observed the interchange between the two women. Samantha had jumped up and moved in front of Sunni. Her ponytail swung from side to side as she shook her head. Her redheaded temper had been ignited again, and her body language not only indicated anger but also intimidation as she stood over Sunni.

"Hmmm. That's a nice story, Sunni." Sam's eyes flared as she jabbed a finger into Sunni's shoulder.

"I'm sure not buying it. You didn't give us even a hint that there was possibly another tracker chip on the dog, but you would have figured that out, I think. Right? Right! You almost got my partner killed last night. And now you say you want us to help you? To protect you? Well, I'm not feeling the love here, honey. Not anymore. You've got a lot more to tell us. I don't think we've gotten the full story, yet. We are keeping the dog here. That's final!"

Sunni sat back in her chair clutching her coat closer. Tears streamed silently from her eyes. She said nothing, but continued to glare at Sam. After an uncomfortable period of silence in the room, Sunni broke away from the stare and whispered, "I'm sorry about your partner."

"Yeah, you should be," said Sam. She turned her back on Sunni and marched to the door, jerking it open.

"Now get your sorry, skinny ass out of here! I'll deal with you later. Dan, Drew, she's all yours."

Drew and Dan looked at one another mirroring concealed smirks. Samantha Atwood had just taken charge. They gathered up several files before pulling Sunni roughly from her seat.

"Let's go!" ordered Dan. Sunni tugged on her wool coat as she walked to the door. Drew grabbed her arm, and she flinched with pain. He didn't withdraw his hand. Dan led the way pulling his keys out of his pocket. The edge of his gun flashed as he lifted up the coat.

"We'll call you when we get there," said Drew as he walked out the door closing it quickly behind them. Sunni Hyun didn't look back.

Samantha stood staring at the door as it closed behind them. Boogie moved to the desk and his laptop. The dog followed him.

"Do you think I could get in to see Quay, yet?" she asked.

Boogie looked at his watch. "Well, by the time you get over to the hospital, it will be close to seven. I imagine they'd let you in." He looked at her blood-spattered clothes. "Do you need to clean up first, Sam?"

Sam hadn't given any thought to her clothes or hair. She looked down at her shirt and jeans. The front of her jeans were stained with dark splotches. The cuffs of her sleeves displayed the same dark stains. Quay's blood. She realized her jacket was probably covered with his blood, too. So much blood.

Yes, she needed a change of clothes. Earlier when she'd realized they were going to be at the safe house overnight, she'd thought about sending in a request for someone to pick up some clothes for her. But she had decided to let it go. Now, she realized she didn't have a change of clothes, and she really couldn't go see Quay looking like this. It was too early to find a store open.

Boogie looked at her. The look of dismay on her face told him what she what she was thinking.

"You know," he began, looking down at his sweatshirt, "I've got this neat Apple sweatshirt. It didn't get ruined. I wasn't running around outside getting shot at. How about you take my sweatshirt. It's big enough it will cover your arms and halfway to your knees. It would cover up the stains. No one will be able to see them. You could go down the hall to the restroom. I think you'd be able to clean up a bit there and pull on my shirt. What do you say?"

Sam looked up at Boogie, and smiled. "Oh, Boogie, you are such a good friend. You know, you really are one of a kind. Nobody else would even think of that. Thank you!"

Boogie was already pulling his sweatshirt over his head. "Here, take it, and go fix yourself up for Quay, okay?"

She grabbed the shirt and impulsively reached up and hugged him before turning quickly to head out the door and down the hall.

CHAPTER FOURTEEN
Quay

Samantha Atwood had mixed feelings as she walked through the hospital doors. She was eager to see Quay. She needed to know he was all right. She needed to see him, to touch him, to talk to him.

At the same time, she wasn't quite sure how she should act. Would Quay be awake? Would he be able to talk? Would he remember what happened? What should she say?

The aftermath of the ordeal last night had brought home to her just how deeply she had begun to care about Quay Thompson, the man, not just the partner. She knew she had come close to losing him. The EMTs in the ambulance and the doctors in the ER had not directly said anything. But she had read their faces. Quay was lucky to be alive. It was more than luck that the bullet had hit neither his femoral artery nor shattered the bone. Thank God he'd survived! Just the thought of losing him made her ache. The reality was that now it was going to be the uphill battle to recovery.

Quay was strong and tough. But he was also beyond stubborn. She had to smile when she thought about him as a patient. He wouldn't be a good patient. He wouldn't listen. He would fight to get back on his feet and back on the job. She knew that before she even saw him.

She reached his room and paused outside the door, listening. Someone was in the room with Quay. She rounded the door and entered. The head of Quay's bed was raised slightly. She took in the scene, sweeping the room in a single glance. Quay lay on the bed covered with a thin and rumpled hospital sheet. Blond tousled hair framed his chiseled, pale face. His mouth seemed fixed in a tight line against pain. A couple days growth of beard stubbled his lined face. An angry, red cut traced down from his forehead to his right cheek and then to his chin. Several stitches lined his hairline along the center of his forehead. Those were the only injuries that were visible. His brow was furrowed as he listened to the man seated in the chair next to the bed. The man was leaning in and talking in a low voice to Quay. Quay was awake and staring at the ceiling.

"Good morning," Sam said trying to sound cheerful.

The big man turned to face her, and quickly stood, extending his hand.

"Good morning, Samantha! I didn't expect to see you here so early. You had a rough night, too."

"Yes, Superintendent, but I imagine Quay was probably having a rougher night. It was good of you to come down. It's awfully early for you to be here."

Superintendent Mike Bergman nodded, and pulled up a chair for Sam. He looked as tired as Sam felt, she thought. Super Mike had not worn his usual suit and tie. He was dressed in a flannel shirt and jeans. A leather jacket lay across the back of the chair. His dark eyes reflected the worry she was sure he was feeling. He was a good man. She knew he fought hard for the well being of his people.

"I took off as soon as I got the call," his deep voice sounded gravelly today. "When my people are under fire, it is important that the BCA supports them. We are family. Quay just woke up a few minutes ago. He's been sleeping pretty much all night. Other than a few groans here and there, he hasn't said much," Mike explained to Samantha. He walked around to the other side of the bed and laid a hand on Quay's shoulder.

"Yes, sir," said Sam as she settled into the chair and put a hand on Quay's arm. "Hey, Quay?" She jostled him lightly. "Are you awake? Are you listening?"

Quay slowly turned his head, focused his eyes, and looked at her. "Hey! How ya doin', Sam?" His deep voice was weak and raspy. She could hear the pain he felt.

His eyes reflected more than his pain, she saw. And there was more than his determination to recover. His eyes softened when he looked at her. The steel blue became darker, deeper, turning less intense, but more direct.

Sam looked at Quay and smiled. "Quay, you aren't supposed to ask how I'm doing. You are lucky to be here, you know? Do you remember what happened last night?"

"Must be trying to forget," he said, giving her a warm smile. "It was a rough one, right? I must have screwed up, big time!"

Both Mike and Sam shook their heads. "No!" they affirmed in unison.

"There's no way you screwed up, Quay. We were just caught off-guard. We had no idea that there was a way they could still track us. The safe house was supposed to be clean and hidden. And we also had no idea how many attackers there were."

Mike sat down and began to fill them both in on the cycle of events preceding the attack. He explained that the conversation between headquarters and Boogie had given them just a few minutes' warning. They believed the killers had possibly sent a drone in to scope out the place before the attack team had even arrived. He assured them that Quay and Sam had done the right thing by leaving the house and forcing the team to divide.

That maneuver may have saved the lives of everyone. What they hadn't been able to predict was the weaponry they carried with them. Considering the expense laid out for a drone and the AK47s, it was pretty obvious that there was money behind this group. Then there was the technology aspect of the chips. Boogie had known that there was a chip used for tracking. What he'd missed was that another chip was on the dog. They'd all thought there was just the one on Sunni Hyun.

During the night and early this morning, they had been able to do quite a bit of background research on Joo Jhim as well as Sunni's mother, June Hyun. With several of the North Korean players sidelined, they were beginning to get a better picture of what they were dealing with.

"It's going to be a very dangerous operation. We will put a full team on this. We will have Samantha, here, head up the group, since you'll be out of commission for a bit, Quay. But you will be kept in the loop, so you can jump right in when you have recovered. I'm assuring you, we aren't counting you out. We know you have a lot invested in this case. But right now, the important thing is to get you back on your feet."

"I agree wholeheartedly, " said Sam, looking intently at Quay. "And Boogie and I have been talking. We have a plan that we hope you will accept."

"Yeah? What's that?" asked Quay with a note of sarcasm in his voice.

"Quay, Boogie is going to stay down here in the Mankato office for now. We will have a lot of follow-up work at the safe house and he can be in constant communication with the headquarters team. He will find a place to stay that will be big enough for the two of you and the dog."

"The dog?" Quay interrupted. "We're keeping the dog? What? Is Boogie in love with it, or something?" He started to laugh but grimaced in pain with the movement.

"Well, I think you may have something there," she said. "But the point is, the dog was micro-chipped with all the stolen data from Cameron Bio-Tech. And it also had another tracking chip implanted on him. That's how they found us last night. We have removed the data chip, and also the tracker on the dog. We will have the data chip secured after Boogie decodes and copies it. The tracker will remain secure at the Mankato office with the dog. We can use it to our benefit later."

"The dog had a tracking chip and a data chip? No shit?"

"No shit! That's what happened. Now, we need to keep that dog under wraps for the time being. The headquarters here thinks they have a place to stay that will work for you and Boogie. It's secure in all ways. And, then you can stay with Boogie. We can have you come in for whatever rehab and medical follow-ups you need here with the doctors. How's that sound?"

Quay looked from Sam to the Mike and back again. They were both nodding in agreement.

"Sounds like you think you've got it all figured out. But I can tell you I don't plan on being sidelined that long. This is my case, you know. It began with me. It's going to end with me!"

Mike began patting his arm. "I understand and agree whole-heartedly, Quay. We will support that completely. But it will take you a week or two to recover. We nearly lost you last night, fella. I don't want you to push your luck."

"Let me talk to the doctors today, and see what they say." Quay was agitated, and a bit worried.

"Quay as long as we're here, and you're awake, maybe we can start with this. What do you remember about the events of last night?"

Quay took a deep breath and began to recall the walk he and Sam had taken into the woods on the path to the lake. He remembered the noise he'd heard. And he remembered thinking they were in trouble. Once the shooting began, he remembered pushing Sam one direction and diving another, just like they had always talked about. That was the last thing he'd remembered.

He was beginning to tire already. He was having trouble focusing on their conversation. Sam and Mike were talking across the bed, across Quay, but he was drifting.

"I'm sorry," he said. "I'm so sorry. I should have protected you, Sam. Instead, I went out trying to be the gunslinger hero. And I almost got you shot, too."

"Don't ever feel like any of this was your fault, Quay," said Sam as she leaned forward looking directly into his eyes and placed a comforting hand on his shoulder, squeezing slightly. "You did exactly the right thing. It was what we'd always talked about. We did our plan. They just had better and more weapons that's all. I'm okay. You're going to be okay, thank God. We'll get them. We'll get them together!"

Mike also reassured him they would get the attackers. It would start with Sunni Hyun. Because Quay had received the initial contact from Sunni Hyun, he had credit for the case. They'd keep him informed. And he'd be back in action in no time to wind up the case.

A doctor walked in just as Mike and Sam were getting ready to leave. Mike introduced Sam and himself.

He took the doctor aside and explained that there would be security for Quay while he was in the hospital. Someone would be here momentarily to begin first watch. If there were any changes in Quay's condition, either Mike or Sam was to be notified immediately. The doctor agreed and busily took notes. Mike walked out into the hallway with the doctor as they continued talking.

Quay closed his eyes and settled back on his pillow, then opened them again and looked at Sam.

Sam looked steadily at him, nodded, and turned to leave, but Quay reached out in a flash and grabbed her hand. She turned back, looked down at their clasped hands, then up into his eyes. His eyes were still and focused on her but with a different expression behind them. The normally steel blue seemed to turn to dark velvet blue, tinged with softness. He looked at her steadily, and there was a moment's hesitation before he spoke.

"You come back soon. I need you."

She looked into his eyes with understanding. "I will. I need you, too. Get well," she whispered. She leaned down and gave him a quick kiss on the cheek and turned to go without looking back. This was a new beginning. This was different. This was the beginning of a new chapter of their story.

Samantha stepped into the hallway and met Mike and the doctor by the nurse's desk. Mike was just finishing up his instructions for Quay's protection. He turned to Sam, looked at her steadily and asked, "Everything good?" She smiled and nodded.

Together they headed out of the hospital to their cars. In the parking lot, Mike briefed her on the plans for

Sunni Hyun. She was to head over to the Mankato office to bring Boogie up to speed before heading up to the Cities. She checked her watch. It was closing in on nine a.m. She'd stop by the grocery store and pick up some food for Boogie and dog food for Chip. They'd both probably be famished, she thought.

CHAPTER FIFTEEN
The Reunion

Boogie was still in the office, feverishly tapping at the keys on his laptop when Sam walked in. He looked up at Sam and his face immediately broadened into a grin when he spied the bags of food she had brought.

"Ah, the female warrior returns with sustenance for the weary and hungry. Thanks, Sam. What'd ya bring?"

"Well, there're some hot biscuits and gravy there for you, and some canned and dry dog food for Chip. Thought we'd try to make you both more productive and happy."

Boogie grabbed the bags from her arms and began opening the tray of warm food. Chip stood, stretched, wriggled his nose, sniffed the air and began a happy dance shuffle. Sam opened the bag of dry food, looked around for a plate or bowl, found one sitting on the console by the TV and poured out the kibbles onto the plate for the dog. Chip looked from her to the dish as if waiting for the invitation to get his food. Sam obliged with, "Come eat, fella!" Chip lurched for the dish on the floor, and began gobbling before she had pulled her hand away.

"Poor guy," she said. "I bet he hasn't had anything since last night. No doubt he's pretty hungry. We'll have to round up that food from the safe house."

She turned to Boogie, "Do you have an address for the place that you and Quay will be moving to, yet?"

"Yeah, just heard from Super Mike before you walked in. There's a house on Hickory Street, not far from here. He said it's pretty innocuous looking, and we can have the dog there. We'll have the house to ourselves. It's a two story. When Quay gets out of the hospital, we'll let him use the downstairs. I can move all my stuff in as soon as I can run up to the Cities and--"

Sam interrupted him, "No, Boogie. You shouldn't have to do that. Why don't you let me do the running to the Twin Cities? I can pick up whatever you need from your place, and I'll also swing by Quay's place and grab the stuff he needs, too. At least, I'll get enough for the time being for both of you. That will also give me a chance to check in with Sunni and Dan and Drew in the new safe house in Maple Grove. I can see what else is new there. Then I'll be back tonight. Would that work for you?"

"Well, I hate to make you do all that driving, but sure, you can if you want. I see your point. You need to see Sunni again and see what else we can get from her. Maybe we can do Face Time when you get there. I can fill you in on what I've learned for sure by then, so she can't slip something by us. We should have any extra facts about her mother, and her background before too long. I'm going to do some digging on this supposed half-sister that Joo told her about, too. It's going to be a busy day."

"Great! I think that will help a lot. We really need to find out who was controlling Joo. Maybe we should look for some North Korean government connections, or even their equivalent of the CIA. That may be something."

"Will do," said Boogie as he turned back to his laptop. She could tell he was already in his element.

Sam left Boogie and Chip settling in at the office. She called Dan on her way to her car and got directions for meeting them. He said they had moved to a safe house in Maple Grove not too far from where they'd first picked up Sunni. Drew had gone to White Bear Lake to pick up Sunni's mother, June Yung Hyun, at the appointed spot near her home. The men providing security for her were bringing her to meet him. Then he was supposed to be returning with her to the new safe house before lunchtime. Sam was anxious to see what the reunion between the two women looked like. She needed to know if Sunni had actually been telling the truth. She thought she could gauge quite a bit by watching them meet. It would take her a little over an hour to get there.

Sunni Hyun was nervously waiting in the new safe house for the BCA man named Dan to return with her mother. Sunni looked around the room, wiped a tear from her eye, and sank onto the sofa. This house was a fairly good-sized rambler with four bedrooms, and a den, and had all the comforts of an upper middle-class home. The flat-screen TV sat back against the wall opposite the sofa. A small gas fireplace was built into a corner of the room. That would be a comfort in the evenings, she supposed.

Sunni saw a remote on the end table next to her, grabbed it, pressed the power switch, and tuned into the local channel for morning news. There was nothing on the news about their misadventure last night. No news of a car chase down the Twin Cities freeway after a murder in a northern suburb's rest area. No news about an attack on a would-be spy. No news about the shooting of a BCA officer in southern Minnesota after an attack on a small country home. It was apparent the BCA had shut down the news line on this. It had to be kept quiet. She'd heard them say it gave them more of an opportunity to lure out the attackers the way they wanted to.

Sunni turned away from the television with an involuntary shudder. She'd told them it wouldn't work.

She'd never be safe here, she'd explained. These people were too good. They would always be one step ahead of the BCA. She'd explained she'd been dealing with this group for over a year. They were terrifyingly good. And, now she also positively knew they were lethal to anyone who crossed them or got in their way.

Her only protection was the chip. She had put all the research data on the chip. And the killers didn't have it! She had to make sure they didn't get it. There were so many reasons to protect that information she'd stolen from Cameron BioTech. In the hands of the wrong people using it from a position of power, the research would be worth billions of dollars. The company or country that owned the CRISPR-Cas9 formula had the capability of so many extraordinary things. But she also knew that most important genome data could be used to create a monster, a superhuman fighting machine, a genius beyond the capabilities of anyone they knew, or a superhuman with demonic, evil, amoral qualities unlike any ever seen in the time of the human race. In a more positive, morally acceptable way, it could create the ability for a cell to regenerate any part of itself. It could help a body cure its own wounds. A person's body would be able to heal its own cancers. The carrier was invincible. It was exciting and at the same time frightening. Cameron BioTech thought they had the data for the creation of the CRISPR-Cas9 model, but they were missing one small piece. Sunni knew what that one small piece was. She had helped develop it. And everyone was going to want it. And they'd have to get her to get it.

She hadn't told Quay and his friends that part of her plan. She wasn't sure if she could. She was scared beyond reason, beyond hope, for herself, for her mother, and for the world, as she knew it. She had no idea who she could trust, and how she was going to get out of this alive. And worst of all, how could she tell her mother?

At half past eleven that morning, Samantha Atwood watched Sunni's mother June as she walked through the door of their new safe house. The small woman, bundled in a heavy winter coat with a wool scarf wrapped over her hair, appeared somewhat confused. Sam had just arrived a few minutes earlier, but she hadn't yet spoken to Sunni. She'd wanted to give Sunni a chance to assimilate what was happening. Sam watched in interest as Sunni looked up, recognized her mother, and her face melted into an expression of relief.

"Mother!" Sunni Hyun cried and flew to the diminutive woman, embracing her in a secure hug before the woman could even put down the bag she was carrying. Standing a full head taller, Sunni looked down on her mother with eyes glistening with tears. June Hyun peered anxiously around Sunni's shoulder surveying the room and the people watching them.

Sunni held her mother away by her shoulders and inspected the small woman from head to toe. "Mother, are you all right?" she asked. Sam noticed that Sunni's mother had stiffened under Sunni's hug. June Hyun looked up into her daughter's eyes searching for answers. She spoke to Sunni in Korean with the tone that appeared to be a question. Sunni shook her head and pulled her mother into another close hug while speaking softly into her ear. Her words were unintelligible to the group assembled in the room watching the two of them.

"Sunni!" Sam interrupted. "Tell us what she is saying. No Korean. From this point on, you will be speaking only English."

"She just asked me what is happening. She doesn't speak a lot of English. I'll translate for you. I just want to be sure she feels safe. She is frightened. There will be a lot to be explained to her."

"We can have interpreters for both of you. If you decide to translate, we will also need to determine if your translation is accurate. Keep that in mind," warned Dan Young. The BCA man was standing behind June Hyun. Drew Thurston standing beside him nodded in agreement. Dan had been the one who had gone to retrieve Sunni's mother. He said she hadn't spoken to anyone.

"You don't need to interpret for me," June suddenly snapped, turning to Dan and Drew. She drew herself up in a movement that made her actually appear taller. Her small, sharp-boned body was rigidly etched beneath the folds of a loose kimono-like shirt draped over loose pants. "I speak English. No need interpret!" Her face and body stance were set in stony defiance.

Sunni stared agape at her mother. Sam observed the interaction between the two women carefully and noted that Sunni appeared to be flummoxed by her mother's demeanor and attitude. There was clearly something in play here that Sunni hadn't seen before. Evidently, Sunni did not realize her mother spoke English fluently. How interesting, thought Sam.

Sam took over, ignoring Mrs. Hyun's indignation and startling revelation. She formally welcomed Mrs. Hyun into the safe house explaining they were there to provide protection for her and her daughter whose life they believed was in danger. Sam introduced Mrs. Hyun to everyone before she led her down the hall to her designated bedroom. She invited her to unpack her few belongings, while explaining she would give her a few minutes to get herself settled, and directed her to where she could find the bathroom and the kitchen. Finally, Sam indicated that she would expect to visit with Mrs. Hyun and her daughter in approximately fifteen minutes in the home's living room.

Sunni Hyun watched her mother and Samantha Atwood disappear down the hallway to the bedroom. Her face was still frozen in an expression of confusion. Dan and Drew indicated she was to stay in the living room while they went to check out the kitchen. Sunni turned and began to inspect the living room. She paced, and then stopped to pull aside the curtain on one of the three windows facing the thick woods standing behind the house. Dan returned in time to see her checking the surroundings. He could almost read her mind. She was thinking, *Woods again. Isolation.* She was learning that this house was isolated even though it was in a populated suburb. He figured she had to be wondering about the wisdom of turning herself in to Quay Thompson. Her mother's presence, Dan believed, would be the one thing that would hold her here.

Sunni turned back to look at the room, ignoring Dan. She was evaluating the place.

The interior of the place was pristine, to the point of looking like a model home, new and never inhabited. The furniture, a sofa, two stuffed chairs, a couple of end tables and a coffee table, also appeared to be new, unused; Dan and Drew had explained that the kitchen was well-stocked, but it looked unused, too, and the bedroom she had been given looked neat, sparse and hotel comfortable.

When she returned, Sam found Sunni settled onto the leather sofa, staring at the fireplace across the room.

"What is going on between you and your mother, Sunni?"

Sunni looked up with a surprise on her face. "What do you mean?" she asked.

"Don't play games, Sunni. I don't have the patience for your games. You told us your mother doesn't understand much English. And yet, it seems she does speak English and understands it pretty well. What's the deal?"

"I don't know what the deal is," Sunni said shaking her head while staring down at the floor. "She's always seemed to have a lot of trouble understanding anything unless I translated for her. I had no idea she understood so much."

"Well, there's obviously much more to this picture. We are going to get your mother out here in a few minutes and get the truth. Do you think she has any idea what you've done?"

"I never told her what Joo was doing, or how he was blackmailing me. I don't think she ever knew or found out."

"We'll see. We need to know everything, Sunni. We don't have time to waste. We will find out what everyone knows; that means you, your mother, and whoever else is involved."

"We're also going to have to check in with Cameron BioTech," suggested Drew who had just walked into the room. He glared at Sunni. "You are in so much trouble, Miss Hyun. There's only one way you are going to be able to help yourself. That's if you help us, and soon!"

Sam's phone buzzed, and she signaled Drew to keep an eye on Sunni as she glanced at the screen and walked away. She answered seeing Boogie's face pop up on her phone. Face time.

"What's new, Boogie?" she said as she walked out of the room.

Boogie began by explaining that the cameras from the rest area hadn't proven anything conclusive about the shooting of Joo Jhim. Although they got the make of the car, they weren't able to get a license plate from the car. Then there was more about the clean up operation at the previous safe house. All had been cleaned up; a cover story had been spread through town via the local grocery stores, gas stations, and bars. Everyone in town would soon be buzzing about the gas explosion at the empty home out on the lake. Many would claim they heard it even if they hadn't. It would be big news for the small town. The paramedics and EMTs with the ambulance crew were sworn to silence. They would agree with the townspeople that they were so thankful that no one had been living there.

The follow-up leads on the attack hadn't gone as well. They hadn't found any IDs on the bodies. They were working on fingerprint identification, but if the shooters weren't already in the database, it wasn't going to go well. They were foreigners.

"Boogie, could we tap into an international data base? These guys are not local. They're probably not even stateside. Got any connections to our counterpart in Korea?"

Boogie grunted. "I'm not convinced North Korea would be accommodating. But South Korea may have something. We'll have to work through the FBI and let them work their links with the CIA. It's going to take a while. Could take up to a week. This case is beginning to develop tentacles."

"I'm not sure we have that kind of time, Boogie. Let's get it started, on our end, at least. We need to know who these guys are. That will lead us to what they are after. I'll work with Dan and Drew here to dig into Sunni's knowledge. She's got something funky going on with her mother. Can you do more deep background on Sunni's parents, too?"

"On it!" he said. "Guess my gaming is going to be on hold for a bit. I was just going to try out some new VR stuff I picked up." He turned his computer screen for her to see.

"VR? Virtual Reality? What the heck, Boogie? Are you going all robotic now?"

"Not quite, yet. But there sure is some cool stuff out there. I'll share it with you when I see you. You'll love it. You can be right on the ground in the middle of fire fight, and not get hurt...oh, sorry." Boogie had just realized what he'd said.

"Yeah. I was in the middle of a firefight, and I didn't get hurt. Quay did, though."

Boogie watched her face on his phone screen. He could see she was hurting. "Sorry, Sam. I didn't mean to throw that at you. Too real. So sorry."

"I know, Boogie. I'll look at the VR when I see you. Just find me something tame like walking with dinosaurs, or something like that, okay?"

"You got it, Sam." There was a momentary pause, and then she heard a crash, and Boogie turned away and began yelling, "Hey! Chip! Knock it off!" Sam heard more crashing sounds from Boogie's end. Then a short woof from the dog. More skittering sounds and rustling ensued, and finally it became quiet. Boogie turned back to the phone slightly out of breath.

"Dang pup! He is a handful, Sam." He turned his phone so Sam could see the pup. "He's a cute dog and all, but he wants to chew up everything in sight. He just pulled my game case off the desk and started taking off with it. He thinks it's a fun game to have someone chase him!"

Sam laughed. It felt good to laugh a bit. "Thanks, Boogie. I needed a laugh. I think I need to spend some time cuddling with Chip!"

"Yeah, well you can laugh. It isn't funny when he's gotten me winded from chasing him. He'll be great rehab for Quay when he moves in. I'll put Quay in charge of the dog."

"Oh great, that'll be fun. We'll hear non-stop griping from Quay. And he'll love it!" she laughed and told Boogie to keep her updated, and that she planned to check in again later. She hung up, took a deep calming breath, and headed back to the living room and Sunni Hyun.

CHAPTER SIXTEEN
The First Deception

Sunni was still seated on the leather sofa. Dan had moved into the kitchen. From the aroma, she thought he must have been making coffee. Drew was seated in a chair opposite Sunni and was busily texting someone.

Sam turned to the hall toward June's bedroom. She found the small woman lying on her bed with a blanket pulled over her, shades drawn, and nothing unpacked.

"Mrs. Hyun?" She walked to the side of the bed and shook the dozing woman slightly. Her dark eyes popped open, and it appeared that she was disoriented. "You are with your daughter, remember? We need you to join us in the living room. Sunni wants to talk to you."

June Hyun nodded, threw back the blanket, and began struggling to a sitting position.

Dan was pouring coffee for the group as Sunni and her mother sat down next to one another on the sofa. Sam pushed the coffee table aside, and pulled a chair up directly in front of the two women. Neither woman looked at her. Sunni was clenching and unclenching her fist, then nervously twisting her fingers. June sat placidly looking at the floor.

"Okay, we need to talk to you first, Mrs. Hyun. Will you give us a brief history of how you first came to this country and what you've been doing since?"

"Yes, I tell you. But first you tell me what my daughter do to you? Why she here? Why you bring me here? She not tell me anything. You tell me, too."

"We will tell you everything we can, but first we need to know about you and Sunni. Some very dangerous men are trying to kill both of you. Do you understand? What you say will help us protect you."

June's eyebrows shot up as she jerked her head up to stare at her daughter. She began a stream of foreign words directed at Sunni that sounded like Korean invective. Sam held up her hands to indicate June needed to stop and calm down.

"No! No!" Sam stated in a firm voice. "You must speak English. English only!"

"Yes, yes! I understand," June answered impatiently. "My daughter lie to me. She to blame for this, yes?" She glared at Sunni.

"We aren't sure. That's what we are trying to learn," interjected Drew.

"It is not my fault!" cried Sunni. "It's your fault for bringing Joo into our house! He caused everything, and you looked away. You are blind, umma!" Sunni had suddenly lapsed into Korean using the foreign word for mother. Then her control returned and she continued. "You trusted that man. He was blackmailing me! Did you know that? And he hurt you. I know that! And you won't admit it!"

The can of worms had been opened. The two women stood and began to scream at one another. Bits of English, interspersed with Korean, made it possible to follow only bits and pieces of the assertions and accusations. It went on for several minutes before Sam decided to intervene. The women had needed to do this, and she'd needed to observe them. It appeared to be an almost love/hate relationship with the daughter needing parental approval, the adult seeking her identity through the perfect daughter. Nothing had popped up in the argument about the supposed love child of Sunni's father. Sunni had held that back. That was also interesting. As angry as she was at her mother, it seemed that Sunni still didn't want to hurt her. She was still protecting her.

The women stopped when Dan and Drew stepped between them and calmly told them to be seated. Now that they had that out of the way, they could begin peeling back the layers.

Sam sat in front of the women, studying each in turn. "June, I want to talk to you first. Were you aware that Joo was blackmailing your daughter?"

June stared back at Sam. She began shaking her head. "Joo no blackmail my daughter. She lie."

Sam continued staring directly at her, watching for any flicker that might give away her doubt or a cover up.

"Why would she lie, June? She was your good daughter, wasn't she? She was a good student. The obedient girl. The smart girl. The girl who loved her parents above all else. She was the girl who lost her father. You lost your husband. Why do you think she would change?"

"I don't know. I don't know. This no good. This bad."

"Yes, June, it is bad. Because, you see, we do believe that Joo was blackmailing your daughter. He was forcing her to steal secrets from the company she worked for, Cameron BioTech. And she was willing to do it only because she was trying to protect you and a sister she had never met nor seen."

The silence in the room hung like a smothering blanket of fog. Sam waited. June needed time to process what she had said.

June opened her mouth to speak, then closed it again and shook her head. 'I ...I ...Joo blackmail? Sister? She no have sister! Who say this?"

June gave the impression of being shocked. If it was true, she hadn't known. Sam looked at Sunni and nodded her head toward her mother. It was time for Sunni to explain the rest of it to her mother.

Sam got up and moved to other side of the room to stand with Dan and Drew. They would let the two women talk for a bit. Sam continued to listen and watch them closely. June simply stared at her daughter. Sam couldn't tell if her expression was one of disbelief or contempt. Sunni's anger had dissipated. Sunni examined her mother's face, pleading, and then she began to silently cry. Now, that the resistance had been broken down, Sam knew they could begin to work with Sunni. She would cooperate. Hopefully, the mother would support her daughter. And with luck, when this was all over, they may be able to track down Sunni's half sister in Korea—if there really was one.

Dan refilled coffee cups and invited the mother and daughter to come to the kitchen table where he had set out some fresh fruit and breads. Sam texted Boogie to bring him up to speed on what she had observed between Sunni and her mother. She thought it looked legit. But Boogie was doing research on his end, and she needed confirmation from him.

She had just pulled up a chair to the kitchen table when her phone dinged with a return text message from Boogie. She nodded to Dan and Drew that they should go ahead and have coffee and a bite to eat while she took the message.

She stepped away to read the message from Boogie.

June Hyun:
-Legal? Check.

-Worked her way up at the Korean restaurant? Check.

-Became the manager? Check.

-Married Joo Jhim? NO! NEVER married!

-No record of the marriage to Joo Jhim!

She read that part of the text three times. Boogie had done his homework on June. Then another text popped up.

-Still working on tracking Joo Jhim's relatives in Korea. Also trying to find a sister who may have had a child with Sunni's father.

-Checking to see if Sunni's father had gone back to South Korea any time after living in the states.

-Lots of red tape with immigration data. Will keep digging.

Sam read both texts and managed to keep her expression unchanged. In her mind, she was shouting, 'Holy Cow! Holy Cow! Holy Cow!' June hadn't married Joo? What was up with that?

The little group had finished eating and taking bathroom breaks when she returned to the kitchen. They settled in again at the table. She didn't want to let up on Sunni. They had momentum. They needed to keep things rolling. They didn't have time to waste.

"Sunni, we have been checking out your story and your mother's. Most of it is true, as you have told us. At least most of what we can verify. We are still working on the background of Joo Jhim."

She turned to June.

"June," she began, "we haven't had the same success with your background story. We have discovered the dates of your arrival into this country with Sunni's father and Sunni. We know that Sunni's father passed away. But you and Sunni both say that at some point a little while after your first husband's death, you met and then married Joo Jhim. That part isn't true, is it? You never married Joo Jhim, did you?"

She paused. The pacing was important. She needed to be quiet and wait now. She needed to let June adjust to the shock of what they knew about her. She wanted June to give a concise answer. Sunni knew this, too. Sunni's head had actually jerked up at this news. It was obvious by the look on her face that she had been surprised at this bit of information. She turned to look at her mother with her mouth open. But she waited, too.

June stared at them with steel behind her dark eyes. Shook her head. Then she quietly whispered, "No. I not marry Joo Jhim."

"Why? Why did you let me think you had?" interrupted Sunni.

"Because he want you believe that. He said important. He said you accept him better if you think we married. He said it important you accept him. I no know why he want that."

There it was, thought Sam. Interesting. Perhaps Joo Jhim had used both women. So who was Joo Jhim?

"Sunni, we need to know more about Joo, but we also need to know why you were so important to him. We know you said you played a huge role in stealing key CRISPR-Cas9 research from Cameron BioTech for Joo. The question is how did he know about you? Who was he working for? What did Joo want to do with it?"

June shook her head again. Her short, dark hair streaked with silver had been combed when she arrived this morning, but straight stringy wisps now fell forward over her forehead and into her eyes. She pushed the hair away, trying to smooth it back. "I hear him talking on phone many time," she said in a confidential tone. She looked only at Sam, not acknowledging her daughter as she sat next to her.

Sunni stared at her mother, mouth agape once again.

"Tell us, please," said Sam, as she leaned in closer to June.

June began telling the story in a soft foreign lilt. She claimed she had, at first, been charmed by Joo Jhim. He had been so helpful. She had very little money. Her daughter had been the light of her father's life. She had promised her husband long ago that if anything were to happen to him, she would always do whatever she could to make sure Sunni had every advantage in life. Joo had offered that support. He'd explained that he had been a close friend of a friend of June's husband, even though she had never met him before. He'd said he knew people. He was a big man, a strong man, who could help and protect them, she said. And he had money.

So, June said, she allowed Joo Jhim to take charge. She said he'd felt that Sunni needed a father, but June knew Sunni wouldn't allow another man to take her father's place so soon after his death. Joo was insistent. He said it was absolutely necessary they give the appearance of marriage. He thought that would open doors for Sunni. It was her husband's wish for Sunni. And somehow, it had helped her get into college. He had connections. He said he could make it happen, and he had.

She turned to Sunni and explained about one of the times she had heard him talking on the phone to someone late at night. He had sounded anxious, almost frightened. He had said something about getting some information. She had also heard him say that Sunni would do it for him. She turned back to Sam, then Dan and Drew.

"I no know what he talking about that time. I try to ask him once, and he say I asking dangerous question." She said he warned her to never ask him again if she wanted what was best for her daughter. She hadn't asked again.

Sam listened to her story and watched the kaleidoscope of expressions flit across Sunni's face. Sunni was, in turns, stunned and hurt by her mother's admissions.

Sam turned to Sunni.

"Sunni, I think now would be a good time for you to explain to your mother and us what Joo did to you. Tell her what he expected of you and what he told you about it."

Just as Sunni turned to her mother and began to speak, Sam's phone rang. It was Boogie. She knew it was important if he was calling this time, and not texting. Sam asked the women to wait a moment, excused herself, and went into the next room to talk with Boogie.

CHAPTER SEVENTEEN
Truth or Dare

Boogie's face popped up again on Sam's screen with Face Time. He was breathless and actually bouncing in his chair. Barely able to get words out, his words were running together.

"Sam, you're never going to believe this. This is crazy. This is big. I don't know what we are going to do with this. Joo Jhim! Joo Jhim, the guy was in a dangerous North Korean subversive group connected to their government. But he was wanted, big time, over there. They've been looking for him. It's big trouble. He has been involved in extortion, assault, and probably murder, although he's never been nailed for it. He was the group's hit man. He must have been controlling Sunni just like she said. She's telling the truth. I'm guessing Joo was also behind her father's death. He probably covered it up, somehow. We'll follow up on that!"

He spilled everything out so fast that it took a moment for Sam to process everything he was saying. She paused a second while he caught his breath.

"Hmmm. You're right. This is an interesting turn of events, Boogie. We thought he might be a North Korean criminal of some sort. But this really puts a different face on everything." She paused again and then continued as she reflected on the information. "So, if Joo Jhim is a North Korean hit man, who was running him? Do you think it really was that North Korean extremist group who was after this genome research? It sounds like the knowledge about CRISPR was out there already. Just had not been patented, yet. That doesn't make any sense. What would they do with it?"

"That's the next big question, Sam. Sunni may have answers on that. We've got people working on it. See what else you can get from Sunni. Maybe she knows something and doesn't know it. You know what I mean? Something she's seen or heard that didn't seem important at the time, but something that may give us some more insight."

"Yeah, I agree. Boogie, thanks for all you're doing. I know you have to be exhausted. Any word from Quay?"

"Yeah, I talked to him a half hour ago. He's feeling the pain, but he's already talking about how soon he can get out of the hospital. They've gotten him a crutch, and he says he's going to try to walk with it tomorrow. Says it hurts like hell. He says he wants to be constantly updated on everything we are doing."

"That sounds like Quay. I'm anxious to get back to see him. I plan on getting back down there around dinnertime tonight. I'll bring your stuff and his. I picked up everything before I came here. Maybe we can grab a bite with him up at the hospital. He can help us walk through all the information we've gathered today. I'll start working on more details with Sunni."

"Gotcha! Later!" Boogie signed off.

Sam thought about the new information on Joo Jhim, and took a deep breath. She pocketed her phone and stopped for a minute to redo the hair in her ponytail. It was the mundane things that gave her time to process facts and next steps.

When Sam returned to the kitchen, Sunni had begun telling her mother about Joo's operation. She was explaining how he blackmailed her and what he wanted her to do for him.

Sam settled in at the table, silently following the conversation. Dan and Drew were leaning back in their chairs also observing silently.

June wasn't looking at Sunni. Sunni seemed to be focused on convincing her mother that Joo Jhim had forced her to steal the data from Cameron BioTech.

"Umma!" Sunni said, again using the Korean word for mother. "You have to understand. I only took that job at Cameron BioTech because Joo insisted I apply to work there. I thought that's what you wanted, too. It was for father. I don't even know how I got the invitation to apply there. Now, I think Joo must have had someone there who opened that door." Sunni's tone was insistent and strident as she spoke to her mother.

Sam pulled out a notebook and jotted down a note about a possible insider at Cameron. That led her to think about Charlie Frank. Charlie had been the security officer turned bad at Cameron BioTech. He had told them he knew someone in Cameron had more inside information about things going wrong there. But his hatred for Quay had been so deep it had difficult to believe him. That was last October. It still gave her chills to think about how close she had come to dying during that case.

When questioned, Charlie had claimed he had been forced to work for Sunni Hyun. This was another twist to that story. Now Sunni was claiming that she was forced to do the dirty work at Cameron BioTech by Joo Jhim. What was the truth?

"So Sunni, you applied at Cameron, got the job, and then what?" asked Dan.

June turned to look at Sunni. She looked as if she was trying to analyze what Sunni would say. She had a huge question mark written all over her face.

Sunni looked at Dan. "I told you before. It was Joo. It was all Joo! He was married to my mother." She stopped herself and looked at her mother. "At least that is what they told me!" Sarcasm slipped into her tone.

Sam interrupted. "Yes, we know that Joo led you to believe they were married. And you said that is why you did what he asked. Didn't you say you were afraid he'd hurt her. And that he said you had a half-sister in Korea that your mother didn't know about. You were trying to keep her from learning that, too, so you did everything Joo asked. Does that just about sum it up?"

"Yes," Sunni whispered.

June gave a grunt of disapproval.

"No sister!" she said, and then paused and turned to look at Sam. "And he not hurt me."

"I didn't know that!" Sunni yelled, abruptly standing and bending over to look directly into her mother's eyes. "I didn't know that," she repeated softly and slumped back into her chair.

Sam decided to take a chance on her instincts. She needed to see who would bite first, Sunni or June.

"Okay. Okay. Let's talk about this," Sam said. She paused to make sure all eyes were on her. "Let's talk about this chip," Sam reached into her pocket and pulled up a small device. "This is a flash drive, June, with all the CRISPR-Cas9 research information Sunni stole from Cameron BioTech. Let's talk about this." She laid the flash drive out onto the middle of the table.

The house became silent. All eyes were fixed on the bright blue flash drive lying on the table.

"I afraid. My daughter. She not good. She in trouble. I take that. Throw it away. All be gone. She be safe."

June stretched her hand out for the flash drive, but Dan reached out and quickly pulled it out of her reach.

Interesting, Sam, thought. She was skeptical. She had a feeling in her gut that June Hyun was not really the innocent old woman that she seemed, after all.

Phones can ring at the most inopportune times. This was one of them. Sam's ring tone startled everyone. As Sam grabbed at her phone, Sunni pushed her chair back and stood. June used the distraction to make a desperate lunge for the flash drive at the opposite side of the table. The sudden lunge upended the table. Sunni leaped for her mother simultaneously trying to wrench the small flash drive from her mother's hand. Cups, coffee, plates, silverware, fruit, bread, and the phone scattered across the kitchen floor in a chaotic crash.

Dan Young and Drew Thurston rounded opposite sides of the upended table in a well-choreographed BCA defensive move; Dan headed to the door, and drawing up to his full height, totally blocked the exit. Drew headed off June Hyun from the other side. Corralling June, he shoved her sharply from behind so that she fell against Dan who grabbed her, whirled her around, and pinned her arms at her side. While Dan held the struggling June, Drew moved in, grabbed her hand, peeled back her fingers and removed the flash drive from her grasp. Sam leapt forward and grabbed Sunni's arm pulling it behind her in one quick move. She body-slammed the young woman into the front of the refrigerator so hard the refrigerator rocked. Sunni melted into a heap on the floor.

Amidst the clatter, Sam's phone continued playing its "Time of My Life" ringtone. Sam lifted the now limp Sunni up by one arm, shoved her back into a chair, and retrieved her phone from the floor. "Stay there!" she ordered.

"Yeah?" she said breathlessly into the phone.

"Hey! What's going on?" It was Quay. "You sound out of breath. Are you that excited that I'm calling?"

"Oh, yeah, right, Quay. Miss you so much. Wish you were here." She let out a breathless laugh. "Just a little bit of a dustup. It's all under control now. So how are you doing, Quay?" She tried her best to sound nonchalant. She glanced at Dan and Drew, nodding so they'd know who had called before she walked out of the room.

"Oh, I'm doing just dandy!" Quay popped a bubble loudly into the phone. Sam grinned.

"Sounds like it, Quay! Got a release date, yet?"

"Nope. They are jacking me around. I'm getting out of here, soon, though. I'm gonna run out of bubble gum today, though. You know what that does to my attitude!"

"I'll be by later tonight to see you. I'll bring you a new supply. I swung by your place this morning and gathered up some fresh clothes for you, too. How's that?"

"That's good. Hope it's something comfy. Sweats would probably be good. I imagine you found some. I could use a visit from you. And I really need to get out of here, Sam. I need to know what's going on. Have you got Sunni Hyun? Is her mother there with you? Where are you guys?"

"Hold on there, pardner," laughed Sam. "You're speeding. Need to slow down."

"Well, I'm going crazy here. I've got a right to know what's happening, you know."

"Yup! And I'll fill you in tonight when I see you. Okay?"

"It'll have to be, I guess. But I've got some news to share, too. You don't think I've just been lying here on vacation, do you?"

"Really? No. I didn't think you were taking a vacation. But you'd better be taking care of yourself, so you can get out here and work with me. What do you have?"

"I'll share with you tonight. I've got some inside info on this CRISPR stuff that Sunni was talking about."

Sam couldn't help herself. She caught her breath; her eyebrows shot up, stomach clenched, and she walked back into the kitchen still holding the phone to her ear.

The disaster she had left moments ago seemed to be now totally under control. Sunni was seated back in her chair, June was seated in hers, the table had been righted, plates, food and utensils picked up and replaced, and the flash drive had been placed squarely in the center of the table once again. Drew and Dan were standing opposite the women, and they were all glaring at one another.

"Quay says he's got some inside info on CRISPR," she announced. She eyed the two women. "Sounds like they don't know as much as they think they do!" she added and watched for reactions from Sunni and June.

Sunni turned to look at Sam. Her face was questioning. June returned Sunni's look, too, but Sam noticed June's face was still a mask.

Sam turned her back to the group and spoke softly into the phone.

"I'll be there in a couple hours, Quay. Hold that thought while I wind up some loose ends here, okay?"

"Sure." Quay's voice held a questioning tone, but he simply added, "I'll talk to you soon. Looking forward to it."

Sam clicked off, and turned to June Hyun.

"Would you please tell me what that was all about? Are you desperate or just a crazy woman?"

June refused to answer or even look at her.

Sam looked at Dan and Drew, raised a questioning eyebrow, and waited. Silence was the only response as Sunni stared at her mother.

"Maybe we should talk to them separately for a bit," suggested Dan. "You could take June into the back bedroom. We'll keep Sunni out here. Mrs. Hyun, you may have a lot more to say, that you don't want your daughter to hear, right?"

June Hyun nodded in apparent agreement. But then as she rose, she emitted what sounded like an anguished, low growl, and she lunged once again for the flash drive. This time, instead of the grabbing only the flash drive she managed a wider arc with the same hand to sweep up a serrated knife that had inadvertently been replaced on the up-righted breakfast table. With equal precision, June managed to seize her daughter's arm with her other hand wrenching the young woman toward her. The stunned group watched as June brought the knife up expertly to hold the blade against her daughter's carotid artery while continuing to cup the flash drive in her fist.

The action had been so swift, so precise, that Dan, Drew, and Sam stood helpless and motionless. Their training and experience taught them to assess the situation first, and then act.

"We will be leaving now," said June. This time she spoke in perfect, unaccented English. "We will be taking a car, and you will not follow if you want me to keep this one alive. She is no good to me now, so it is entirely up to you."

Sam's eyebrows shot up as she listened to June's bold, and now precise English. Sam chanced a couple steps forward, testing the situation, but June pulled Sunni tighter against her chest, pressing the knife blade against Sunni's neck causing a thin, red line of blood to form. Sunni remained still. She did not struggle against her mother's grasp; instead, huge, silent tears had begun to roll down her cheeks. Immediately, Sam realized that Sunni really had not known the depth of her mother's deception. It was suddenly quite clear that this whole scheme had to have been June Hyun's.

June spoke defiantly as she watched Sam begin to move toward her and her daughter. "Stop! You will not prevent this! Not this time! Mr. Drew, you reach very carefully and slowly into your pocket and pull out your car keys. Toss your keys to the car over here. Sunni will catch them, won't you my daughter?" Her derisive tone brought more tears from Sunni. Stifling sobs, Sunni nodded weakly.

Drew reached slowly into his pocket with eyes steadily focused on June, and pulled out a set of keys. He held them up for her to see and tossed them to Sunni, who caught them handily.

"Very good, daughter. You finally did something right!" June laughed with another derisive snicker.

June continued to sidle back toward the door still clutching Sunni to her chest. Then she turned Sunni slightly toward the door and instructed her to open it. Sam, Drew and Dan watched unmoving. As the two women backed slowly out the door, Sunni stumbled slightly.

It was just enough. June tightened her grip on Sunni, but while clasping the knife more tightly, she lost her grasp on the flash drive. As the flash drive fell, June looked down, and two men who had been stationed outside as guards quickly appeared behind her. June hadn't expected the guards. She whirled, pushing Sunni into them as she ducked under the grasp of the young guard, snatched up the small drive from the floor in one fluid dive, and flew out the door and around the side of the house. Sunni and the two guards tumbled off balance into a heap in front of the door. Sam turned and ran for the back door. Dan and Drew followed June out the front door.

Just as Sam ran out the back door with gun drawn, June was rounding the corner behind the house heading for the garage. Sam raised her gun, aimed, and shouted, "Stop! June!"

June stopped for a millisecond, screamed, and launched the knife at Sam in a professional arc. Sam ducked to the side and fired her gun as the knife whizzed past her.

June crumbled to the ground moaning, and still clutching the flash drive to her chest.

Sam ran to her, bent over her, slamming June's body flat against the frozen ground.

"Well, I guess you aren't who you wanted us to believe, are you, June?" Sam yelled. "Who are you working for? You couldn't be smart enough to be working alone," she concluded as she ripped the flash drive out of June's hand.

June wilted under Sam's grasp. "You stupid woman. This flash drive was just a decoy. It's blank," Sam was still running on adrenalin. She shook June and continued shouting at her. "We weren't going to let you have anything, you understand? Nothing. We just needed to see who you really were. And I guess we did, didn't we? You just destroyed your life and your daughter's life for nothing. And we aren't even close to being done with you!"

June looked up into Sam's eyes with disdain.

"Not for nothing," she whispered. "We will still win." She smiled.

Then June's head fell back as she slipped into unconsciousness. She was out. Sam collapsed, sitting down on the frozen ground next to June. The reality of the cold winter air hit her, and she began shivering. She wasn't sure, though, if her trembling was from the freezing cold or from an adrenalin rush. She knew June Hyun wasn't dead. Sam had been diving to avoid the knife as she fired. Her shot had hit June in her shoulder. June would have been dead otherwise. She hadn't meant to even fire. But in the heat of the moment, training kicked in before reason. She'd been under attack. June had meant to kill her. She was glad June would live. There was more they could learn from her. The EMTs would be here in a minute.

The plan had been to push the two women as hard as possible to see who would blink, so the BCA team had prepared for something like this. Dan and Drew had posted two guards outside the front door. One more was posted in the garage by the car. Drew had picked up a flash drive that looked exactly like the one they had shown Sunni earlier. She would have thought it was one that they had used to copy data from Cameron BioTech chip. But it had been June, not Sunni who had blinked first. Now they needed more information from June; Sam was pretty sure Sunni didn't have all the answers they needed. She had only been the tip of the iceberg.

Maybe Quay had some ideas. She hoped he'd be able to talk with her. Sam rose as the EMTs arrived, gave brief instructions for security, and headed inside. Time was short. She needed to help Dan and Drew organize this mess and get Sunni settled before taking off for Mankato to follow up with Quay and Boogie.

CHAPTER EIGHTEEN
Filling in the Blanks

Quay lay propped up in bed; a Vikings football game played on the TV on the wall opposite his bed. The crowd's cheering and sports commentary filtered softly into the room. His eyes were closed.

He was in a dream sleep. The game refs on TV had called for an instant replay. Quay's own instant replay flashed in his mind. He watched his deceased wife Karen's smiling face look down from the podium at him. Karen nervously began the press conference. He was standing in the crowd watching proudly. He didn't even hear the shot. Only saw the blood blossom on her chest as she crumbled in slow motion behind the podium. Fear! Panic! Shouts for help and 911. He couldn't move. He tried to get to her, but his feet seemed to be caught in quicksand.

Then the scene changed. Sam's laughing face appeared as she rode next to him heading to a crime scene. He'd just told her another Ole and Lena joke, and she broke into laughter. She loved those jokes.

Another change of scene and another flash of memory. Charlie Frank, Cameron BioTech's crazy security guard had grabbed Sam and was backing through a door with her in tow. She was struggling against his grip. The madman held a gun to her and dragged her to his truck. Quay watched helplessly as they sped away. Once again he had the overwhelming feeling of walking through a bog. His feet wouldn't move. He futilely reached out. It was slow motion.

Then the scene shifted again, now moving into a fast forward blurred stream of images. The location and time changed again. Another memory scrolled to a time before. Sam was with him at his brother John's home in

Lutsen near Lake Superior's north shore. She was laughing with his sister-in-law Sharon. They had just shared an inside joke about Quay. Sam had needed a change of clothes and ended up using Sharon's clothes. There'd been jokes about Quay's bubble gum addiction. All of them had laughed at his nephew Adam's Ole and Lena joke. He heard it clearly, the whole dumb joke.

His nephew Adam had begun with the usual, "Did you hear the one about Ole on his deathbed?" They all stopped to listen as Adam continued.

"Ole was upstairs on his deathbed. Lena had been baking cookies. The aroma of the fresh-baked cookies came up the stairs, and Ole has to get to the cookies. He drags himself out of bed, crawls to the stairway, bumps down the stairs, and gets to the kitchen. He pulls himself up onto a chair, grabs a cookie and begins to munch away. 'Mmmm, deese is so goot, Lena,' he says. 'Ole!' Lena shouts. 'Yew can't eat dose! Dey are for the funeral!'"

Young Adam's Ole-Lena dialect was pretty good. They'd all laughed. Quay's mouth twitched into a slight grin in his dream sleep as he reviewed the scene.

Then it all suddenly changed again. He heard Sunni Hyun's high, determined voice. Her dark eyes stared defiantly at him. He frowned. Anger flowed through his body. Then Sam's voice rose again. It was an urgent demand. A look of terror filled her eyes. Sam was pulling him close. "Hang on, Quay! I've got you! Hang on! Help is coming!"

"Quay! Can you hear me! Quay, open your eyes, you're okay now."

Quay struggled to wake from the dream. He heard, "Touchdown for the Vikings!" from an excited TV announcer. His eyes opened into slits. Blue eyes looked up into green eyes. Sam. Recognition filled his eyes.

"Hey, Quay. You were having a bit of a dream there, fella," Sam said. "Seemed like you were laughing one minute and groaning with pain the next. Dreaming about the safe house?" Sam asked, her tone filled with understanding. She was sitting on the edge of his bed and holding his hand in hers.

It took him a bit to return to the present. He had been so deep in the dream sleep. But seeing Sam's smiling face brought him around in seconds, and he broke into a huge grin.

"Yeah, I guess so," he said. He paused, mentally shaking his head before he asked, "Did you bring me anything?"

She happily noted the old twinkle still there in his eyes. She pulled her hand away from his and dug into her coat pocket pulling out a full package of his favorite bubble gum.

"Did you really think I'd forget?" She held it up for him to see.

"Well, I figured you must have been pretty busy today."

"You have no idea!" she said. The day's events tumbled out as she unwrapped his first piece of gum for him.

Samantha had just finished with the story about Sunni and June's attempted escape when a furry, light gold animal trailing a leather leash streaked into the room and ran straight for Quay. Chip's tail was wagging so hard his entire back end was swaying from side to side. The dog laid his head on the edge of the bed near Quay's hand and began alternately licking and frantically nudging his hand. Quay laughed and looked up as Boogie walked into the room.

"They said they thought it'd be okay if I brought him in to see you, as long as I kept him leashed. I couldn't hold him once he saw you. I think he actually remembers you!"

"You know they say dogs never forget. I'm glad to see him, too," said Quay looking from Boogie to Chip. He patted the dog's head, rubbed his ears, and said, "Good to see you too, young fella! How are you holding up?"

"The question should be how am I holding up!" said Boogie. "He really has been a bundle of energy!"

They were all smiling as Chip continued to chase from one to the other in an excited, tail-wagging greeting. His friendly antics had brought much-needed cheer into the room.

Quay pulled himself up into a straighter upright position while Sam plumped his pillows behind him. Boogie pulled up a chair by the bed next to Sam's. Chip was determined to snuggle with Quay, so they gently lifted the pup onto the bed. He curled up with his head on Quay's chest and settled happily in as Quay continued to pet him.

"Well, what have we learned about CRISPR-Cas9?" Sam asked Quay. "You told me you had a bit more info. Let's start with that."

"Sure. While you two were out fighting the bad dudes, or dudettes, in this case, I was in here diligently working on recuperating, and at the same time using my connections with Cameron BioTech. I still know some people there from our run-in with their crazy security guard Charlie Frank. So, I called over there today and got in touch with one of the head researchers. I explained who I was. He had to verify my creds, of course. Had him call our boss, Super Mike. Mike gave them permission to share anything and everything with me.

"The head researcher's name is Dwight Davis. He has been on the research team at Cameron for several years. So he has all the background stuff. What he shared with me matches up with the information Boogie found online and with what Sunni told us. The basics in layman's terms are that everyone is born with some bad or flawed genes. You might have some genes that would indicate a possible predisposition toward such diverse problems as schizophrenia, diabetes, heart disease, cancer."

"That's quite a broad spectrum," Sam commented.

"Yes, and it's quite a big deal! It would be natural to want to protect your baby from any of those things. But with this CRISPR-Cas9 technology, you could do all that, and on top of that, someone could also digitally design a baby. There would be no disease carriers. You could tweak genes to determine eye color, hair color, even a widow's peak or prevention of male baldness. How about that? You could compare it to our use of antibiotics when it comes to disease. You can imagine there must be some boundaries set to prevent misuse. That's why Cameron is being so careful about crafting the patent. Cameron wants to make sure this research doesn't get into the wrong hands."

"So Sunni, being a researcher at Cameron, knew about all of this?" asked Sam.

"Yes, she was one of their top CRISPR researchers. She had access to everything. If Joo Jhim was really blackmailing Sunni Hyun, and I say IF with a question mark, then Sunni had to have known she would be placing all of that incredible data in the hands of a terrorist group who wanted to create their world with digitally perfected children. That could mean super humans. And she also had to have understood that the many other aspects of CRISPR-Cas9 would provide enormous power to whoever had control of the patent. She claims she didn't give Joo all the correct research data. And the research hasn't been released, yet, but she may still have it in her possession. That's what we need to find out. Cameron doesn't want this released until they have complete safety profiles in place. Of course, our boss man Super Mike is worried. We need to get this cleared up before any of this to gets out to media. That would be the real danger!"

"So do you think your wife Karen was going to make an announcement about this when she was shot?" asked Boogie.

"I think that was part of it. I believe, and so does Mike, that the North Koreans, aka Sunni Hyun and company, wanted to prevent the announcement. They wanted to keep it under wraps until they could discredit Cameron's research, and then siphon that same research out via Sunni, patent it, and claim it as their own. Shooting Karen gave them enough time to create a diversion of Cameron's plans. They wanted to have enough time to spirit the research away and distort Cameron's research. They'd keep the good research data, and make sure Cameron had errors in their work, so they couldn't patent it."

"Okay, that clears that part up, Quay. Now, what do we know about June Hyun, Sunni's mother?" asked Sam as she turned to Boogie.

"So glad you asked," said Boogie. "Here's what I found out today."

He paused just long enough for Quay to rearrange himself more comfortably and pull Chip closer. Chip didn't seem to mind the extra affection as he lifted his head to give Quay a light doggie kiss on the chin. Quay smiled and bent forward to snuggle with the dog. Chip's tail wagged happily.

"He sure is a nice dog. Hate to think about what he's gone through. He seems to be coping pretty well, though. Pretty laid back dog!"

"Ha! You haven't seen him on one of his puppy tears," retorted Boogie. "That dog tucks his tail and runs full blast from one end of the yard to the other for a full ten to fifteen minute tear without stopping. Then you need to throw a ball for him for another fifteen minutes. Then he might settle down a bit. You are just seeing him at the end of the day. He's tired now. That's the only time he's laid back!" Boogie's tone in telling the story betrayed the actual affection he felt for the dog. "Just wait until you settle in with us, Quay. You'll find out!"

"I'm looking forward to it," smiled Quay.

"So, you asked about the background on Sunni's mother," began Boogie, getting back to business. "She's not all that Sunni apparently thinks she is. In fact, I believe June Hyun's the actual brain behind this operation. From what I can find out, she isn't even actually Sunni's mother!"

Sam and Quay both raised eyebrows. Boogie nodded and continued. "Sunni Hyun was born in South Korea. That part is true. Her father, Hal Hyun, was married in South Korea to a woman named Jaemee Park. Jaemee Park died in childbirth. Hal and his baby girl, Sunni, came to America alone. We think he thought he would have more opportunities for his daughter if he moved to the United States. He met June shortly after moving here. She became the nanny for the little baby. Couldn't find any proof that they'd ever married. The baby grew up calling June mother, and her father must have never told her otherwise."

"You have got to be kidding! So Sunni thought June was her mother, but June hadn't married her father, and not only that, she thought June had married Joo Jhim, and she hadn't. This June is quite the woman!"

"It seems that June is actually a North Korean operative. It also appears that Hal and Sunni were unaware of this. They were not a part of her conspiracy. Her Korean name is Jun Kim. You spell Jun without the e. This plan has been in place for years, it seems, even prior to the development of CRISPR. The information I was able to get from the people in Washington is that operatives from North Korea have been on the lookout for any type of research in America they could steal to help North Korean advancement. They seem to have been looking for the quickest way to world domination. Their agents were looking for anything and everything; that included advanced research in space technology to nuclear weapons to disease control.

"June hit a bingo when she heard about Cameron BioTech, the research lab so close to where she was living with Hal Hyun. Sunni was very bright, and she encouraged Sunni's father to groom his daughter for a role in research. They had the time to wait. In fifteen years, they had their road mapped out for them. Then, she had to have had Hal Hyun killed to get him out of the way."

"Killed? What? Sunni said he died of a heart attack!" said Sam.

"Yeah, well, my guess is she had to get rid of him so Joo could move in. We can have the body exhumed and checked if we can't get a confession out of her. But that is the most plausible explanation for the sequence of events."

"What about the bruises and abuse that Sunni said she saw on her mother...I mean June? Do you think Joo actually beat her?"

"If she's as badass as you're describing, I'm guessing June did some kind of a make up job on herself to gather Sunni's sympathy and make her more susceptible to Joo's threats!" ventured Quay.

"Exactly what I'm thinking, " nodded Boogie.

"Well, we have put a lot of the pieces of the puzzle together. Right now, we have to get a confession from June what's-her-face. And we need bring Sunni up to speed. I'm thinking she'll cooperate once she realizes the full scope of how she was played, especially if we include the information that June may have been behind her father's untimely death," said Sam.

"Yes, but we also have some bad North Korean operatives out there that we need to shut down," added Quay. "We need to follow up on Joo Jhim's connections around here. They got him out of the way. They are still a threat. Maybe June or Sunni can help in that area, too?"

"I think we can call in the feds for that work. How about we wind up the case here with Cameron BioTech and Sunni Hyun? We can let the feds work on the international stuff. I think we're almost there!" Sam's voice was tinged with a bit of relief.

"Oh that sounds so good!" agreed Boogie. "Let's get this report filed with the boss. We've put in a full day."

"Yup! I agree. Quay, here, needs to get some recuperative rest. We all need to get a good night's sleep. How about that?" Sam turned to look at Quay.

"I guess I can agree with that. I'm hoping I've only got one more day in here. I can still work the phone here. You guys can work on Sunni tomorrow. Where are you going to stay? And where's Sunni?"

"She's still in the safe house in Maple Grove," answered Boogie. "June is under guard at the hospital up there. She'll be moved to lock up when they release her. And Sam and Chip and I are going to head to the safe house here. It's just down the hill from the hospital here. It's got enough room for all of us and a fenced yard for Chip. We'll get some sleep tonight and check in with you and Dan and Drew in the morning. We can maybe do a conference call and map out our strategy with Sunni Hyun and June."

Boogie was in organization mode, thought Sam. "Don't mess with him when he's knocking out the Vultures," she laughed.

"Vultures?" asked Quay.

"Oh, you wouldn't understand," said Sam. "I'll explain another time. Get some sleep, Quay!"

Boogie grabbed Chip's leash and started to head for the door. Sam moved closer to Quay, bent over his head and placed a quick kiss on his forehead. "Sleep well, tiger!" she whispered, and patted his chest.

Quay smiled, and leaned back on his pillow, blew a huge, pink bubble and popped it as he watched her walk out the door. He listened to Boogie's laughter echoing down the hall.

CHAPTER NINETEEN
Bombs and Blizzards

Samantha and Boogie loaded dog food, new dog toys, and Chip, into Quay's truck. Earlier in the day with instructions from Quay, Boogie had gone to the police lot to retrieve Quay's truck that had been picked up from the safe house. Sam grabbed her bag that she'd packed earlier at her place before she'd headed back to Mankato late in that afternoon. They loaded the truck with their bags, Boogie's computer, and the few groceries they needed and headed to the BCA house on Hickory Street.

Chip was delighted with the new digs. He inspected each room of the older three-bedroom house before settling comfortably onto the sofa in the living room with his new stuffed bear. Sam joked that Boogie must have a soft spot for the dog, because he'd bought so many toys and treats for Chip, and had minimal clothing and supplies for himself.

"I can get by on just a toothbrush, toothpaste, and a change of underwear," Boogie said seriously. "But this dog has been through so much, he deserves to be treated with a lot of special love and attention!"

Chip seemed to understand that Boogie was talking about him, and walked up to Boogie, sat in front of him, and raised his front paw. Boogie clasped Chip's proffered paw, and bent down to Chip's level so that Chip could happily place a big kiss on Boogie's cheek. Then Chip happily danced away, spun in a circle, and lay down in the center of the room, his tail wagging like a dust mop on the wood floor.

Later after unpacking her few things in her room, Sam found Chip and Boogie in the kitchen. Boogie had already hooked up his computer and was working frantically at the keyboard. She could tell he was in deep thought because he was hunched so far over the computer that she could only see the top of his head. Boogie had bent low, leaning close to scrutinize the screen; his long hair fell over his face, and his brows wrinkled into a frown.

"What's up, Boogie?"

"I think we may have something. One of the guys in Washington sent me some background on Joo Jhim. They already had a file started on him. They've got some evidence that points to June managing Joo. He wasn't managing June. It was just the reverse! They've laid out a hierarchy in the stuff they've sent. It shows that relationship. I think when we get back to talking to Sunni, we need to talk to her about some very specific conversations she had with her mother."

Sam's phone went off. "It's Quay," she said, as she tapped it to answer.

"Quay! I thought you were going to get some sleep?"

"Yeah, that's what I thought, too! I actually slept a little while earlier today. But I just got a phone call from Claude Bartholomew Ayres aka Swivel. Remember him?"

"Oh, right! I remember! Your 'favorite' snitch. What brought him out of the jack-in-the-box? Pardon my pun." She remembered Quay joking about how this particular paranoid snitch popped his head up and swiveled side to side always looking for spies.

"He says he's got some dope on someone named June Yung Hyun. Said he thought I should know. Of course, he's hoping there's something in it for him. He claims he has sources who are saying she's hired someone to plant a bomb at Cameron BioTech."

"A bomb? What? Damn! You're kidding!?! June Hyun is planning on bombing Cameron BioTech? No way! That's too far up the ladder! Hold it! I'm going to put you on speaker, so Boogie can hear this."

She nodded at Boogie, who had stopped typing, looked up at her, and listened intently. She tapped the speaker and laid her phone on the table so they could both hear. Quay backtracked and repeated what he'd just told Sam.

"This is not good. Are you sure we can we trust Swivel? I've met that guy," said Boogie." He's a meth head. If I remember the guy correctly, he speed talks, always licks his lips, and smells like a mixture of dirty sweat socks and Cheyenne cigarettes!"

"You've got that right, Boogie," said Sam, adding more explanation, "Remember, Quay dubbed him Swivel because his head always seems to be on a swivel. He's constantly looking right to left thinking someone is following him. He's paranoid as all get out. He always has a bottle of Dr. Pepper with him wherever he goes. Doesn't he also have spider web tattoos covering both elbows?"

"Yeah, you're both right. He has those tattoos in addition to SS lightning bolts on his neck. He's a real prize."

"So we're supposed to believe this paranoid, Nazi doper's reports?" asked Sam.

"I know it sounds crazy. But I think Swivel may have good Intel on this one. It just rings true. He's got specifics. He has background on June as well as on Joo. It goes back more than a year. Says he has friends who know June, too. They agree with him that she's a tough cookie. They claim she's involved with some bad people. He thinks she uses her restaurant as a front. He says other things that line up with what Sunni told you. He shared things that make sense, Sam.

"So I've already put a call in to Super Mike. He's going to have Swivel picked up and just placed in protective custody. We believe he may be in danger now that we've got June, and Joo's dead. Who knows who else he's talked to. By now June's friends could have figured out that Swivel's got info that could put everybody in their group in jeopardy. So Mike is having Swivel picked up within the hour. Tonight, right now, we have a bomb squad going out to Cameron. They are going to go over that place with a fine tooth comb. Mike got the ball rolling on that, too."

"Okay," said Sam. "What do you want us to do? Should we head up to the Cities?"

"I want you to get me out of here. Now! I need to head back to the Cities with both of you tonight! I've got to talk to Swivel. He won't talk to anyone else. He only trusts me. And he's going to be pretty upset that I had him picked up.

"Next, we need to talk with June. And we need to have Boogie go over any tech stuff that she and Sunni have. Get the computers. We've got to track her emails, track her phone calls, find out who she's been in touch with. And we also need to get Joo Jhim's computer and his phone. We have to track all communications from and to these three. And..."

"Quay, slow down. You can't possibly be ready to do that! You are recovering from a pretty bad gunshot wound remember? You're insane."

"I'm fine! This isn't going to be a lot of physical stuff. It's armchair work. My brain isn't recovering, you know!" he was sounding belligerent and was definitely exhibiting his stubborn side, Sam thought. She knew she should approach it differently with Quay when he got like this, but right now she was more worried about his recovery.

"We need to get going on this stuff, Sam!" Quay was insistent. "It's possible we've got a bomb sitting somewhere at Cameron BioTech. We've got a foreign group involved in some sort of sabotage with this damn futuristic research, and we can't waste time! My little injury isn't anything compared to what's going down right now."

"You're little injury isn't so little, Quay. You are in no shape to travel, yet!" Sam pushed back at his argument. "Boogie and I and the rest of the BCA will work on it. You just can't overdo, or you'll be right back in the hospital. Your doctor won't release you."

"He will. I'm going arrange it. I can travel. You're not going to stop me, Sam. Pick me up in my truck. You drive. I'll sit in the back of the cab with my leg up on the seat. And that's final! I will be going with you!"

"But you haven't been checked out of the hospital. The doctor will need to see you, and he won't be around again tonight," she reminded him.

"I can handle the doctor. I'll be ready to leave in an hour or two. You can count on it!"

"Quay, let's just wait until morning." Sam pleaded. She was thinking ahead, hoping she could slow him down a bit. She continued before he could interrupt her. "Super Mike has got Dan and Drew and the BCA crew covering things for now in the Cities. We can leave early in the morning if the doctor gives you the okay. In the meantime, we can use the time to coordinate with the guys up there. That'll give you a wee bit more time in recuperation, too."

Boogie interrupted with a cautionary tone of his own.

"Well, it looks like we won't have much of a choice. We definitely won't be leaving tonight. And it will probably be a slow ride in the morning, too," he said with a tone indicating both resignation and alarm. Sam turned to see Boogie staring at the television.

"Why?" Quay asked sharply. "What's going on, Boogie?"

Boogie glanced at Sam, and they turned to watch as the local weatherman on TV pointed to a huge weather map showing central and southern Minnesota covered with shades of deep blue. The words 'Blizzard Warning' were scrolling across the bottom of the screen.

"It's the weather, Quay. I'll turn up the sound so you can listen to the weather guy on TV," said Boogie.

The weatherman was forecasting a winter blizzard.

"This is going to begin in the next hour with steady freezing rain. That will be followed by several inches of snow and high winds later tonight. This will be a typical January blizzard, folks. Unfortunately, this one will be the type of storm that will keep everyone in the area off the roads for at least tonight and maybe a part of tomorrow. Just plan ahead, and stay inside."

The weatherman noted that it had already begun to rain, and the temperature would be dropping from a balmy thirty-eight degrees to a low of five degrees by morning.

"Oh, great!" Quay grumbled. "How many breaks can this mob get? They must have fortune cookie luck. First, they got away with killing my wife, and setting up a bunch of other crazy people to take the fall. Then, they continued pulling the wool over our eyes with Sunni Hyun and her mother. And now, they get the benefit of a winter storm to hold up our follow up with a possible bomb at Cameron BioTech! How does that work? Somebody up there must really have it in for me! Damn!"

"It's not you, Quay. It's just a typical January in Minnesota. Relax! If we're not going anywhere, neither are the bad guys, right? It buys us a little time to do some more research and get all of our facts straight. We can use this time to have Boogie do some more background work. We can Face Time with Boogie's tech crew in the Cities. They dig into the computers they confiscated to look for and feed us any useful information."

"That's true," agreed Boogie. "I can call Lex Ellingson tonight and see if he can pick up the computers before the storm hits. He could work on them from home tomorrow, if he needs to."

"Well, that at least sounds like a decent plan," Quay agreed begrudgingly. "But how do we know they haven't already set the bombs at Cameron?"

He was thinking through his strategy as he spoke. "Okay, you two do what you need to do to get more background information on June and company. I'll work the phones here to follow up with the international connections. I'll see what I can find out about the North Koreans. How's that sound?"

"That sounds like a much better plan, Quay," said Sam. "I think you need to get a good night's sleep tonight, though. No one is going to be around tonight. You can get on it in the morning. With luck, you can join us at the house here in Mankato by mid-morning tomorrow. Then we can all put our heads together before we head north. What do you think?"

"I suppose." The tone of Quay's voice revealed his reluctant acceptance.

"We'll get going as soon as the roads are ready for travel," Boogie assured him. "I don't imagine that will be much before noon, at the earliest. It depends on how fast this storm moves. But, you can be sure we are going to get there in time to settle this thing. We can coordinate a lot from here before we leave."

"Yeah, I know. It's like we keep getting roadblocks thrown up at us at every turn. I'm just so tired of feeling like there's a yoke around my neck," muttered Quay.

"We all understand, Quay," Sam said. She could tell from his tone how frustrated he was. She was, too. So was Boogie. They all needed to tie up the loose ends of this case. It was going to take perseverance and working one step at a time. Planning was the key to the solution, she thought.

"Looking ahead, I'll call Dan and Drew and see what they can pull out of June and Sunni. Anything will help. Maybe we can get June to slip up."

"Okay. Let's get going!" Boogie was on his feet rearranging his computer and workstation. "If we find anything that really stands out, we'll share it immediately. Let's see if we can complete this puzzle!"

"Talk to you later, Quay! You need to get some rest tonight if you think you're going with us tomorrow!" ordered Sam.

Quay popped a bubble loudly into the phone and disconnected. Sam and Boogie chuckled. The team was in business!

It was nearly nine o'clock that evening when the storm winds really began whipping up. The rain had finished, turned to ice, and the snow had begun. Forceful winds rattled the windowpanes with insistent surges. Samantha peered out the dining room window toward the street. The street light across the street revealed thick, hazy, white sheets of snow blowing in tornadic swirls. Drifts had already begun accumulating around the cars parked at the curb. Judging by what Sam could see, the magnitude of the storm was everything the weather guy had predicted.

"It's a good thing you let the dog out before this storm really got going," Sam said. "He wouldn't want to be going out now. Nobody would!" Sam turned from looking out the window to look at Boogie who was hunched over his keyboard in a freeze frame of the same position he'd held for the last hour.

Sam walked into the kitchen, put her partial cup of coffee in the microwave, and pressed reheat. "Boogie? What have you got? You've been pretty quiet for a long time. Anything?"

"Huh! There's so much stuff here. The stuff that Lex was able to pull off June's computer is confusing. It's a mess to try to put together in any coherent order. I'm working on it using a Dynamic Binary Code, but this stuff is in an odd kind of code that I don't have a lot of experience with. Usually there's a pattern. With this one, there's not a clear pattern. There are a lot of gaps. I'm going to have to modify the program to teach it to fill in the gaps. It's gonna take some time."

"Yeah. Sure. Okay," said Sam. Boogie was speaking in a foreign language as far as she was concerned. All she could do was agree with him and commiserate. "Uh, but can we take a break for a few minutes and talk it through?"

Boogie looked up at her, stretched his arms and arched his back. "Yeah, I think I need to rest my eyes and brain for a bit. It's all running together."

"Want a cup of coffee? There's beer in here, too."

"No, I think I'd just like to grab another Coke."

Boogie took the pop Sam offered and called Chip over. The dog stood and stretched, wagged his tail, and moved next to Boogie to receive some of Boogie's attention. As he laid his head in Boogie's lap, Boogie began to absently stroke the dog's back. Sam pulled a chair up to the table.

"You know, I've been thinking about June," began Sam. "If June is really the one behind all of this, she has to have had some tech knowledge, or she knows someone who does. She must have a community she's working with. It appears that she's been sending and receiving coded messages and money, right? She's paying people. She has to be the person who is setting up not only the kills, but also is the one who's running the communications with North Korea. I think we could dub her the Great Coordinator/Conspirator. Since you're working on the attachments of the messages, I can start with June's bank accounts. Let me put in a call to Super Mike. We need to track the money. Then we'll see where we can go from there."

"Okay. I want to check in with Super Mike, anyway, to see what's happening with the Cameron bomb crew."

Over the next hour, Sam and Boogie worked the phones from the safe house while Quay used his cell phone from his bedside at the hospital. Quay found himself embroiled with federal red tape and an old friend named Joe Joyner.

It was almost eleven, when Quay finished his conversation, switched off his phone, and lay back onto his pillow. It had been good catching up with Joe. Quay had stayed in Minnesota after college and had been eventually hired by the BCA. His friend Joe had been eager to move out of state and up the ladder. He worked in the BCA for a couple years before being picked up by the CIA. He moved to Virginia and now had a nice little office in Langley.

When Quay explained the BCA history and investigation into Sunny Hyun and her mother June, Joe Joyner had immediately recognized the names. He had been able to fill in some pieces, but not all of them. The information Joe was able to give him was troubling. Joyner said June had come under the eye of the CIA just in the last year.

He provided some background information explaining that the CIA had been tracking a group out of North Korea that identified itself as NKUNA. Joe said it supposedly stood for the North Korean United National Army. But they weren't a military group. They just referred to themselves as an army. An army of what, they weren't sure. It appeared, in turn, they were connected to a company called Hang Sun Research in North Korea.

Quay remembered Charlie Frank mentioning that name. In his confession Charlie had said that he believed Sunni was streaming out Cameron BioTech's research data to Hang Sun Research. Charlie said that Cameron was ahead of all other research labs in the world, and Sunni Hyun intended to stop them. But the BCA hadn't been able to successfully track anything back to Hang Sun Research in North Korea since they hadn't been able to capture Sunni Hyun.

The CIA wasn't sure yet if the NKUNA group was a security risk, either. They had just begun maintaining surveillance recently. The plot at Cameron had ended, they thought, when Sunni Hyun disappeared. She wasn't at Cameron. She wasn't a danger to them. Then, June Hyun had appeared on the radar when they began seeing regular correspondence between June and a researcher at Hang Sun. The emails hadn't meant much. They appeared to be generic in content on the surface, detailing June's daily living in Minnesota and her work at the restaurant. She had spoken of a man named Joo Jhim in disparaging terms more frequently in the last month. She labeled him as a failure at her restaurant.

Interestingly, she had also mentioned the dog Chip. One email in particular, had described the dog and had even included a picture of him. She had explained in detail that she had had the pup micro chipped for ID in case it was lost, but added that the dog was with either Joo Jhim, Sunni or herself at all times. It had seemed an innocuous statement on the surface. But, considering the people she was corresponding with, it seemed to be information that wasn't necessarily relevant. Joe had highlighted that email when he read it.

Quay had also found that interesting. He shared the information Boogie had been able to uncover on June and Joo and the discovery of the extra chips they had discovered on the dog. Now, the NKUNA group was a new wrinkle.

Quay had listened, had time to think about the case, and summed it up saying, "The NKUNA group may be our link to the theft of the genetic research at Cameron BioTech. It sounds like they are probably connected to Hang Sun Research. In fact, I'm thinking June Hyun is likely the leader of that group."

Joe's voice had changed when he answered. Quay had noticed Joe became brusque, more business-like. There was an urgency in his voice when he said, "I agree, Quay. This sounds like something that we should move on quickly. Let's see if I can come up with more info on NKUNA. They may be more dangerous than we had initially thought. If this CRISPERCas9 research is as advanced as you say, we could have a major world terrorist group working right under our noses." He'd said he'd get on it and get back to Quay in the morning. Quay responded saying it sounded like Joe was going to be pulling an all-nighter. They'd ended the call with more questions than answers.

Quay mindlessly moved his leg, grunted in response to the sharp pain it caused, and breathed through it. He wondered what they had gotten into? He had a feeling they'd literally opened Pandora's box, and tomorrow was going to be an even longer day. His first stop had to be with Swivel to find out what he knew about the bomb and June Hyun. Tense, sore muscles knifed through his body interfering with his thoughts. He pushed the pain away and forced the aching muscles to rest. Closing his eyes, Quay blocked out the echoing hospital sounds in the hallway, and allowed himself to drift away into a restless sleep.

CHAPTER TWENTY
Breaking the Code

Sun swallowed up the night, and the morning broke clear and cold. Like most days after a blizzard, sunlight pushed through, bouncing off the glistening drifts with searchlight intensity. The fresh snow blanketed the small city muffling the echo of the one or two vehicles crunching along the streets. A neighbor's snow blower thrummed in an active struggle to clear a driveway.

As promised, Quay had summoned his doctor to his bedside early in the morning and had persuaded the man to release him into the care of Samantha Atwood. Sam received the call from a clearly disgruntled doctor at six-thirty that morning and had promised she would do everything possible to maintain Quay's care and control his activity.

Sam pulled Quay's truck up to the hospital entrance just after ten. A few cars had ventured out, but the streets were still mostly empty. Plows had begun their work as soon as the snow quit at dawn. Boogie stayed back at the safe house and busily organized the packing up of the computers, their supplies and the dog, while on speakerphone with Cameron's head researcher, Dwight Davis.

Boogie had risen just as the sun began to peek through the blinds of his bedroom. He had immediately gone to his computer, determined to find the source of the enigmatic code and fill in its gaps. When Quay called about his hospital release, he was anxious to tell Boogie and Sam about his conversation with Joe Joyner at Langley. That led to Boogie following up with a call to Joe and asking him to share what Langley had in the emails from June Yung Hyun. Now that Boogie had a burgeoning idea of who and what June Hyun was, he was moving on to talking with Dwight Davis and the researchers at Cameron BioTech to share what they'd learned with them. The next step would be to first find out if, and where, bombs had been planted at Cameron, and then deactivating them. That was a case of no news being good news. No bombs had gone off over night. A BCA crew would be over there this morning. Sam and Quay were going to take that on. It was Boogie's job to use the coded messages from June to determine just exactly how June and NKUNA were planning on using the CRISPERCas9 data. There were so many tiny pieces to be put together. Sam said it reminded her of trying to put together her mother's favorite broken teapot after she had dropped it on the tile floor in their kitchen. The fragile pieces had to be arranged and rearranged to make it right. She'd shed tears as she'd glued the tiny shards in place and presented it to her mother.

A friendly nurse wheeled Quay into the lobby of the hospital. Sam stared at the weary, pale face of Quay as he struggled to sit up straight in the chair. His injured leg was supported straight out on the chair rest with a special brace. She realized the jacket he wore must be one that had been supplied by Super Mike when he visited. It was a standard issue, dark blue BCA thermal jacket. She briefly wondered what had happened to Quay's other jacket. She noticed the nurse had pulled a dark knit cap down to cover his ears. Then she noticed the fresh blue denim shirt and jeans under the coat, and winced, realizing what his clothes must have looked like when he'd entered the hospital. Tousled hair curled out from under the cap in a shaggy mess over his forehead. She glanced up at the nurse who shook her head slightly in disapproval. This wasn't going to be easy, she thought. But for Quay, she would make sure it worked.

"Does he have medicine to take with him?" she asked the nurse.

"Yes, his meds are in this bag," she held up a white, paper bag. "He had his pain and antibiotic meds at six this morning. He should get another pain med at noon. He can take up to four a day. The antibiotics are to be taken once a day. There are two kinds of antibiotic pills. The rest of his clothes and personal effects are in this bag." She held up a large plastic bag identified with the hospital logo.

"Thanks, so much," Sam nodded as she took the things from the nurse. Quay mustered a confident thanks and nod to the nurse.

They braced for the cold air as they moved through the doors to the truck. Puffs of white exhaust fumes plumed from the rear of the truck. Sam's muscles tightened with the cold. She imagined they were all feeling the clutch of the subzero cold this morning.

Loading Quay into the rear seat of the extended cab pickup took Sam, the female nurse and another male nurse to make it happen without reopening Quay's wound. Quay's face creased with the exertion, but he made no sound during the transition process. Sam had brought a pillow to put under his leg and another to put behind his head and back so that he could sit up with his back to the opposite door and his injured leg extended on the seat. He rested his other good leg off to the side, foot on the floor. She pulled a blanket over him and buckled him in.

"How's that feel?" she asked.

"Oh, just peachy keen," he smiled at her before he turned to look back with a little wink and smile at the two nurses. "Thanks again to you both for everything," he said. "And please tell the doctor and the rest of the team how much I appreciated their care."

They nodded and waved them off, as Sam climbed into the driver's seat.

Quay settled back against the pillow. "Now, I could really use a piece of my gum, if you please."

"You are going to have to wait until we pick up Boogie and Chip. All the supplies are back at the house." Sam's answer was clipped and to the point. She still wasn't happy with Quay's demands for early release, much less his attempt at playful banter.

Quay let out a muffled groan. He was covering the pain he was feeling from all the jostling of the move. He just wasn't going to admit it.

They loaded the back of the truck with their clothing and supplies securely packed in a large Rubbermaid tub; Chip settled on the floor of rear seat next to Quay happily gnawing on a new rawhide bone; Boogie climbed into the passenger seat with his tablet already using his Wi-Fi to get online, and Sam settled into the driver's seat, put the truck in gear and pulled onto the street. She was a competent driver, well acquainted with Minnesota's winter driving. Her BCA training had included instruction in a variety of driving skills. One such training had included using a simulator for winter driving tactics. She had aced that training. She wasn't worried about the drive as long as the roads were somewhat cleared. The roads around town had been cleared to at least a single lane. Sam was hoping the freeway would be better. She knew MNDOT crews got out early.

The defrosters worked full blast when they first took off, as the outside frigid temps competed with the interior warmth of the truck. She had turned the heat up in the truck to warm not only herself and Boogie, but also to provide some comfort for Quay in the back. The eastbound lanes of Highway 14 had been cleared sometime during the night. They rode in silence for the first half hour before they bypassed Janesville, and she recalled the safe house battle north of the town. The memory was too stark and too fresh. She closed it down.

Samantha refocused on the road conditions. The right lane remained fairly clear, while blowing snow drifted into a hem of cottony patches on the edges of the left lane. Chip must have settled in back on the floor, she thought. She hadn't heard or seen him since they left Mankato. She assumed he was sleeping. What a good dog he was. He was going to be a great pet, she thought again.

Occasional bursts of wind whirled the fresh snow across the lanes causing brief white outs. She was thankful that only a few brave souls had dared to attempt traveling this morning. An occasional car or truck in her lane forced her to cautiously move over into the icy, snowy drifts of the left lane. She didn't want to use her brakes for fear of a skid. Better to slow while moving into the left lane, and then speed up a bit when carefully proceeding around the other cars. She occasionally stole a glance in her rear view mirror to check on Quay. He had dozed off shortly after they reached the I35 freeway in Owatonna. His pale face looked composed and at ease. The creased wrinkle of a frown flashed across his forehead and disappeared. The meds were working, she thought.

As she looked behind them, she noticed another vehicle, a van she thought, following them. It had followed her into the left lane as she passed the other vehicles. She decided they were using her lead to clear the lane for them. It wasn't unusual for vehicles to travel together in weather like this. Because it was a larger white van, it was difficult to even see the vehicle when the snow blew across in whorls between them. Remembering the tracking chip they were carrying to BCA headquarters, she still had to wonder if they had awakened June's group. She'd keep a close eye on the van, she decided.

Boogie had his ear bud in place and was intently listening to someone on his phone. She heard him saying something softly. She wasn't sure he was talking to himself or to someone else. He was so intense. He stared at his iPad and typed in something. Then his lanky frame seemed to straighten and tighten all at once. She looked at him.

"What? What's going on, Boogie?"

"I think I've got it. I think we have an answer. When we get to the Cities, I want you to take me to see June Hyun first, okay? She's going to answer some very specific questions!"

"Okay, I think we planned on heading there, anyway. The Double D team, Dan and Drew have been talking to her. They pulled her out of the hospital and have her in lockup at County. They've also got Swivel there under protective custody. Quay wants to talk to him. What do you have?"

"It looks like we've got a break in the code. I need to talk to her, and we can both talk to Swivel, too. We can corroborate everything with the info I have. How long before we get there, Sam?"

"I think I can have us there in a couple hours or less. We aren't going to win any races today, but the pace is a steady fifty. The plows have opened up one decent lane. I can put the bubble lights on top, too. That would help, if you need me to."

"No, that's good. We probably won't get there much faster. I think we could wrap this baby up today!"

"What's going to happen today?" Quay's voice broke in sleepily from the back.

"We're going to get you closure. Then you are going home to recuperate! That's what's going to happen today!" said Sam.

"Tell me what you've got," demanded Quay. He pulled himself up a bit, groaning with the movement.

Boogie turned to face Quay. "It looks like the coded emails June was sending went to someone in NKUNA in North Korea. According to what I can see, she told them how she had used Joo to set up Sunni for data recovery from Cameron BioTech. She assured them she would have all the information for them by the end of January at the latest. Earlier emails from December expressed her dislike of Joo Jhim's handling of Sunni. She spoke disparagingly of him, and the return email instructed her to 'handle him'. We can assume that she took that literally, and she decided to get rid of Joo. She no longer had any use for him, since she must have realized that Sunni wasn't going to be able to get any more information for them from Cameron. Sunni has been on the run since last fall."

"That sounds about right. So does June actually mention CRISPR?"

"Yeah, I think that was part of the missing code in the messages. When I get it put together, it's funny. She talks about getting lettuce from the store for use at her restaurant. It's such an inane comment in the midst of the email about family. I think lettuce is CRISPR and the store is Cameron BioTech."

"You've got to be kidding! That simple?" Sam asked.

"Well it sounds simple, but decoding this mess with all the holes in the coding wasn't so simple. It was just filling in the blanks until I could put the message together. They were really careful to cover as many tracks as possible. This is a crazy, huge operation."

"Sounds like it," said Quay. "We always thought there was something a lot bigger there. Does she mention any other names or people she's working with?"

"Not really, but we can track the emails now. I'm ready to send the decoded messages back to CIA. They can start casting the net."

"Okay, let's get it to Joe Joyner. Can you send from your iPad?" asked Quay.

"Sure. I want to do a couple other things first. I want to see if she's got something she sent to local people about the bombs as Cameron."

"Good idea. If you can get that, we can send it to Super Mike. He already has a crew at Cameron with bomb sniffing dogs," said Sam.

"How do you know that?" asked Quay.

"I talked to him this morning before I came to the hospital to get you," said Sam. She was smiling as she looked at Quay in the rear view mirror. "See. I do manage things for you while you're laid up. I've kept all the plates spinning, Mr. Thompson."

Quay laughed. Then groaned. "Don't make me laugh. It hurts when I move any part of my body. You would think it's just the leg. But the rest of me is still stiff and sore."

"Yeah. No doubt," said Boogie. "What you went through will take its toll."

"Say, how long has that white van been behind us?" asked Quay as he looked out the rear window. "I thought I saw a van like that back at the hospital when we were loading up."

"I don't know. I first saw it when we were on 14 just past Janesville. It has kept up with us since then. I just figured we were making travel easier for those behind us. Why?"

"Nothing. Maybe I'm just being suspicious for no reason. Could just be coincidence. I just can't imagine a vehicle staying with us for so long. Where are we?

"We are just coming into the south end of the Twin Cities. We're just coming up to the ski slope at Buck Hill. It'll take another half hour to forty-five minutes to get to our destination."

"Well, let's just keep an eye on that white van. If they stick with us, we may need to invite some company to pull them over."

"Okay. In the meantime, just lie back and relax. How's our pooch doing?"

"He's got his head on the edge of the seat. Happy fella, aren't you?" Quay said, talking to the dog.

Boogie's cell phone rang. He answered with an abrupt, "Yeah? Whatcha got?"

He listened intently as Sam and Quay watched and tried to glean the content of his conversation.

Boogie's voice changed becoming almost a whisper. "That's not good. Okay, I'll tell them. Thanks."

He clicked off and sat silently staring out the window.

"Well?" Sam prodded. "What was that all about?"

"It was Super Mike. It's not good news."

CHAPTER TWENTY-ONE
Loose Ends

"So let's have it," said Quay. His voice was resigned with a steely edge.

"Well, it's about the guy you know as Swivel," he paused, obviously reluctant to continue.

"Yeah, what about him? What happened to him?"

"Super Mike put Swivel in protective lock up at Hennepin County. Somehow somebody got to him. They found him bleeding on the cell floor with a shiv stuck in him. They took him to HCMC, Hennepin County Medical Center, but they don't know if he's gonna make it."

"Oh dammit! Dammit! Dammit all to Hell!" Quay yelled, pounding the back of the driver's seat, and then pulling himself up and forward a bit. Before he could get completely turned around and up, he fell back again, groaning in pain from the jolt of his sudden movement.

"Sit back, Quay," said Sam glancing back over her shoulder. "Just let it go. There's nothing we can do right now. Super Mike will handle it. We'll be there before long. You can talk to Mike."

"But I need to talk to Swivel. Awww, geez!" he rolled back onto the seat. Chip sat up panting, and let out a short whimper, and slurped Quay's hand. "I'm okay, Buddy," Quay said to the worried dog, patting it on the head. Chip reached up and continued slurping Quay again on his arm. Quay leaned forward a bit to receive another slurp on his chin. "Yeah, I know, fella. You want to make it all right, don't ya?" He continued petting the dog. "This dog is actually trying to comfort me," he said. Surprisingly it did seem to comfort him.

After several moments silence, he said, "Sam, this is no good. This is entirely my fault. Swivel would have stood a better chance if we'd just left him alone. He could have run and hidden, at least. Ah shit, Swivel! They got him! Damn!" Quay laid his head back on the seat and stared at the ceiling.

"Well, Super Mike did say he talked with Swivel for a few minutes before they took him in to lock up," explained Boogie. "Swivel had some names. He didn't remember all of them, but he told Mike quite a bit. Mike thinks Swivel heard names of some of the people in that NKUNA group. That's a big help. They must have figured out he had something incriminating that they didn't want him to share. But he's already done it. So if it's any consolation, Swivel has done a bit of good after all."

"Now all I want to do is talk to June," said Sam. "I want to lay that woman out on a table, hold her down, and pull her fingernails one by one out until we get every bit of information that she has."

"Yeah, well, something like that, I guess," agreed Quay.

The roads coming into the Twin Cities had been sanded, and the ice was melting as the temperatures rose and increasing traffic wore down the snow pack. The wind had died down a bit. The storm was moving out. Things would be back to normal by late afternoon. Just in time for rush hour, thought Sam.

Sam sped up a little and followed the split of 35W onto I94 near downtown Minneapolis. Several skyscrapers dwarfed the old Foshay Tower that used to be the tallest building in Minneapolis. The IDS tower loomed behind the imposing black structure of the new US Bank Vikings Stadium. The skyline was still one of her favorites, she thought.

A few more cars were merging from the ramps onto the freeway. She glanced in the rear view mirror and saw the white van still following behind them. She decided she wouldn't mention it just now. She didn't want Quay to be more upset than he already was.

"Boogie, is June at Hennepin County lockup, too? Did Mike tell you?"

"She was, but Mike pulled her out after Swivel got knifed. He's got her locked up in quarantine over at BCA headquarters. We can just go straight there if you want. That would be easiest, I guess."

"Okay, good. I think we should do that. I'm just going to take the exit on Highway 36 and cut over to Snelling and go up that way. There may be less traffic," she explained. She looked at Boogie, hoping he would look at her so she could signal with her eyes for him to look behind them.

Boogie picked up on the look and glanced out the side passenger mirror. The white van was still behind them. He realized that was why Sam was taking an alternate route. She wanted to see if the van would follow them, but she didn't want to upset Quay. He'd forgotten about it. Boogie looked back at Sam and nodded, silently saying, "Good idea." Then he bent to his iPhone and began a text message.

The van followed them onto Highway 36 heading east. Sam was carefully maneuvering toward the left lane so she could make a left turn going north onto Snelling when she heard the sirens behind her. The light changed, and she moved cautiously through her turn as two St. Paul squad cars pulled in front of and behind the white van following them, preventing it from making a similar left turn. She continued on Snelling watching in her mirrors as the police jumped out of their cars and approached the van, guns drawn. Boogie was busily texting again.

Sam looked at him. "Any new info?" she asked.

"Yup! Got 'em! That was a good call!" said Boogie. "Man, you are so good!"

Sam smiled. "Yes, I am!" she said. "Did you hear that, Quay?" Boogie thinks I'm pretty good."

"Oh, really? Why?"

"Well, we just got rid of our tail! I alerted Boogie, and he texted it in to dispatch. SPPD came to the rescue. They have a couple interesting perps in custody as we speak. We'll find out more when we get to Headquarters."

"That's great! Interesting. At last we've got some good news!"

"That's not all," said Boogie. "I just got another text from Super Mike. He's been working on June pretty hard. He's got some info on the bombs at Cameron BioTech. They aren't explosive bombs, he says. June admitted they are dirty tech bombs dumped into the computers in the research area. They are meant to infect the research by dropping a major virus into the whole system. She claims we are too late."

"That's not good news! Has Mike called that head research guy, Dwight Davis, at Cameron?"

"All done. Davis is working on it. I'm going to head over there while you guys go up to see Super Mike. The Cameron people want me to help dig through the files to stop the dirty bomb in the research lab. My guess is, that June Hyun had Sunni use a flash drive to not only retrieve information, but also to plant a virus in the system. It probably has a timer on it. Now that I broke the code she was using, I think I can back it out of the system. It's important that I get in there before that timer goes off, though."

"Good news, Boogie," said Sam. "I'm so glad you've been working this with us! What would we do without our number one Tech Guru Boogie? You are going to be the Vulture this time, right?"

"I guess that's true. The uninvited guest comes in to do some damage and ruin their fun. And I'll get to take all the credit! I think this is going to be a good challenge," he said, smiling.

"Do you want me to just drop you off by your car, Boogie? Is it still in the parking ramp at Headquarters?"

"Yeah, that's cool," said Boogie. "I've got everything I'm going to need." He was gathering up his laptop, iPad, cords, and tech equipment as she pulled into the BCA Headquarters ramp.

"Keep us updated, Boogie," Quay said. "We'll need the information you get to help tie things up with June and Sunni."

"Will do." Boogie was out of the truck loping toward his car as Sam drove out of the ramp toward Quay's reserved parking space near the back entrance.

"Boogie already contacted Super Mike to let him know we are close to headquarters. He's got some guys coming out to meet us, Quay. I've got to get the wheel chair out of back. You wait with Chip, until I get it set up." Samantha Adkins was taking charge, and right now, BCA detective Quay Thompson was relieved to have it that way. It was two-thirty in the afternoon, and his body felt like it was two-thirty in the morning. He was physically exhausted.

Sam saw Super Mike, Dan, and Drew coming out to meet them as she pulled into Quay's reserved parking spot next to the door. Chip had perked up as soon as the truck slowed. Quay talked softly to him, assuring him, and the dog sat patiently.

"He is the best dog," Quay said. "I hope we can find a good home for this fella."

"Don't worry, I think there are already plans for him," Sam answered cryptically. "Let's get the two of you out of here."

With the help of the three men, it only took a few minutes to transfer Quay to the wheel chair and move inside. Happily alert, Chip pranced with excitement, tail wagging high. Samantha couldn't help but think that Chip was demonstrating the emotions they all were feeling. They were closing in. Chip tugged at his leash, pulling Samantha off to the side into a snow-cleared area.

"Um guys, I think I'll meet up with you inside. Chip has some business he needs to take care of."

Mike nodded. "We'll be up on the second floor in the conference room. I picked up some lunch for us."

Sam let Chip lead her around the edges of the snowdrifts until he found a spot to relieve himself.

Super Mike had reserved a wood-paneled conference room. He was pouring coffee for the group when Sam and Chip walked into the room minutes later. "Mission accomplished," she announced. Mike's secretary Barb had set up a spread of sandwiches, chips, plates, and napkins in the center of the table. Two large pots of soup awaited their choice.

"Lunch is courtesy of the Panera down the street. The sandwiches and soup are labeled. Choose whatever you want."

"Drew and I brought some food for Chip," said Dan. "We figured he'd need something."

"Good idea," said Sam.

Sam grabbed two extra bowls from the table and opened the bag of dog food. She poured the kibble into one bowl and water into the other and called Chip to come to her. They all watched as Chip began gobbling his food. His bushy tail wagged in gratitude. The small group couldn't help but smile as they watched his happiness.

Sam pulled up a chair next to Quay, dished up a bowl of soup, and grabbed a sandwich and chips for him.

"You better take the pills they sent along, Quay," she reminded him. "It's past noon. Take them with your lunch. It'll help with the pain."

Quay looked at her, smiled, and muttered something about her being his mother.

After Chip finished eating, he settled and curled into a ball in at Quay's feet, buried his nose under one paw and promptly fell asleep.

Sam looked around the table as they ate. With the exception of Mike in his clean cut, button-down shirt and striped tie, they looked like a rag-tag crew. Quay's body language made the effects of his shooting and subsequent surgery apparent. His pallid face and tense posture couldn't hide the ever-present pain he struggled to conceal as he leaned forward placing his elbows on the table. He'd managed to comb his hair, but thick stubble covered his cheeks and dark circles had formed beneath his blue eyes. Dan had plopped down on the chair opposite Quay with a sigh. His rumpled shirt, with open collar were obviously yesterday's clothing. He ran a hand through his hair trying to smooth his unkempt mess. The older Drew settled into a chair next to Sam. He also wore yesterday's clothes, stains and wrinkles revealing the extended wear. Deep lines had set in around his weary brown eyes. Each of them exhibited a scruffy two-day growth of beard. Sam didn't even want to think what she looked like. They were all exhausted, she thought as she surveyed the group.

"Okay, let's have it!" demanded Quay in a gruff, gravely voice. "What about Swivel? How is he? And what do we know, and what do we still need to find out?"

Mike began shuffling through some papers in front of him. He looked first at Quay and then the others before beginning to speak.

"First of all, let me tell you the most recent good news. The men in the white van following behind you on the way in have been detained. They claim they were hired to follow you and report back. They say they didn't know anything else. They had a throw away cell that they picked up at a drop box. That's how they communicated with their control operative. They were from a Korean community. We believe they had connections to June's restaurant. The payoff was supposed to be left in a drop box, too. The phone line is closed. There is no way of following up or tracking with it. But we have other options, beginning with the restaurant. We'll start flashing some pics around."

He continued, "Then there's a bit more good news. The CIA guys out east are going to let us work this end. That's mostly because they think they've got bigger fish to fry with the international espionage activities from NKUNA. We were able to give them enough from the bits of information we gleaned from June and Sunni Hyun. Also, Boogie was a tremendous help. When he broke the codes used in June's emails, he shoved the door wide open for the CIA to dig deeper into NKUNA and their activities."

He took a deep breath and continued, "Our focus now will be to nail down the facts to make a case stick. We need to tie up all the loose ends into a nice, sweet package. Then we pass it all along to the Feds."

"But are we getting credit?" asked Quay.

"Yes, we are being given big creds, and we will be brought in on everything in the final run."

"Okay, I guess we can live with that," Quay said as he surveyed the rest of the group and saw the nodding heads. "So, what about Swivel? I need to know he's all right."

The superintendent took over. "You can all relax. I just learned minutes before you came in that Claude Bartholomew Ayres, aka Quay's snitch, Swivel, is out of surgery and in recovery. He explained that Swivel had been conscious when they'd brought him in to the hospital.

Quay leaned forward expectantly. "What did he say?"

"Nothing, really. He said he wouldn't talk to anyone but you, Quay. He said he doesn't trust anyone else. But he did claim he has a lot to tell you about someone called June. –His words."

"Huh! He must have been pretty sure he was going to survive," joked Drew.

"He's a weird duck," agreed Quay. "It took a while to earn his trust. He's a mess, and a meth head, but he's also extremely intelligent. When can I see him? What's the word?"

Mike was nodding. "I think we can arrange to get you over to HCMC to see him. That will kill two birds with one stone, so to speak. Might be a good place for you, too. The doctors there can check you out while you're there!"

Quay groaned.

"It's a good thing, Quay," Sam assured him. "If Swivel sees that you've taken a hit from these guys, too, it will let him know that you two are on common ground and all that. He might be even more willing to talk."

"I suppose that's could work," agreed Quay. "But I want to see him first thing when I get to the hospital. Then after we talk, maybe they can find me a room down the hall from him to rest while I'm waiting to be checked out. I want constant access to him."

"We can work on that," Mike assured him. Mike turned to Sam next.

"Sam, bring us up to speed on what else you've got."

Sam shared Boogie's plan to work with Dwight Davis, the head researcher at Cameron BioTech, and the rest of their tech people. She told them about Boogie's excitement as he had broken the codes found on the computers they'd gotten from June and Sunni. She explained that Boogie was sure there was a timer on the virus release. Boogie had told her that the knowledge of the code system used by June would allow him to go into the virus lodged in the system at Cameron BioTech. He was confident he could stop the release of the virus before the timer went off and dropped into the research system at Cameron.

"You know he's a gamer, too," explained Sam. "He looks at this as one big competition. And knowing that Boogie doesn't like Vultures who try to steal his thunder, I can safely say, he will meet and surpass the expectations of the group at Cameron. He said he will be in touch with me as he continues to work with the crew at Cameron, if that's okay with you, Super Mike," she asked, turning to look at the Superintendent, and then realized what she'd called him. The detectives didn't use his nickname to his face. She gulped and attempted to cover it by quickly continuing, "I meant Superintendent Mike. If we get it soon enough, we can use that information when we meet with June."

Mike smiled at her slip. "It's okay. I kind of like the moniker of Super Mike. Yes, have Boogie keep in touch with you. You can coordinate and share the important stuff with the rest of us."

Sam looked over at Quay. She realized he was really hurting.

"How are we going to coordinate all of this?" asked Quay. "It's going to be a tight time table."

"We'll work that out," said Mike. "While you are visiting with Swivel, I'd like to have Sam sit downstairs here with Sunni Hyun, first, and then visit with her mother June. Let's try to get a good handle on exactly what Sunni knows about her mother before we go to June. We need to determine if she's told us all she knows, and of course, try to decide if she's telling the truth. Then we can use that when we work with June. Dan and Drew have pretty much exhausted their chances with June. She's shut them out. But she may respond to you, Samantha, especially if she knows you have talked with Sunni. The woman factor will help, I think."

"I'd be happy to visit with 'the Ladies,'" Sam said with a note of sarcasm.

Mike turned to Dan and Drew next. "Let's have you two firm up our leads with Joe Joyner at CIA. Tell them what we've gotten out of June about NKUNA so far and see if they have anything more. What gaps can we fill? Sam, you'll need to keep a fluid line of communication open with Dan and Drew, too."

The atmosphere in the room changed from one of chaotic, confusing leads, to a cohesive, charged force. The group began to feel they were closing in. They had their assignments. There were clear directions to the final goal: the arrest of June Hyun and her group of infiltrators. The espionage at Cameron BioTech would be thwarted. The CRISPR-Cas9 research would move forward with the patent secured by Cameron. The multiple murders connected to the case could be closed. They needed to move together now and act to make it happen.

"Who's going to take care of Chip?" asked Drew, as they stood to leave. The group turned to look at Mike expectantly.

"I think my secretary Barb would love to keep him here for a bit," he said. "Don't worry about Chip. He'll be fine. Since Dan, Drew, and Sam are going to be in the building, they can come back and get him when they're done."

Chip heard his name and ran to Quay, laying his head in Quay's lap while giving him multiple quick slurps on the hand.

"You're gonna be fine, fella. You're going to stay here," said Quay as he looked into Chip's eyes and gave the dog an affectionate pat on the head. He leaned down to Chip and said softly, "I'll be back to see you later, okay?"

The dog seemed to understand and turned back to Dan and Drew. Dan patted his thigh motioning for the dog to come to him. Chip did a happy high-stepping prance across the room and promptly sat next to Dan.

"I think he's adopted all of us," laughed Drew.

Sam said goodbye to Quay, giving him a hug and ruffling his hair as she handed him three packs of bubble gum. "You're probably going to want these. I think this should be enough to last you until I see you later," she grinned.

Quay looked up with a tired smile, palming the gum, "Always planning ahead aren't you, Sam?"

"Trying to!" She laughed. "You go talk to Swivel. He's got some good stuff. Then see if you can grab a bed and get some rest, okay? I'll check in later after I talk to the women."

"I'm on it," he said.

Sam turned, hurrying out the door before he could see her face. It was difficult watching the normally strong, take-charge man she'd come to admire, take this job sitting down, she thought. She couldn't help it. She was worried about him. It was just too damned hard to see him like this.

CHAPTER TWENTY-TWO
Spinning Plates

Samantha Atwood felt like the center point of a juggling plates act. The plates had been set spinning on poles, but if one should stop it would fall, and the rest would surely follow. As she'd told Quay, she was trying to keep them moving.

She took a deep breath as she entered the elevator to the basement. The elevator felt close and stale. Just her nerves, she thought, as she took another deep breath and shook out her arms. Sunni and June were being detained in two separate rooms, under guard, in the basement of the BCA building. The door opened to reveal beige walls lit by florescent light strips in four-foot intervals above the limestone-tiled hallway floor. Her booted footsteps reverberated down the hall as she approached the door numbered twelve. A solitary man reading a magazine sat on a cushioned chair between rooms twelve and sixteen. Sam flashed her badge, and simply said, "Mike sent me." He nodded and rose to unlock the door.

Sunni Hyun was lying on a cot pushed against the back wall of the room. A small table and two chairs sat near the bed. Sunni looked at Sam as she entered, but didn't rise.

Sam pulled up a chair next to the cot. She said nothing, but stared intently at Sunni for moments before saying, "Hello, Sunni. How are you doing? Are you comfortable?" It was evident by her tone that she really didn't care. Sam was angry, fed up. "Let's talk a bit, shall we?"

"Where's my mother?" Sunni demanded in a sullen tone as she glared at Sam. Sunni hadn't had a change of clothes since Samantha had last seen her at the

Maple Grove safe house. One side of her fine, black hair was pulled behind her ear and held in place with a large flat barrette. The other side fell across her face in long, wayward strings.

"You know where she is," Sam answered in clipped speech.

"I know you have her. I know you shot her, but I don't know much more than that."

"Well, let's see. Your dear mother is recovering from the gunshot wound. My shot hit her in the shoulder. It was a minor injury. She's lucky I didn't kill her. I could have, you know. Like I said, she's lucky."

Sam paused, stood and looked around the room. "We've got your mother just a few doors away. We thought you'd like to be close to her." Sam paused to let that sink in.

Sunni stared at her with a mixture of contempt and fear.

Sam stood over Sunni and continued in almost a whisper, "It appears that mommy dearest isn't the sweet, innocent woman you presented her to be. She is actually a very dangerous woman. What I don't understand is, how do you fit into this family picture? Are you like her?"

"I don't know what you're talking about. Everything I did was only to protect my mother, my family." Sunni looked directly into her eyes.

"And tell me again exactly what you did," demanded Sam as she sat down again across from Sunni.

"I told you already. I stole the research for the CRISPR program from Cameron BioTech when I was working there. I was forced to get it for Joo Jhim. But I didn't give him all of it. He couldn't use it without the parts that I withheld. I needed to hold some back to protect my mother and myself. It was my failsafe. He threatened me. He threatened my mother. We would have been killed, if I hadn't done what I did!"

"Okay, that's the story all right. I heard all that the first time. But now tell me about the work you really did for your mother, because your mother obviously has a different story to tell."

"I don't know what she was talking about back at the safe house. I've never seen her like that. My mother was never like that. And she never spoke much English. I don't know what's going on with her. And now," she paused as her eyes began to fill with tears, "and now, I haven't been able to talk to her since she ran, and you shot her. I just don't understand. She's not the same. Something is wrong. She must be scared of something. Please believe me. Let me see her." Sunni's voice had risen into a pitchy plea.

"We'll see. Let's go back over what your mother told you about Joo Jhim. How did she introduce you to him?"

"I was young," Sunni's voice had become a dead monotone. "I had just lost my father. Suddenly this man Joo Jhim was always hanging around."

"Back up. How did your father die?"

Sunni looked surprised. "How did he die? Why? You don't think Joo had anything to do with that?"

"No, probably not, but maybe your mother may have!"

Sunni let out a defiant shriek. "No! No! No! That's not possible! My father had a heart attack. That's what happened. Umma was there. She called me and told me about it."

Sunni began to sob.

Sam looked at the crumpled girl sobbing for her lost parents, stood, and walked away. When Sunni's sobbing began to subside, Sam decided she had to push a bit harder. As hard as it was, she needed to see if she could generate more doubt about June.

"Not long ago that woman held you hostage and threatened to cut your throat, Sunni," Sam began. She spoke softly at first, and then became more forceful. Sam's training had helped her develop some good questioning techniques. Now was not a time for weakness.

"What makes you think she wouldn't have been responsible for your father's death, Sunni? It would have been very convenient for her. Think about it. Your father's death cleared the way for Joo Jhim to enter your lives, didn't it?"

Sunni sat back on the cot. She brought her hands up to her cheeks. Tears continued to stream down her cheeks. She angrily swiped them away. Sam waited.

It took ten minutes of tears and silence. Sunni finally pulled herself together and looked at Sam.

"Why are you doing this? Why are you destroying my life?"

"I'm not the one destroying your life, Sunni. It seems to me that between you and your parents June and Joo Jhim, you guys have done a pretty good job of that before we ever got involved."

"But I didn't want to be a part of any of it. Joo was the one. And, Joo was not my parent. Joo forced me, threatened me!"

"Yes, that's what you've said. But why should I believe you? You've been in all the right places at the wrong times during every aspect of this case. We know you were actively employed at Cameron. You played a major role in the CRISPR research there. You also have had North Korean connections through Joo Jhim and June Hyun. There's more.

"Our contacts suggest June received communications from a contact in North Korea on a regular basis. We have the texts. We were able to track all of them.

"It's time you take a long, hard look at June, Sunni. Think about this. If, as you say, you were used, you need to think back to remember each of the times you were given orders. Think about the times June may have actually been the one who gave Joo orders or even placed demands on you without you realizing she was doing it. What proof can you give us that you were an innocent pawn in all of this?"

Sam watched Sunni closely. Her expression was guarded now. Sunni was thinking. She seemed to be processing what Sam had said, but Sam couldn't tell if she had made an impression on the woman.

"You've got to come up with something fast, because as we speak, Quay is talking with a source who says he has information about June and her friend Joo. And our buddy Boogie, you remember him? He is working another angle with the lead researcher over at Cameron. They are working as we speak to clean up any viruses that you may have dumped in the system there."

Sunni's head jerked up at this. Sam realized Sunni probably hadn't known about the addition of the viruses into the Cameron system.

She continued, "Yes, viruses! You dumped viruses into the system. Using a flash drive provided by Joo Jhim, I suppose. Didn't you know that? And then there are the patents that North Korea wants so badly. They aren't going to get any patents on anything. North Korea is not going to win this round. And neither are you. We are! Cameron BioTech is also going to prepare those research patents for CRISPR-Cas9 and expedite the processing, so that the research is safe here at Cameron and out of the hands of North Korea. NKUNA isn't going to get anything. On top of that, Dan and Drew are working with the CIA to track down the North Korean United National Army operatives in North Korea. They will be blocked, tracked down, and arrested for international corporate espionage and probably murder.

"It's all finished, Sunni," Sam said, raising her voice. "This was all part of a plan June put into motion years ago. If you were a part of this, you know it's over. If you weren't a part of it, and you were just a pawn in their game, you need to think about that. You may have a few pluses going for you. You said you didn't give Joo all the data, because you didn't want it to fall into the wrong hands. That tells us that you may have had a tiny bit of conscience. Then you called Quay for protection. That's another plus on your behalf. But you need to add more to it before we are going to be willing to trust you and give you any leeway."

Sam paused, watching Sunni closely. She examined Sunni's face and body language, watching for any miniscule changes in her facial expression or her eyes that might indicate a defection.

It was a waiting game, now, and Sam decided she had time to wait. She sat back in her chair, crossed her arms and stared intently at Sunni. Sam could easily read the combination of fear and indecision in the emotions flashing across Sunni's face. Sunni had had to assimilate a lot of information in a short amount of time. But Sunni was a smart woman, and Sam figured she'd come around, if she were a smart as she thought she was. Sam just wanted to give her time to put it all together. She was feeling pretty positive Sunni would see there was no other way out.

"What do you want me to do?" Sunni finally asked. "Do I have to meet and talk with her in order prove it to you?"

"That's actually a very good idea. You could meet with her. Have a conversation with her about how this has made you feel. Get her to talk to you, and we'll see if she trips up. What do you think? Can you do that?"

There was a long pause before Sunni said, "I think I have to do that. I can't continue to live like this. I can't live with these lies. I want my life, my real life." Her demeanor had changed. Sam sighed with relief as she realized Sunni had made up her mind. Sunni was going to help them end this.

"Let me see my moth...June." She stopped midsentence, shifting from saying mother to using the woman's name.

Sam smiled at the change in Sunni's wording. Sunni was so hurt she couldn't any longer refer to June as her mother. "June is three doors down the hall on the left, she said.

Three Doors Down, Sam thought. How ironic. That was the name of the group that Quay used to listen to. The group's song "Here Without You" had been especially meaningful to Quay after his wife Karen's death. The lyrics started with, "A hundred days have made me older/Since the last time that I saw your pretty face." She'd heard Quay sing along with the song so many times as they rode to a job together. Three doors down. She hoped the meeting of June and Sunni Hyun would tie it all together for Quay. Three doors down and a couple hours more. Then it could come to an end.

Sam stood and waited for Sunni to collect herself. She understood this must be a very difficult thing for Sunni. All these years, Sunni had believed that June was her mother. In addition, June had let Sunni believe her mother was a weak woman who had actually been abused at the hands of Joo Jhim. Sunni had only seen June as a withdrawn and quiet woman. It must be clear to Sunni now that it had all been an act. With the evidence Sam presented to Sunni, and June's attack using Sunni as protection at the safe house, Sunni must finally realize that June's personae was all just a facade. She had been playing the abused woman very effectively, while instead, she had been the woman in power. She had run the operation and was the control operator for Joo Jhim, not the other way around. June had quite probably ordered the murder of Sunni's father, and had seen to it that it looked like a heart attack. June had probably also been behind the order for the murder of Joo Jhim, after it appeared he was bungling the operation. Sam decided to hold that last bit of information back, for now.

"Sunni, I will let you go into June's room alone. But I will be observing from the next room via a camera and a microphone from June's room. Before you go, you need to decide on how you want to handle her. She may want to attack you again. Are you ready for that? We will make sure you are safe. But there is that possibility."

"Yes, I am ready. I won't be her fool any longer! I will fight back!"

"You also need to decide what approach you will use to get her to talk," Sam coached her. She needed guidance to make this work. "We need her to talk, Sunni. We need to have her open up and give you names and dates. It doesn't matter how you get her to do that. If she's angry and blurts it out, that's great! That will probably be the best approach. Get her so mad that she won't think about what she's saying. She's smart. It will take persistence. That means you will have to bring up specific events and demand that she tell you what happened. I suggest you start with the first murder last fall at Cameron BioTech. That was the time when Karen Thompson was shot by the sniper in front of Cameron. Push her on that. Hard! We assume it was an attempt to scare off possible investors and put blame on Cameron for their research endeavors. But we need confirmation."

"I understand."

"Then you need to follow up on June's plan for the CRISPR research. Who was going to get the data from your flash drive? What were they going to do with it? Egg her on. Make her feel stupid. She's been trying to do that with you for years. Turn the tables. Drop it on her that you used her by withholding information. Tell her she didn't get all the research. Tell her she's a failure. That will probably do it."

"All right. All right. I can do it. I'm so angry. So sad. I'm so hurt. Just let me go." Sunni shook her head, straightened, and smoothed her hair.

Sam's cell phone buzzed. The caller ID said it was Quay.

She looked at Sunni. "Can you wait just a moment? This is Quay. He may have more information that will help you." Sam motioned for Sunni to sit back down on the bed. Sunni collapsed onto the bed with a sigh as Sam stepped out to answer the call. She hoped Quay had some important news for her.

Superintendent Mike himself had dropped Quay off at the county hospital. He assisted Quay as he moved into the wheel chair, and then pushed him into the hospital. One of the BCA security officers met them in the entry.

The superintendent had quickly introduced Quay to the BCA officers and explained the proposed meeting with Swivel.

"Good," the security officer said. "You can come with me. He's been asking for you. I told him you were on your way. That seemed to calm him down a bit."

Mike nodded before saying, "Quay, I'm going to stop at the desk and let them know you are here. They are expecting you and have a room ready. You are to see Dr. Hanson at 3:30. That gives you about an hour with Swivel. Will that be enough?"

"I think so. I'm not sure I can stay up any longer that that," admitted Quay. "Let's go see him," he said to the officer.

When Quay entered the darkened room, he saw a shrunken form covered by a light sheet, curled into an 'S' on the bed. A rolling hospital tray perched on the opposite side of the bed. The hospital smells of cleaning disinfectants and a variety of body fluids surrounded him. At least here in the hospital, Quay wasn't met with Swivel's usual overpowering stench of drug-soaked, sweat-filled clothes that seemed to follow him like Peanuts' Pig-Pen.

"Hello, Swivel. I'm here to listen to your story," said Quay as he entered the hospital room. He wheeled his chair close to the bed and nudged the thin body.

A shaking, bony hand reached out placing itself flat on the bed to work as a fulcrum to support, lift, and turn his body. Dark brown hair pressed in straight strands against the sides of a colorless, sunken face. Swivel's eyes were rimmed with half-moon purple circles.

"Hey, Thompson. You came!" Swivel almost shouted in a surprised, raspy voice. "Oh, God, man! You came! I can't believe it!"

"Yeah. I heard you wanted to see me. Sounds like some of the bad guys got to you in lock up, huh?"

"You could say that," he rasped. "I don't think they wanted me around. I guess I saw and heard things at that restaurant I worked at, that I wasn't supposed to see. It wasn't my fault. I just worked there, ya know? How was I to know?"

"I understand. Let's talk about what you saw."

"Wait a minute! What happened to you man?" Swivel stretched his neck up like a periscope and looked left and right and back to the left again. His Swivel nickname was truly an accurate moniker, thought Quay. Swivel's paranoia controlled every movement of his head as he snapped it left to right.

"Are we alone?" Swivel's eyes pierced Quay with an accusing look. Then his eyes scrolled down to Quay's leg. "Hey, why is your leg all wrapped up like that? Why are you in a wheel chair? Did they get to you, too, man?"

"Yeah, I got in a bit of a gun fight. It's okay, they can't get us now, Swivel. We're alone. We're safe, now. I came out of the fight with a little nick. Nothing too bad. Sort of like you, Swivel. They can't really take us down. Right? We're the tough guys, right?" said Quay redirecting Swivel back to the two of them and their conversation.

"Right! We can do this. I'm gonna help you, you know, man? I gotta tell you a few things," Swivel lowered his voice to almost a whisper, "but I've gotta have some protection here, man," he said glancing again at the door. "What are you gonna do for me, huh? Are you gonna take care of me? Do I get paid? Can you help me, man?"

"We'll work something out," Quay assured him. "Maybe after you get cleaned up, we can set you up with a real job. Maybe we can work out something for you with us, since..," Quay paused for a moment before continuing, "since you know so many people."

Quay intentionally left the possibilities open, hoping that Swivel would be enticed enough to bite. Swivel had almost been killed. Swivel knew now that Quay had been shot. He knew how dangerous this group was. He was sure there were others out to get him, too. But Swivel had some skills. The BCA might be able to use him, if they could get him off the meth and cleaned up. But right now, Quay could see that Swivel was a mess.

Even though the room was cool, Swivel was sweating profusely. His blankets revealed the sharp edges of a very bony body. Swivel flopped back on his pillow and closed his eyes, claw-like hands pulling the sheet up to his chin.

"Swivel, I need to know everything you know about June Hyun and Joo Jhim. I understand you knew them. And I need it all in the next half hour. We don't have time to waste. Like I said, you will be protected. You trust me, don't you?"

"I guess so," sighed Swivel. "But I'm so tired. All I want to do is sleep right now. You're the only one who has ever listened to me or even cared what I thought, though."

"You're right. I remember when you were just fifteen living on the streets. I remember when your mother died a couple years ago and left you all alone. I was the one who picked you up on cold winter nights and took you to shelters for food and a warm bed. I tried to help you Swivel. Remember that?"

"I know. You did help. I just couldn't get away from the stuff, Quay. I don't know if I can now. It's been too long. I think I'm sick." He closed his eyes and sighed deeply.

"You are sick, but you aren't going to die. You will get well, and you will get stronger. You're in the best place. The doctors will help you. We will help you. But right now I need your help, Swivel. "

"Hmmm. Right." Swivel closed his eyes, yawned, then opened them again and stared intently at Quay. "You sure as hell have a lot of confidence in me."

"I do. I know you're smart Swivel. In fact, I know you are almost a genius. You didn't think I knew that did you? But I do. I just hope you haven't fried too many of those brain cells already. We can use you, Swivel. You can count on it."

"Okay," Swivel let out a deep breath. It seemed as if he had been holding his breath for a long time. "Let me tell you what I know. I'm very tired. I've got to get it out, before I fall asleep."

"I'm listening."

Between intermittent bouts of shivering, coughing, and yawning, Swivel began to spill out his story.

He had begun work at June Hyun's Chinese restaurant as a dishwasher in October. It had been steady work and gave him the money he needed to continue his 'lifestyle'. He thought June Hyun was very stern boss, and she was also very removed from the work at the restaurant. She didn't seem to really care about the restaurant operations at all. She left everything to several other designated workers. She spent a lot of her time on her phone at her desk in a small office at the back of the storage area. She disappeared for two hours every

Monday and Wednesday afternoon always after receiving a phone call. When the call came, she didn't talk, just listened, and then left. Joo Jhim came in and picked her up for each of these 'trips'. She would first take him off to the back appearing to explain something to him, before loading up her laptop and disappearing out the back door with Joo in tow. They usually came back after a couple hours with Joo following June back into her office. Then they would sit with heads bent together in deep conversation. Swivel thought they spoke in Korean, because he couldn't understand anything he heard. June would have her laptop open, and many times Swivel saw that she had a flash drive inserted in the laptop.

One day, they had left the door ajar when Swivel heard June yelling at Joo. From what he could hear, June had demanded that Joo push Sunni into getting some kind of information by the following Saturday. Joo countered that he couldn't do it. Joo had balked saying something like he thought Sunni would be too suspicious. June began yelling at Joo in Korean, picked up a book from her desk, and threw it at him. He ducked, and the book hit the door slamming it shut. Swivel ducked away and had pretended he hadn't seen or heard anything.

Another time, he said he had heard June's phone ping with a text message while he was working in back. She'd left her phone on the counter where they loaded the dishes for the customers' meals. Swivel had been standing nearby and saw the screen. A partial message showed on the screen. He remembered that the message said, "NKUNA chief expects delivery by January 15th."

He had stepped away as June came back for her phone. He saw her read it, shake her head, and erase the message.

He had seen one other message. It was the last one and the most recent. June had once again left her phone unattended. It pinged, and Swivel read a message that said, "Remove J today. Weakness perceived." It also said something about a crisper being incomplete. Swivel didn't know what that meant. He didn't think it was referring to a lettuce crisper, but he thought it was important. That word was all in capital letters. When June read it, she erased it, seemed to swear in Korean, and then made a call. She was angry that time. There was no doubt considering her tone. She spoke in Korean, but Swivel had heard Joo's name mentioned and something about the car that he knew Joo drove. She also said something about Maple Grove. That was last week.

Then he had heard Joo was dead. Swivel put it all together and figured that June was responsible. He was pretty sure June had ordered a hit.

"That's when I decided to quit. I wasn't going to work for any hit woman! That woman is crazy! But she must have figured out I knew something. Because those guys came after me in the jail. They scared the hell out of me, man! They said something about it being from June, when they shoved the blade in me. I thought I was dead, man! I don't want anything to do with them!"

Quay had listened in silence as Swivel worked his way though his story. Swivel paused occasionally to sip from the water bottle next to his bed. Each time he'd stretch his neck up and glance about the room and at the door.

When Swivel finally finished, he looked at Quay and asked, "Will that help? Did I help you, Quay? Will that help me?" His tone was almost pleading and at the same time frightened.

"Yeah, I think it will help both of us, Swivel. The information that you heard and what you saw may be circumstantial in some respects, but there is enough meat there with the names mentioned, that I think we can build a case. Our top tech, a guy by the name of Steve Schroeder, we call him Boogie, is working on the laptop owned by June. We are following up on her phone calls and emails. I think with the combination of your information and Boogie's work, we've got enough to put June Hyun away. Because you remembered the date, we will be able to track June's phone call to the people she hired to do the hit on Joo Jhim. We will also use the information from you to back track the call she got ordering her to get rid of Joo. If NKUNA was mentioned anywhere, the CIA will move in and settle that detail."

Swivel rested his head back on the pillow and let out a long, relieved sigh.

"One more question for you, Swivel."

"Yeah?"

"Did you ever get the sense that June's daughter Sunni Hyun was a part of this?"

"No. No. She acted like she was afraid of Joo. And she was always taking care of her mother. Seemed worried about her.

"June changed when Sunni came in. She would begin acting like she was afraid of Joo, too. And then she'd moan and hold a part of her body, like her arm or stomach. I knew it was all a show, but I don't think Sunni ever caught on. She loved that woman!"

They both settled back, Quay in his chair, and Swivel against his pillow. Quay's eyes crinkled at the corners, a smile growing. "Thank you, Claude Bartholomew Ayers!" he said. "You done good!" It was his usual way of confirming with Swivel that he appreciated his help.

Swivel nodded and smiled weakly as another involuntary shiver traveled over his body.

"I'm going to be down the hall if you need anything, Swivel. I'm going to be doing a little convalescing myself. We'll both have security outside our rooms here. Get some rest," he said, and then added in afterthought, "and for God's sake eat! You need to get some meat on those bones if you're ever going to recover and work for me!"

"Thanks, Quay." Swivel smiled and gave a small wave to Quay as he turned away.

Quay rolled out the door, pulled his phone out of his pocket and called Sam. He was telling her the story as he reached his new hospital room. That hospital bed looked incredibly inviting.

When Sam had answered her phone, she could hear the exhaustion in Quay's voice. She had listened quietly as he shared the full scope of his conversation with Swivel. It took several minutes for him to lay it all out.

"He's credible, Sam. I think we can count on him. He's smart, and he's got a memory like an elephant. Now, if Boogie comes through with the facts to verify what Swivel says, I think it will tie up a lot of loose ends. We just need Sunni to break her mother. Do you think you've got her ready?"

"She's waiting for me right now. We're going to talk to June. She's going in alone. I'll observe from next door. We've got cameras and mikes in June's room. It'll be good, I think!"

"Great! Let me know what happens, okay?" Right now I'm headed to bed. The doc is supposed to be stopping by in a few minutes. He'll check on my meds and then I'm going to catch a few winks. But don't be afraid to call me about any of your stuff there."

"You've got it. By the way, how's your gum supply?" she asked with a short chuckle. He knew she was asking about how he was feeling.

"You know, I'm so tired, and so relieved at what Swivel told me, I haven't even thought about it until you mentioned it right now."

"Oh great! Now I suppose your gum addiction is going to be my fault!"

"Nope. I think I'm good. We'll see how I feel when I wake up." Quay gave an audible yawn. "You gotta stop worrying about me, Sam. I'm good. I just need a little rest."

"Okay, I hear ya. Take care, Quay, and get your rest. I'll talk to you later when we know more."

Sam clicked off, and turned back toward the door to Sunni's room. The door stood open. Sunni had obviously heard the conversation with Quay.

"So you really are going to be watching and listening when I go in to see her?" asked Sunni.

"How else can we protect you? My God, Sunni, she is dangerous. Don't you see that?"

"I don't know. I just don't know." Sunni shook her head and turned away from Sam. "I thought I knew her. I thought she loved me. I loved her. I thought she needed my help. I felt guilty that I wasn't there for her. I thought Joo was hurting her." She stopped suddenly and twirled around, stomping her foot. "My entire life has been a lie. I had a great job, I thought I had a good family, and now I find out none of it was real!"

"Your job was real. You got that on your own, Sunni. You are smart. Some experts fooled you. They knew what they were doing. They used you. Now you have a chance to turn the tables. Go in there and talk to June. Threaten her. Make her believe that you haven't told us anything. Maybe you should tell her that you are going to expose her if she doesn't cut you in on the deal. Tell her you've worked for her long enough. Tell her she has screwed up. Now she has to work for you. Get her to give you names, phone numbers, contacts, everything. If you do that, Sunni, you are buying your freedom. Can you do that? Can you turn the tables on this woman who has used you all your life? You should be furious, Sunni! You have a right to be angry. Show it! Use it! Use her!"

Sunni stood with her fists clenched at her sides. Her dark eyes had a murderous look. There was no doubt that she was angry. Just how angry was the question. Sam needed Sunni to be so angry she couldn't think of anything else. She wanted her to forget about mother/daughter love. She wanted Sunni to forget about protecting a mother. She wanted her to feel that curtain of red rage flow down over her eyes. But she didn't want to tell Sunni that June wasn't her biological mother, yet. If this worked right, June would tell Sunni herself. She opened the door and stood to the side directing Sunni to leave.

Just then Sam's phone beeped. A text had come in. Sam glanced at the message. It was from Boogie.

-*Stopped timer. Retrieved virus. All good at Cameron. Call when you can.*

Sam looked up at Sunni who had waited with her eyes on fixed on Sam.

"Sunni, there's one more thing you can use against June. Tell her the virus at Cameron has been stopped. It didn't work.

Sam smiled as she escorted Sunni into the hall.

CHAPTER TWENTY-THREE
Full Disclosure

Sunni walked into the hall, looked right and then left. Sam pointed to June's door. "Three doors down on the left," she said again. Sunni turned and marched down the hall, angry footsteps reverberating off the walls. A portent of the storm to come, thought Sam as she watched Sunni's determined march.

Sunni came to an abrupt stop in front of the third door and waited as the security guard reached for the keys on his belt chain, selected the right one and turned his key in the lock. He had barely finished rotating the key before Sunni pushed in front of him and shoved the door open so hard it slammed with a thwack reverberating against the interior wall.

"June! You and I need to talk! Now!" Sunni enunciated each word in a commanding voice that clearly revealed the depth of her anger.

June's head jerked up, and she jumped up from the edge of her cot, quickly backing away from the furious Sunni.

June recognized the intense red rage in Sunni's eyes. She realized Sunni knew. Composing herself and staring defiantly at Sunni, she paused before she answered.

"I wondered how long it would be before they sent you in here to talk to me," she sneered in clear, inflectionless English. "You certainly don't believe you can get me to tell you anything. I can see you are now just a sniveling dupe of the BCA. A worthless, disrespectful..."

Sunni interrupted June's diatribe, her voice rising in an accusatory arc, "You! You have the nerve to speak to me like that? You used me! Your daughter. At least you had me believe I was your daughter." Sunni paused and took a deep breath. "But your little act back at the safe house turned everything around, didn't it? I'm thinking you aren't even close to who you said you were. You aren't even really my mother, are you?" Sunni paused, and then began again in a quieter, menacing voice. "You lied. How could you do that, June? What kind of a woman does what you have done?" Sunni stopped and then spewed a string of invective in Korean. Switching back to English, she asked, "Did Dad know? Was he part of this, too? Did he want me to be your spy, too?"

"Your father knew nothing." June sneered. "He never did anything but dote on you." June spoke with sarcasm.

"So you admit that it was all you?" asked Sunni.

"He was a waste of my time. He was supposed to have been my conduit to you after your mother died. That was all. I waited years for you to become useful. I groomed you. I taught you. I directed you. And you followed. All your life, you followed! You were a good daughter." June chuckled as she spit out the word 'daughter', shaking her head as she turned away from Sunni. Her small frame slumped as she braced her hands on the back of a chair.

"I did nothing for you. Not for you! Not because of you! I wanted to make my father proud." Sunni paused and let the silence sit between them. Then as she began processing the events in her mind, she suddenly changed her tone from accusation into one of thoughtful observation.

"So you used me. Now I'm going to use you. I'm sure this plan you initiated is worth a lot of money. I've given my life to you. So, you owe me, June. You owe me a lot. Now I want my due. You are going to share with me. I have a way to get us both out of this. You used me, and I want a part of this now."

June was surprised. Her face registered incredulous astonishment before dropping the mask down to cover her surprise.

"Do you understand what I'm offering you? Do you understand what kind of trouble you are in?" demanded Sunni.

"Yes! I understand fully. But you must listen to me," June answered. She was pleading now. "You are making a huge mistake if you join forces with Quay Thompson and his group. It will mean your death. And mine. You need to follow me, Sunni! You need to listen!"

June's face had turned to expressionless granite. She stared at Sunni judging the success of her words. She waited.

After a long pause, Sunni answered. "And why should I do anything you wish? I have my own plan. I know so much more than you think I do, June."

June's eyebrows shot up as her narrow, dark eyes searched Sunni's face to see if she was being truthful.

"Oh, yes! You thought I was smart. Smart enough to steal the research and to cover your tracks for you," Sunni continued. "But you didn't think I was smart enough to know what was happening, did you?" chided Sunni.

As June continued staring at Sunni, a flicker of uncertainty passed over her face, and then quickly washed away.

"You see, about the time you steered me toward the research facility at Cameron BioTech, I began to realize how focused and overly determined you were on making sure I got that job. When you brought Joo in," she paused, and then asked, "You did bring Joo in, didn't you? It wasn't the other way around as you wanted me to believe, was it? You brought Joo in to take the place of the father I'd lost."

June gave an almost imperceptible nod. She waited for Sunni to continue, staring at her with piercing eyes.

"But, you see, I was also smart enough to read the signs. I began to suspect that Joo was doing your bidding. He was so demanding, so pushy, that he almost seemed afraid that I wouldn't follow his orders. That's how he gave himself away. That's when I decided I couldn't give him all the research from Cameron BioTech. So," Sunni paused a moment for effect and then continued, "I withheld some of it. The data that I gave you isn't complete, June. It won't be complete unless you work with me. I've got all the data. I've got the chip with all the information you need. You can't do anything without my help. You see? I'm much smarter than you thought."

Sunni stood proudly at the foot of the bed, with a satisfied smile on her face. Sam watched through the two-way mirror in the adjoining room listening to the conversation. She was amazed at how well Sunni had pulled herself together. Sunni had deftly turned June's threats around to be in her favor without giving everything away at once. She had set the trap up so very cleverly. She was right. She was one smart woman. Now all she had to do was snap the trap.

There was slight tap at the door of the adjoining room, and Sam turned as Super Mike walked in with Chip prancing beside him.

"How's it going?" whispered Mike.

"Great, right now. She has set June up. We'll see how this plays out!" Sam said as she reached down to pat Chip who was nuzzling her hand.

They turned to watch and listen together.

June leaned back against the headboard of her bed. "You are very smart, Sunni. But I'm not sure you are smart enough. You may have all the information, but do you realize that we are both dead if you don't deliver it. It's not just me, Sunni. I have dealt with this organization for many years."

"Who are they?" Sunni interrupted.

June paused before answering. She looked at the door and then toward the window.

"We are alone. No one's listening," Sunni assured her seeing June's hesitation. "You can talk. So, who are you indebted to?"

June stood, and paced to the door and turned to face Sunni. "NKUNA." June said and then read the question on Sunni's face. She continued. "You don't know about them, I see. It's a patriot group in North Korea. The North Korean United National Army. They call themselves NKUNA. They intend to use the patent for CRISPRCas9 to provide legitimacy to our country. Using the CRISPR data, they will develop a super blood cell that will reject all disease. Then we can inject it into our people and ourselves. Next we spread a new disease into select populations and hold the CRISPRCas9 as a cure. Just like that, we can change power in world order. Don't you see? It's so simple.

"North Korea wants to become, and will become, a recognized world power. Therefore, you see, NKUNA operatives will kill to get their hands on this research, Sunni. They will kill us if we don't get it to them."

"But if they kill us, they won't have it, will they? At least, that is, if they kill me. You won't matter, because you don't have the complete research data." Sunni added matter-of-factly. "I do."

June sucked in a breath. "You wouldn't do that to me." She had moved closer to Sunni, a shadow of fierceness crossing her face.

"Why wouldn't I?" Sunni lifted her chin and stared directly into June's dark eyes. Her voice was steady and determined as she continued. "I have nothing to lose. You were not a mother to me. Were you ever my mother, June? I was a baby. Were you my real mother? I want to hear it. I want you to tell the truth for once."

"I was the woman who raised you, Sunni. That's what is important."

"That's not what I want to know. I want to know what happened to my real mother."

"Your real mother's name was Jaemee. She died when you were born. You never knew her. She never saw you."

Sunni crumpled onto the chair next to the bed, then recovered her composure. "So, I never had a sister, like Joo said. Then when did you come into the picture?"

June stood stiffly erect near the door. "Sunni, we don't have time to do a full family history. We need to plan."

"I WILL do a full family history, or you will have nothing," said Sunni forcefully.

June sighed and sat back down on the edge of the bed. "All right, so what do you want to know?"

"Did you plan to meet and marry my father?"
"Yes and no."
"What do you mean?"

"Yes, I planned to meet him, and no I never married him."

In the next room, Sam and Mike looked at one another and gave each other thumbs up. "Score one for Boogie," said Sam, acknowledging Boogie's research on June.

"You never married my father?" Sunni was aghast now. "How did you manage to keep that quiet all those years?"

"We just never mentioned it. Then when he died, I began working at the restaurant, and Joo joined me. He was put in place by NKUNA, too. We worked together to put you in place at Cameron, although you didn't know it."

"So, in actuality, you were the boss of this whole thing?"

"Yes, I was. And I still am, Sunni. You need to listen to me. You may think you have all the answers, but you don't."

"I need one more answer, first. How did my father die?"

"How did he die? What do you mean? He just died. That was all. He just died." June was curt and clearly not interested in reviewing more family history with Sunni.

"No, I think there's more to it. He died at a very convenient time for your operation, didn't he? It helped your control over me, didn't it? You killed him, didn't you?"

"Sunni, it doesn't matter now. That's not important anymore. What is important is that we are running out of time."

Sunni stared at June with raised eyebrows. "What more are you planning?

"There is a virus that we placed in the Cameron BioTech computer system. Actually you placed it there when you used the last thumb drive. The virus was preset to reprogram the system as soon as it loaded onto the computer. The 'dirty bomb' in the virus is on a timer. When it begins, it will destroy all the research in Cameron BioTech's labs. It is set to go off soon. It was meant to destroy any hopes for Cameron BioTech to use CRISPR. But if we don't get out of here with that last bit of data that you withheld, everything is lost. We must get out of here before that virus is downloaded. Before they find out. Tell me what you have done with the data, and then we can work out a deal. You said you had it. Where? We can tell NKUNA it was Joo who set the whole thing up without our knowledge. That's what went wrong. We'll tell them I was only trying to protect you."

"No!" Sunni interrupted. "I'm afraid not, June. That's not going to happen. We aren't going to work out any deal." Sunni spoke very calmly and quietly.

"What? You must! There's no..."

"I said NO!" Sunni stood and shouted, interrupting June's plea. "I'm not going to help any woman who murdered my father! I'll tell you what I am going to do. I'm going to help Quay Thompson and Samantha Atwood throw you in jail for a very long time. You are a treacherous traitor. Your precious plan to destroy the research at Cameron BioTech has failed. Your virus isn't going to be released. They are on to you. They have all the information they need. They just needed confirmation. And now, thanks to our conversation, they have it! You are done, you monster!"

June lunged at Sunni knocking over the chair between them. She clutched Sunni's shoulders, pushing her small frame against the mirrored wall. Sunni's head flew back and hit the mirror shattering it into pieces. She struggled to push June away, screaming, "Monster! Monster! You are a Monster!"

In the adjoining room, Chip jumped up and with a fierce, deep growl began barking ferociously at the door. Sam and Mike flew to the door, sprinted out of the room, and rushed into June's room. Chip, in determined protection mode, pushed past them. The dog sprang through the air in one giant leap, and landed with his front paws punching squarely onto June. June fell away from Sunni, tumbling off balance, and landed on the floor with the dog on top of her. Chip growled ferociously as he grabbed her shirt and began shaking it.

June screamed, "Help me! Help me! Get the animal away from me!" while Sam put an arm around Sunni's shoulders and carefully escorted her from the room. Chip turned to look after Sam and Sunni. Mike surveyed the room smiling at Chip as the dog stood over June.

"Good boy, Chip! You got her! Come here, fella!"

Chip stopped and looked up at Mike, then looked at June once more before backing away from her. He pranced over to Mike and received a pat on the head and a special treat Mike had brought with him. Mike tapped Chip on the collar, and as they turned to leave the room, he looked back at June.

"You are one cold bitch," he said to her. As he turned away and walked out with Chip trailing after him, he instructed the guard, "Let's move her to another room."

June Hyun lay back on the floor surrounded by bits of shattered mirror. She felt a long, thin shard at her fingertips, lifted it, turned it in her hand and with one swift move, jabbed it into her neck. Arterial blood spurted in measured arcs from the carotid artery in her neck. The glittering shard now covered with blood clattered away as June Hyun's hand fell back to the floor.

It was nightfall before the team was able to meet again. This time they joined Quay in his hospital room at HCMC. After he had finished his interview with Swivel, he had contentedly checked himself into a room for further observation. With special permission, Chip was allowed to join them.

Quay had propped himself up in the bed, pillows three deep behind him with scribbled scraps of paper littering the top of his bed. He was on the phone when Samantha Atwood walked through the door followed by Superintendent Mike Bergman, Boogie, Dan Young and Drew Thurston, and one very happy golden retriever. Quay quickly ended the call with what sounded like a muttered order and clicked off before Chip once again pushed ahead of the group, giving out a happy whine as he ran to Quay. The pup placed his big front paws on the side of the bed and stretched his head up to nuzzle Quay on his neck. His wagging tail and swaying hips gave evidence of his happiness. Quay laughed. "What a happy dog you are!"

"I guess Chip is pretty much speaking for all of us," said Mike. "We're very relieved to see you are taking our advice and resting comfortably, Quay!"

"Yeah, I'm gonna need to take a little more recovery time now, I guess," Quay said smiling at the group. "God, it's so good to see all of you! It's so good to have this done! Over with!" He reached out stroking the dog's back repeatedly. "And this dog was a walking evidence file! What a stroke of luck!"

"I think Chip is going to be more than that," said Sam. "I think we have a new BCA mascot! It's just a matter of who gets to keep him and help train him!"

"We can settle that with no problem," said Boogie. "I think he stays with me at the office when Quay is on a case. That way we can all enjoy him. He'll be our therapy dog. We need him to reduce our stress. Chip will be great for that. Then the rest of the time, it's obvious, he'll be Quay's buddy! He lives with Quay. Will that work?"

Boogie's suggestion was met with a chorus of yups and yeses, and hands stretched out to pet the dog. "As long as we get to see him when we come up to the main headquarters," inserted Dan. Drew nodded.

"Mike?" Quay asked. "Will that work? I wouldn't mind having Chip around. But what about at headquarters?"

"I don't see why not. If Boogie wants to be in charge of him at headquarters, I don't see a problem with that. We can get Chip trained to do some work for us, too. We could use a good canine officer. Let's do it!"

A universal sigh of happiness settled over the group.

"Now, I hate to be a downer, but let's debrief a bit on this case," said Mike. "You all had separate parts of this. It was a big case. But I think we can finally put it to bed. June Hyun is dead, but we've got enough information to bring closure. We video recorded the last conversation between her and Sunni."

They nodded, looking from one to another.

"Yeah," agreed Boogie. "Cameron BioTech is happy to know that their research is protected. I worked today with our other tech guy Lex Ellingson and their techie Dwight Davis. I turned over the thumb drive and the chip that Sunni had created. They were relieved to receive that. Since I broke the code on the virus, we were able to get into their system and stop the detonation timer. There is no way they can destroy the research that Cameron BioTech has for CRISPRCas9. Dwight was working on finalizing the patent application as I left, so they will have everything secure before the end of the week. There's no chance that NKUNA can get their hands on anything. What Cameron finally decides to do with the CRISPER Cas9 research is anyone's guess. But I think we can be sure that it won't be used to hold the rest of the world hostage. What I do know is that we can be prepared for some pretty amazing changes in our world in the years ahead, thanks to the CRISPR research team."

"Yeah, I agree. That is a relief," agreed Quay as the others nodded. "And my snitch, Claude Ayers, aka Swivel, gave enough background on June Hyun to provide us with probable cause in the entire investigation. Even though we already had quite a bit, Swivel filled in the missing pieces. We can get a search warrant to go through everything she owned."

Quay shared his conversation with Swivel and his promise to help Swivel get clean.

"I think Swivel is a smart guy. With his background and knowledge, we might be able to use him, if he can get cleaned up. I'd like to try to continue to work with him," Quay explained.

"Sounds okay," said Mike. "We'll look into that. Now, let me fill you guys in on the last piece. Samantha and I had an interesting day with June and Sunni Hyun. Sam met with Sunni Hyun first, and was able to convince Sunni that it would be in her best interests to get June to share what she'd done so we could get it recorded. Sunni turned out to be masterful at eliciting a full confession from June. Unfortunately, June went ballistic when she learned that Sunni had conned her. She attacked Sunni before we could get her out of the room."

Mike went on to share the rest of the events surrounding June and Sunni with the team, adding a description of the protective attack on June from Chip.

"The dog has proven himself several times in the last few days. I'd say he's been the key player in this entire case. And now, since June Hyun took her life, we'll need to gather a bit more information to fill in the blanks.

"There's Sunni Hyun. She gave us a lot. What happens to Sunni Hyun will be up to the courts. After contacting Quay, Sunni provided willing assistance in getting the full confession from June Hyun. That will weigh heavily in her favor in court. She was an unwitting and ultimately an unwilling dupe for June. That may be enough to give her only probation. We could ask that we have the option of calling on her for help as needed also. She's smart. But probation will probably be her best hope. The courts will decide.

'And finally," Mike continued, "I received word late this afternoon that the FBI and CIA have rounded up the NKUNA players here and abroad. That includes those organizing the attack on Joo Jhim. We will not have to worry about further attacks from them. They are finished. We can finally and completely close the last Cameron BioTech murder case and the attempted murder on Quay. We now know, Quay, that ultimately it was NKUNA who ordered the murder of your wife at Cameron. They had hoped to use the sniper killing and the protest groups to discredit the work Cameron BioTech was doing. It is done, Quay. I know that will be a relief to you. And we thank you for your work!" He turned to look at the rest of the group, and added, "Thank you all, too!"

Quay nodded. He looked up at Mike, reaching out to shake his hand. "Thank you, sir! You have no idea how that makes me feel."

The room became quiet. They had watched Quay Thompson suffer and grieve since the murder of his wife in front of Cameron BioTech. They all understood the magnitude of this moment.

"I'm ready to move on," continued Quay. "This is the closure I needed. And yes, thank you, all of you," he said again looking around at the group of faces. "You know, you are my family. I don't know what I would do without you."

Samantha looked at him with tears in her eyes. She smiled, patted his knee, and said, "You're probably going through bubble gum withdrawal now, Thompson!"

It was enough to break the somber moment, and they all laughed when she pulled out a wrapped bubble gum package from her pocket. Chip sat up at attention next to Quay. Ears up, the silky fur of his chest puffed out, tail dusting the floor in repeated wags, Chip waited expectantly for his treat, too. They laughed again as Quay laid aside his package of bubble gum, and opened another small package, and then flipped Chip a bit of dog treat from the package Mike had brought in.

"We share our treats, now," he laughed.

EPILOGUE
The Question

It had taken more than a month of rehab, exercise, and determination for Quay Thompson to recover fully from his wounds. While Quay had enjoyed the company of Chip at home, he'd also had an expert trainer come in to work with the dog. As expected, Chip was an eager, smart trainee. Quay had been assured that it wouldn't be long before Chip would be a full-fledged canine officer.

Another change in Quay's life was the addition of Samantha Atwood to his family life. Sam had become a regular visitor, checking up on him and encouraging him. Their bond grew stronger as the days and weeks passed. It had begun with a brush of a good-bye kiss as she'd left one evening. Shortly after, they admitted to each other what all their friends already knew: they were more than partners. They'd made it official in early March when they opened up to the team at work that they were dating. Super Mike agreed that, for now, it would be all right. Quay wasn't officially back to work. He said he would decide later how to approach their partnership and courtship. He admitted that he hated to break the team up, but said he'd have to look at it.

All in all, they agreed it wasn't just the work that drew them together. It had been their private conversations and shared beliefs about life, work, and family. They had a lot in common.

Usually, weather permitting, they spent their time together walking or hiking along cleared trails. It was good for Quay's leg, and gave Chip the exercise he needed, too. The hikes also gave them an opportunity to just be with one another. Sam would loop her arm through Quay's, and they'd stroll along arm in arm for a while, before breaking into a racing sprint that left them breathless and laughing with Chip happily dancing around them.

Over the weeks, they'd reminisced about all they'd shared over the last couple years: Karen's murder, Quay's grief, Sam's lost child and divorce, Sam's kidnapping, the wild chase up north to rescue her, the capture of the first people involved in the Cameron Case, as it was now called. The lives of those initial deceptive villains, Charlie Frank and Ernie Elson, had required several discussions to dissect their personalities and stories. Then came the final deception with Sunni Hyun. They agreed that was a whole 'nother story. It had been a shocker when Sunni had called Quay begging for help. The ambush at the safe house in southern Minnesota and Quay's shooting would leave neither of them the same. And then, the last surprise came in the form of Sunni's 'mother', June Hyun.

Over the last year, the tenuousness of life had been presented to each of them again and again. Life was too short to take for granted, they agreed. They needed one another. They wanted one another. And it was on that note that Quay finally asked Sam to stay the night.

"I think I need a woman," he'd said. "I think you're the one. And besides," Quay assured her with a twinkle in his blue eyes, "you're not too bad to look at." She laughed at his backhanded compliment and gave him a playful shove.

"You flatter me, sir," she said in an exaggerated Southern drawl flipping her ponytail and batting her eyes. "Guess you're not so bad yourself, Gumby," she joked. She'd started calling him Gumby since he'd had awkward moments of flailing around during rehab. His leg would flip out and back in what she'd teased as being Gumbyesque moves.

Then of course, there was the bubble gum. Sam and Quay teased one another mercilessly about his use of bubble gum to help with nicotine withdrawal, mostly because he blew huge pink bubbles at the most inopportune times. It was just at that moment he came up behind her and blew a huge bubble popping it next to her ear as he threw his big arms around her in a bear hug. "Yes, I do flatter you, Samantha Atwood, and I will continue to do so every chance I get. That is, if you'll let me?" It was a question that was answered as she turned in his arms and raised her lips to his for a kiss.

Their first night had been one of hesitant moves. Starting slowly, they had used the urgent desires of their bodies to guide them. Quay explored Sam's long, lanky limbs, running his hands over and around her breasts, marveling aloud at her toned body. Sam ran her hands through Quay's thick hair, exploring his body and kissing Quay's scars, murmuring over and over again that she was sorry, before he pulled her up to his lips, pressing his naked body against hers. It was several hours later before they were finally spent. They giggled as they viewed the disaster of the room strewn with discarded clothing, pillows and blankets tossed onto the floor; and they laughed as they welcomed a delighted Chip who jumped onto the end of the bed wagging his tail and snuggled between them in obvious approval.

As their relationship grew, Sam and Quay enjoyed a constant, easy banter. Others had to smile as they listened to them, too. Then Quay had taken Sam up north in the spring to Lutsen to visit again with his brother John and sister-in-law Sharon. She'd been welcomed by the family in her new role as Quay's girlfriend, and the stories between the brothers kept them entertained throughout the weekend.

Later that spring, they'd spent a weekend fishing together at one of the North Woods lakes, playing cards with Quay's nephew and niece, Adam and Allison, now in their teens, and then watching movies together next to a cozy fire. Samantha began to feel like she was a part of the Thompson family. Since she really didn't have a family of her own, Quay's family was a welcome, comfortable addition. Quay's brother John was especially happy to see Quay joking around again. This was the brother he remembered and loved. He agreed with his wife that Samantha was good for Quay.

It was late in April when Quay and Sam returned from a weekend road trip down to southeastern Minnesota to watch the eagles on the river near Wabasha followed by lunch at Slippery's Bar made famous in the movie *Grumpy Old Men*, and from there over to Mankato to visit with Dan and Drew. They'd had a great time over drinks and an evening meal catching up with them and their families. Chip had gone with them, and they were happy to be reunited with the new canine officer-in-training.

It was late Sunday evening when Quay turned into his driveway, and turned to Sam. "What do you think about summer weddings?"

Samantha blinked. "Oh, I think summer weddings are so much fun. Why? Who's getting married this summer?" she asked.

"How about us?"

The silence hung between them. Sam didn't move. Quay realized he was holding his breath when Sam finally turned to look at him.

"Really, Quay? Do you think we're ready?"

"I think I'm ready to give it a go. I think we do pretty well together."

Before she could say it, he added, "and I don't just mean as partners, Sam."

"Is this just a slick way for you to get me into bed again?"

"No. I've got better lines for that," he said as he blew a huge pink bubble and popped it. Sam laughed.

"You do, do you?"

"Yup!"

"Well, I guess we can give it a whirl. Let's try for late summer. And the wedding has got to be up north. What do you say we find a spot along the North Shore?"

"See? We are already on the same wavelength. I like that idea!"

"Do you think Super Mike would give us time off? At the same time?"

"I've already talked to him about time off for us. He said he thinks he can arrange it."

"Quay!" Sam laughed. "You really are something, Mr. Thompson!"

"Yes, I am! Yes, Miss Atwood, I am!" Quay laughed as he reached across to put an arm around her, pulling her close.

"And you'd better not forget it!" He smiled as he bent to kiss her.

ACKNOWLEDGEMENTS

There are so many people to thank for supporting me in this endeavor.

Thanks, first, to my countless interested readers who have been so patient and have kept asking, "When will the next book be done?" I appreciated your hanging in there for me. I hope *The Final Deception* was worth the wait.

Thank you to the following special people in my life:

For always being on call to field questions related to law enforcement procedures, weaponry, and criminals, thanks to our son, Matt Cowdin, Director of the Law Enforcement Academy at Missouri Southern State University in Joplin, Missouri,

For advice and knowledge of life-saving responses in the field, many thanks to my sister-in-law Ann Cowdin Gerdts and her husband, Jason Gerdts, Emergency Medical Responders for Waseca County, Minnesota, and to my nephew, Brad Cowdin, a firefighter/EMT with the Cedar Rapids Fire Department in Iowa. You were always ready when I called.

To my first editor and friend, Chris Baker, who waded through a terribly rough first draft and provided excellent questions, comments, and support.

To my final editor and long-time friend and fellow teacher, Olivia Bastian, for completing multiple reads and offering just the kind of concise plot evaluations and suggestions I wanted. You are a true friend! Thank you! (And yes, I meant to use the exclamation points there.)

And finally, I must give special thanks to my husband, best friend, and chief cheerleader of more than fifty years, who has supported my whims, no matter where they led, as well as my creative need to tell stories, written and otherwise. He has patiently listened to my ramblings about genome research, to crazy chicken stories (read my blog about that one), to insane character descriptions, and for always being willing to read and reread my writing. I know I can always count on you to give me the right advice. You have my love... always.